DIVIDE THE NIGHT

DIVIDE THE NIGHT

WESSEL EBERSOHN

PANTHEON BOOKS

NEW YORK

Library of Congress Cataloging in Publication Data

Ebersohn, Wessel.
Divide the night.

I. Title.
PR9369.3.E24D5   1981   823   81-47194
ISBN 0-394-52076-9   AACR2

Manufactured in the United States of America

FIRST AMERICAN EDITION

For Elizabeth,
who expects much from life and seems likely to have her
expectations realised.

FROM THE PLACE where Cissy stood in the shadow of the used-car dealer's sign, watching, she could see the door clearly. She had passed it coming down the road and it had been open then. Through the narrow opening she had been able to see the pockets of potatoes piled against the far wall and the stack of biscuit boxes that did not seem to have been opened yet.

The light inside came indirectly from somewhere above, allowing only the faintest glow along the edge of the far side of the door frame. By this light she had just been able to see into the room. The biscuits were what interested her most. A box of biscuits would not be too heavy. If she could grab one quickly she and Billy would run all the way down to the gardens behind the station and hide in the bushes there. There would be enough in a box like that for both her and Billy and plenty left over for tomorrow.

The room where the boxes were kept was long and narrow so that even though the door was only a little way open she had been able to see almost all of it. She had not been able to see behind the door and the shadows down that side were dark, but it just seemed like a room where there was nobody. Who would sit there in the darkness, Cissy asked herself. It would take only two counts, maybe only one count to dash in and get a box and dash out again.

"Cissy," the little boy said. "Cissy. Cissy." His voice was tired and plaintive, whining almost. "Cissy, what we doing here?"

"Quiet, Billy." She was thinking and did not want to be disturbed. He was enough trouble without bothering her now.

"But what we doing, Cissy? Why can't we go home?"

"Because there's nothing at home. Now shut up, Billy."

"I'm tired, Cissy. I don't want to stand here all the time."

"Shut up, I said. Don't be a baby." The boy pulled his hand

7

free of hers and sat down with his back resting against the wire fence.

The street was narrow with small stunted oak trees close together on either side, their remaining autumn leaves filtering the light from the street lamps until little reached the pavements. Most of the ground floor windows on either side belonged to business premises and were in darkness. Above the ground floor almost all the buildings held apartments and through the leaves Cissy could see light in some of the windows.

If I go quietly, she thought. If I go quietly and we run away quickly, no one will see us. I know it's a sin, but the Lord will not punish us if we are so hungry. There's nobody. If I go quickly nobody will see.

Cissy Abrahamse was fourteen years old, but because she had been poorly fed all her life her growth had been retarded and she looked more like a wasted under-nourished eleven-year-old. She was wearing a thin cotton dress that came down just below her panties and a filthy woollen jersey that was its original green colour only in patches now and had large holes both back and front where for years the stitching had been unravelling. Her brother, Billy, was five and, in appearance, like any other five-year-old, somehow having escaped the physical effects of being part of the home that had produced them. It was a home that had ceased to exist two nights previously, when their mother had gone out and not come back. Neither had eaten since then. Neither would ever know that their mother had died after being run down by a motor car on the night when they had last seen her. The methylated spirits she had drunk that night when she had not been able to interest a customer, and there had been little left to interest customers, had induced a state that had made it almost impossible to come home across the city safely. Deep in her drugged brain had been the knowledge that she must come home to the children. It had been that knowledge that had killed her.

The night was cold with the hard sharp cold of Johannesburg's winters. Neither Cissy's thin dress nor her tattered jersey were protection against it, but she did not feel the cold. There was room in her senses only for the crack in the door through which she had seen the biscuits.

Billy was also not feeling the cold. He had toppled over onto

8

his side and was asleep, leaning against the wire fence of the used-car dealer's yard, his limbs loose and relaxed and his face untroubled as if the situation was entirely normal. She reached out her hand to wake him, but withdrew it. It would be better to let him sleep until she came back with the biscuits.

Leaving Billy asleep on the pavement, she moved carefully down the block, keeping close to the buildings and deep in the shadow of the trees. Through the leaves she saw that there was light in a window above the door, but her view was obscured and that was all she could see. A few blocks further on a man in a sweater and jeans came out of a building and went straight to one of the cars parked against the pavement without looking to either side. Cissy stood quite still and waited until she had heard the engine start and seen the car move away up the road, the tail lights flicking on just before he turned at an intersection. Then she started forward again, keeping so close to the stone front of the building she was passing that her right arm rubbed lightly against it.

She stopped just down the road from the open door at a break between two trees. Through the break she could look into one of the lighted windows above the shop. All she saw were the whitewashed walls of a room and against one of them an old marriage portrait in faded colours of a man and a woman. When she had been much smaller they had once visited her Auntie Esther and she remembered that her aunt had had just such a portrait in just such an oval frame. She wished she knew where her Auntie Esther's house was so she could go there and take Billy there, but it had been a long time before and she had only gone once.

She waited for a while, looking at the open window, watching for any sign of movement, but there was none. A few more steps brought her opposite the door. By the light from above she could see again the cartons of biscuits, neatly piled on top of each other near the far wall. Against her conscious wishes Cissy's saliva glands started pumping the unwelcome fluid into her mouth. She could feel her heart beating strongly from the top of her throat into the back of her mouth. The top of her forehead felt hot and she knew that her hands were shaking.

There's nobody, she thought. There's nobody. I can go in and take a box and nobody will see. It will only take two counts and

9

I will be out again. The Lord Jesus will not make it a sin. Me and Billy are too hungry. He will forgive us. And there's nobody.

She looked up at the windows of the apartments on all sides, but she could see little through the branches. They also won't see me, she thought. I will go quickly. It will only take two counts and nobody will see me.

Looking up and down the street one last time to ensure that no one was watching, Cissy walked slowly across the road, stopped in the doorway and, carefully, very slowly, so slowly that it hardly seemed to be moving, she pushed the door open wide. To her right another door opened into the darkened shop and next to that a flight of steps led to the floor above. The stairs were unlit, the only light coming from somewhere beyond the landing. The little room was a store. On her left the rows of shelves fastened to the wall reached all the way up to the ceiling. It was too dark on that side to see what was on them.

From the stairs or the landing above she heard a sharp click, not loud but clear as if someone had dropped something small and hard onto a stone floor. Cissy waited, the outstretched fingers of one hand still touching the door as she had pushed it open, listening for the sound to come again or for footsteps or any sound at all. The moment passed and everything was as it had been before: the silent storeroom, the dim light coming from the stairs, the sacks of potatoes and the cartons of biscuits . . .

She looked quickly at the stairs for one final reassurance, then moved across the room, her hands outstretched before her. The pile of boxes was higher than her head and she had to reach up on tip-toe to take down the top one. She had started back to the door before she realised that the box had come away too easily and rested too lightly in her hands. She shook it once and then put it down on the floor. The second one was also empty, and so was the third. Pushing carefully against one of the boxes near the bottom of the pile and feeling them all move, she knew that they were all empty.

The pockets of potatoes were nearby. She pulled at the top one, but it was too heavy and how would she and Billy cook them. Perhaps there was something on the shelves. She had turned towards the shelves and was running a hand along the smooth surface of one in the darkness when she heard the sound. It was small, quick and muffled, possibly the sound of a footstep on a carpet. Then there were sounds from the stairs, not the sounds of footsteps, but the creaking of an old wooden staircase as the weight of a body is transferred carefully from step to step. For a moment she was motionless, held fast by the sound, her eyes fastened to the bottom of the stairs, the open door an invitation in the corner of her field of vision. To reach the door she would have to run past the bottom of the stairs. Whoever was on the stairs would possibly already be able to see the bottom and the door.

She moved quickly into the narrow opening between the biscuit cartons and the wall, dropping to her hands and knees, her head hanging low, ashamed that she might be found in this place. She had waited only a few seconds when the light came on. Somehow she had not expected the light. It came as a shock, her shoulders jerking once, then held rigid by the fear within her. She heard a movement from the door and listened for the sound of it closing, but it did not come. Instead she heard the voice of a man, deep and stern. "I know you're behind those boxes. Come out of there."

Cissy closed her eyes tight and prayed silently. "Please, Lord Jesus, make him go away. Make him go, please Lord." She had attended Sunday school once for a short time and remembered being taught that faith could move mountains. She only wanted it to move the man whose voice she was hearing. "Please Lord . . ."

"I know you're there. Come out right away and it will be better for you." The voice was stern and righteous, the way she imagined the voice of God would be. Listening to its sound made her even more ashamed of where she was and what she had been trying to do.

"Come out. I'll come and get you if you don't come out on your own."

The cement floor was cold beneath Cissy's hands and feet. She heard the man's feet move on the floor, a few shuffled steps and then silence. "Come out. I don't want to play games with you. I don't like people who make trouble. I don't want any trouble."

The voice was strong and angry, but not harsh and at last Cissy did what she knew she would have to do. She pushed the boxes away and scrambled out, half-rising, her hands clasped together in an attitude of supplication. "Please, Mister. Please,

11

Mister. Me and my brother are very hungry."

The face she saw was long and pale, the eyes frowning beneath a high broad forehead that receded into thin grey hair combed neatly back over the top of his head. The head was held upright, the chin pulled back, like a soldier she had seen in a picture. She looked straight into his eyes. They seemed to be full of tears. She could see the dampness all round the edges. Over his fingers he seemed to be wearing some sort of little leather gloves, each glove covering just one finger. "Please Mister, me and my brother . . ."

Then she noticed the gun in his right hand. The flash of light from his hand, the sudden sharp sound, the blow in her stomach and the awful pain, all came at the same moment. "Mister . . ." Cissy sank down to her knees, bending her head forward to look at the blood flowing from her stomach in wonder and horror. Somewhere far away she thought she heard the sound of Billy calling her name. She was not aware of the shadow in the doorway. The second bullet killed her.

ONE

THE LIGHT ON Yudel's desk was flashing furiously. He knew that at the other end of the circuit Rosa, his wife, was pressing the button that caused it to flash and she would certainly be furious. The little red light set into the surface of his disordered desk was the way she was supposed to draw his attention while he was with a patient. The light was positioned so that the patient would not be able to see it if he was in the chair across from Yudel or prostrate on the couch, having his soul laid bare.

Yudel slid the book he was reading over the light to hide it from himself. His patient was a lean dark-haired boy in his early teens and he was prostrate on the couch, but he was not having his soul laid bare. In fact he was sleeping. The light on the desk had been flashing in short bursts intermittently for the last half hour. Yudel had noted with interest that the intervals between bursts of flashing were growing smaller by what seemed to be an even rate. He wondered absently if any learned society would accept a paper on the linear rate at which his wife's agitation grew.

The disorder on Yudel's desk was its normal condition. He told himself that its disorder existed in inverse proportion to the orderly nature of his thinking. The worse his desk looked the better he was thinking at any particular time. Or so he told himself.

At the present time its entire surface was littered with bits of scrap paper covered with scribbled notes concerning his patients' problems. Some of the notes were on magazine covers or in the margins of old newspapers. One very brief reminder—Mrs P. Deep depression. Some husband. Not surprising—was written on the back of an empty cigarette box Mrs P. had left on his desk. As a filing system Yudel's desk was something less than perfect. It was fortunate that his memory was very near to being perfect and the notes were largely superfluous.

13

He was still trying to read, but the flashing light that he knew to be behind the book was turning out to be a problem. It was almost worse than when he could see it. Concentrating on the book had become nearly impossible. For all he knew the light might be flashing continually now. Rosa might have reached detonation point.

He removed the book and saw that the light was out. Perhaps Rosa had given up hope and sent the other patients away. It turned out to be a brief hope. Before he could go back to his book the light was flashing again.

Yudel's study had two doors, one that opened into a short passage that, in turn, led to the living-room where the next patient would be waiting, and a sliding door that opened onto the garden. He sighed tiredly and went to the first of the two doors, opening it just enough to look out. Rosa shoved her head past him to see what was happening inside the room. "What's going on in here?" she wanted to know.

"Psycho-analysis," Yudel told her, stepping back for her to enter. "Psycho-analysis is going on in here."

"Don't be funny. Do you know how many patients are waiting for you in there?" She gesticulated angrily in the direction of the living-room.

"No," Yudel said truthfully.

"Three," Rosa filled him in. "Mrs White, Mrs Rosenkowitz and Mrs Atkins."

"Nothing wrong with any of them."

"They pay, Yudel. Isn't that important to you? If it's not important to you, it is important to me." Rosa was speaking in a hoarse aggravated whisper, trying to keep her voice low enough so that the patients would not hear while keeping it sharp enough to get through to Yudel. "And I thought psychologists' patients were never supposed to see each other. You always say that it should never happen."

"They don't qualify as patients, Rosa. They're only customers."

"And him? What's wrong with him? Can't he sleep at home?" Rosa glared at the sleeping boy on the couch. "His mother's out there, frantic. She keeps asking me what you're doing to him. Do you realise that he started a half-hour appointment two hours ago?"

"He's sick, but there's nothing wrong with those women."

"Well, cure him on his own time. He's only sleeping. Why does he have to sleep here?"

"Rosa, you listen to me." Yudel tried to look and sound superior. "I am the psychologist. You are the wife and the receptionist. Let me do the curing and you do the receiving and the accounts and so forth."

"There aren't going to be any accounts at this rate."

"Nevertheless . . ." Yudel shook his head. He was still trying to sound superior, but he could find no suitable way to finish the sentence.

"Yudel, please." Rosa went over to pleading. It was a pleading that held within it the exasperation of an intelligent long-suffering person dealing with a mentally-crippled husband. "Please, Yudel. You've got to see the way those women are looking at each other. They're all acquaintances, you know—perhaps not Mrs Atkins— Mrs Rosenkowitz and Mrs White are though, and they didn't know that each other went to a psychologist. You should see how uncomfortable they all look. It's awful. They even tried to make conversation. That was worse. You should have heard it." The scene that Rosa was describing suddenly presented itself very clearly to Yudel's imagination. "Stop grinning, Yudel. It's not funny." Rosa's whisper took on an even greater urgency. "You're supposed to see that something like this never happens."

"I'll tell you something. It'll probably cure all three of them."

"What do you expect me to do?" She looked again at the boy asleep on the couch. "Can't you get rid of him? Why don't you wake him up?"

"He can't be woken now." Yudel realised that he was still grinning and tried to rid his face of the amusement.

"What's so funny?"

"Nothing's funny." With an effort of will Yudel got his face straightened out. "He's a sick boy and I can't wake him."

"What must I tell them?"

"Tell them they can wait or they can go home."

Rosa marched purposefully out of the room, swinging the door closed hard. Yudel had been expecting it and had followed her to catch it before it slammed and woke the boy. He sat down at the desk again and picked up his book. He had only read a few lines when the light was flashing again. Yudel sighed, more

15

deeply and with a more profound resignation than before, and went to the door again. This time Rosa did not burst into the room. "They're all waiting," she said grimly.

"Okay," Yudel said. He closed the door, but this time he did not sit down. Instead he stood at the glass-panelled sliding door that opened out into the garden, looking down the hill over the rooftops of the houses below. Evening was approaching and the pale bleached colours of the African day were deepening into subtler fuller shades. Behind him he heard the boy on the couch stirring, rising slowly from his sleep. Then the door of the study opened and closed again. Turning, Yudel saw that the boy's mother had come into the room. "What do you want?" he asked.

She was a small neat dark-haired woman and, to Yudel, she was one of the two people responsible for her son's condition. Her mouth was compressed into a severe little line and her eyes were tense and anxious. "What are you doing to my boy?" she asked, swallowing heavily. It was clear that she was surprised at her own impudence.

"I'm undoing all the bad things you and your husband have been doing."

Her eyes seemed to stiffen at the words. "Well I never," she said.

"And there's a great deal that needs undoing," Yudel added.

"I certainly won't bring him to you again." Her voice was shaking with anger at Yudel, anxiety for her son whom she had left in the hands of this strange wild-haired little man, and tension because of her own effrontery. "Once was enough," she said.

"The wise thing will be to let him decide whether he wants to come back to me or not."

"His father and I make such decisions." The woman started towards the couch where her son was pushing himself up on one elbow.

"Mrs Roberts," Yudel said. There was a quality of sharpness in his voice that stopped her and she turned to face him. "You are in my consulting room now. You have no authority here. Stand over there please." Yudel pointed towards the door.

The pinched severity of her mouth became still tighter, the eyes more rigid, but she went to the door and watched her son from there. Yudel went to the boy on the couch and laid a hand on his shoulder. "How are you, Graham?"

"I'm all right, Mister Gordon."

"No headache or anything?"

"Nothing, Mister Gordon."

"I want you to come back next week to see me again. All right?"

"Yes, sir. I'll come."

The boy got to his feet and Yudel turned to look at his mother. She was looking at her son's hands, at the absence of the little nervous movements that she had seen there during the last three years. Yudel led the boy towards his mother. "I'll look forward to seeing you next week, Graham."

"Yes, Mister Gordon."

"Now you wait next door for a moment while I talk to your mother." He let the boy into the living-room and closed the door quickly before his mother could escape. "You noticed a change?" Yudel asked.

It was a little while before the woman answered. "I have to grant you that he appears different. His hands . . ." The words came out grudgingly.

"Yes. Well he's not cured—far from it. What you can see are the effects of the hypnosis. I shall need to see him often and I shall need to see both you and your husband."

"My husband would never . . ." Her tone of voice showed to what extent she felt affronted.

"We'll see about that," Yudel said. "For the moment let the boy decide if he wants to come."

Yudel escorted Mrs Roberts to the living-room where Graham was waiting. "See you next week," he said to the boy as they went out. Then for the first time he noticed that there was no one else in the living-room. He found Rosa sitting at the kitchen table, staring grimly at the opposite wall. "Have the ladies left?" he asked gently.

"What did you expect?"

Yudel was about to say that he had fostered no particular expectations on the subject, when he thought better of it. Instead he returned to his study where there was now nothing to do except perhaps file the notes scattered around his desk. He knew he was not going to do that. He was aware of Rosa in the kitchen or possibly roaming the house, waiting for him to come out so that she could discharge her pent-up agitation on him. Somehow Yudel's wife considered his study to be out of bounds.

The light was off and the sliding door was still open, letting the lovely clear cold evening into the room. Yudel loved the feel on his skin of the sharp dry evening air before the cold of the night arrived properly. Through the open door he could see a corner of the brown stone face of the Union Buildings on the far side of the valley and between himself and them the more or less random scattering of apartment buildings and houses interlaced with the jacaranda trees that had such a softening effect on this part of Pretoria. Absent-mindedly he ran his hands through the clutter of papers on his desk, sometimes glancing vaguely at one in the half-light without reading it and replacing it among the others. Yudel loved the approach of evening. If it had been possible he would have reserved every evening for just watching the day end. One of his hands, still wandering among the pieces of paper, touched the edge of a more orderly pile. He withdrew a number of pages, all the same size, clipped neatly together, and tried to examine them in the quickly diminishing light, but it was already too dark. He reached out and switched on his desk light. In his hand he was holding his accounts of the previous month. They had been buried under the residue on his desk and had never been posted. No wonder nobody paid, he thought. Yudel admitted to himself that in some matters Rosa had cause for complaint.

The door to the passage opened at that moment and Rosa took a step into the room. She was frowning heavily. Her eyes and the area around them seemed to have grown darker in the last hour. Perhaps it was the light, Yudel thought. "There's someone to see you," she said. "You'd better close that door. It's freezing in here." The words came out with difficulty, as if there was some sort of severe obstruction blocking their path. Yudel knew that this was the restrained Rosa, a high-pressure boiler within and all the steam valves shut off tight. He reasoned that perhaps he should be glad of that. The one with the valves open was a problem.

Her eyes fell on the accounts in Yudel's hands. "What are those?"

Yudel had to suppress a momentary impulse to hold them behind his back. "Accounts," he said.

"Which accounts?"

"Last month's." He felt like a victim of the Inquisition admitting to heresy, knowing that down below in the dungeon the rack was waiting.

Rosa drew herself up and her eyes became darker still. "No wonder nobody paid," she said.

"That's just what I was thinking," Yudel said.

Rosa withdrew quickly without saying any more and Yudel closed the sliding door. She ushered the new visitor in and closed the door hard behind him. She did not slam it, but it was closed purposefully enough to leave Yudel in no doubt as to what her feelings were.

The new visitor was a man in the latter part of middle age. He carried little excess weight and stood less than average height, but because he held himself very neatly erect with his head back and his arms straight down at his sides he seemed taller than he was. Yudel's first momentary impression was one of great dignity, as if the man he was looking at understood his own worth and valued himself highly, but without arrogance. It was an impression that was reinforced by the stern expression of face and the way he looked straight into Yudel's eyes. But it was an impression that was dissipated as soon as Yudel first looked into the watery eyes in the long oval face. They were the eyes of a desperate and despairing man. He could see in them the sadness of a man that was close to surrendering every interest he had in life.

Yudel knew that surrender was rarely a condition that related to one object or one aspect of life only. Especially in the old it was a state of mind that affected a human being's behaviour in every respect. Also it was not a condition that overtook a man suddenly. There was a long period in which it grew and all the time the sadness of defeat and the knowledge that there could no longer be any resistance would be enveloping the personality. Eventually it showed in everything he did, in the way he walked and held himself, in the expression of his face and the nature of his conversation. Most of all it showed in his eyes. The other man had imposed a calm and dignity on his bearing and his face, but it was the eyes that revealed everything.

19

Yudel got to his feet and held out a hand. "I'm Yudel Gordon," he said. "How do you do?"

"I'm Mister Weizmann," the man said. He made no move to take Yudel's hand.

Yudel glanced involuntarily at the other man's hands. His fingers were sheathed in leather sleeves of uneven lengths, very few being of normal length.

"Will you sit down, Mister Weizmann?" Yudel gestured towards the chair opposite him. Weizmann sat down and his bearing when seated was as carefully erect as it had been when he was standing. It was a studied production that had as its purpose the convincing of others, but most of all the convincing of himself. He wanted all to know that he was a worthy and dignified man. And he too wanted to believe it. "Now how can I help you?" Yudel asked him.

"I've been having trouble in my shop," he said. "It's my shop you always read about in the paper." He spoke softly, almost casually, and the severity of his expression had softened.

"What sort of trouble?" Yudel asked.

"I've been having people breaking into my shop. Twenty-seven times people broke into my shop. Youngsters, blacks . . . twenty-seven times . . ."

"Twenty-seven times? In how long?"

"In two years." He paused as if expecting Yudel to question him. When Yudel said nothing he went on: "I don't like people who make trouble. All these youngsters are thieves. I'm a peace-loving man. If I'm left alone it's all right." The sound of his voice was still calm and conversational, but he no longer looked directly at Yudel as he had done when he first came in. Now he was looking down at the edge of the desk or the floor next to his chair or at his hands that were resting in his lap, the fingers tucked away as if he was hiding them. Yudel tried not to look in the direction of Weizmann's fingers. He had had little medical training and few possibilities presented themselves to his mind. He settled for leprosy. Weizmann had stopped talking, apparently not knowing how to continue. At length he spoke quickly. "If they keep breaking into my café, I'll shoot them dead."

"Have you had cause to shoot at them in the past?"

"I have shot at them. I'm not saying I haven't shot at them. But every time they were breaking into my shop. You have to protect your own place." He had dropped his head, his chin almost resting on his chest, but there was still something of the worthy bearing about the way he drew in his chin and tried to keep his mouth firm. The casualness had left his manner of speech entirely. "White youths have become criminals. They are falling in with bad company. They'll all land in jail."

"Have you ever hit one that you shot at?" Yudel asked.

Weizmann continued as if he had not heard the question. "I want to stay out of trouble. I'm a peace-loving man. You can call me honest Weizmann. I don't want any trouble, but if I get trouble I can look after myself. My brother always used to say, Johnny, if they look for trouble with you, they can be sure they'll get it." Ever since Weizmann had introduced himself his name had been scratching at Yudel's memory and now that the christian name had been added it seemed even more familiar to him. Johnny Weizmann. He had heard the name before. It could not have been important to him at the time. It's my shop you always read about in the papers, Weizmann had said. But Yudel's reading of newspapers was normally perfunctory and unreliable.

"You have a brother?" Yudel prodded the conversation in the direction he wanted it to take.

"I had a brother. They killed my brother."

"Who killed him?"

"I don't know. How am I supposed to know? Youths. Blacks. I don't know."

"How did they kill him?"

"They beat him to death in his flat. He was unrecognisable. I couldn't recognise my own brother the way they beat him up." He was speaking quickly and angrily, but Yudel could detect little horror in his voice for the act he was describing. "I saw him the day after he died. The doctors said he died of a heart attack, but what caused him to have a heart attack is what I want to know. They can't tell me anything. I saw his body and I know what he looked like. He was unrecognisable."

"I can see you were very attached to your brother."

"Oh yes. We did everything together. He sometimes helped in the shop. He was always round at my place."

"Where is your shop?"

"Hillbrow. Lower Hillbrow."

"You came all the way from Johannesburg tonight?"

21

He nodded quickly in affirmation. "My shop is the Twin Sisters Restaurant. I've got twin girls. The young one got married last week. She's only a few hours younger than her sister. They're both married now. They're big now."

"When thieves break in do you find evidence in the morning or is there an alarm?"

"I hear them. They never get in without me hearing them. I'm a very light sleeper. Before they get in sometimes I'm awake. I'm a peace-loving man, but I can look after myself." Weizmann lifted one of his hands and placed it on the edge of the desk. The thumb was intact and was not wearing a leather sheath. All the others wore leather sheaths and of them only the little finger appeared to be of normal length. The fore finger was the shortest, just one joint still remaining. It took only a moment for Weizmann to become aware of his hand. He plunged it down to his lap again, shielding it from sight between his legs. "My damn hands," he said. It sounded like a curse, but he said nothing more about them, probably assuming that the sight of them was explanation enough.

In spite of himself and his inner professional chidings, Yudel was fascinated by the other man's hands. If this man felt that so much was against him, clearly the condition of his hands would reinforce that feeling. It was not this that fascinated Yudel though. It was simply the sight of them, the stumps of what had presumably once been normal fingers and their leather caps. He wondered again what it was that the leather hid. With an effort of will he directed his thinking back onto a more professional course.

"You always hear them breaking in?"

"Always. I always hear them. I'm a very light sleeper. All my life I've been a very light sleeper."

"You sleep in the shop?"

"We've got a flat above the shop. I always leave the door to the shop open. Then I can hear them come in . . ."

"And sometimes you shoot at them?"

"I'm not saying I don't shoot at them. I can look after myself."

Yudel repeated an earlier question to test whether the reaction would be the same. "Have you ever hit one?"

At the question he seemed to bend further forward, determined that he would not have to look at Yudel's face. And the reaction was the same. "I like helping the police. I often help the police. When there was still a police station near to us I was very well-known to the police. They all liked me. I had a lot of friends among the police. I often tried to stop robbers when nobody else would help. The police know me well. They call me honest Weizmann. Now they've taken the police station away it's much worse . . ."

"Are you Jewish, Mister Weizmann?"

"No." The voice was decisive. "No, not any more. Not since I've been an adult. I stopped that years ago."

"Was there a reason?"

"I'm just a South African now. I'm a patriot. I try to do my duty. I help the police. That's what's important. I do my duty like a good South African."

Making what seemed to be a great effort, Weizmann raised his head, seeming to consciously square his shoulders and lift his chin, but he turned his face away so that he would not have to look directly at Yudel. Now Yudel could see his eyes again. They were so wet that at first he thought that the other man might be crying. "Are there burglar guards on the windows?" Yudel asked.

"No. Why should I spend my money on burglar guards? I can't afford it. I'm not a rich man. I had to spend a lot of money on lawyers. Nobody helped me. I had to get an overdraft from my bank." Yudel noted that this admission answered his earlier question. "I don't look for trouble. It's not fair I should have all this expense."

"Perhaps if you had burglar guards you would sleep better."

"I'm a poor man. I can't afford luxuries like burglar guards. Other people can afford things like that, but I can't. The real trouble is the youth today. They have fallen in with the wrong company. That's the real problem." It was a refrain that Weizmann had repeated often. It was one Yudel was sure he would repeat many times in future.

Yudel looked at the defeated man on the other side of the desk, defeated and yet holding up his head, somehow still going through the motions of dominance and worth. He asked him the only question that seemed of immediate importance. "Mister Weizmann, why did you come to see me?"

23

"They told me to. They said I had to."

"Who said so?"

"Colonel Jordaan said so. He said you would be able to help me. They forced me." He paused for a moment and his voice became indignant and unsteady. "I don't think I need help. I can't see it. Why is it me that must have help? If they leave me alone there's no trouble."

"You know, Mister Weizmann," Yudel said, "everyone needs help some time or other—me, you, everyone . . . Maybe you do need it now. It's nothing to be ashamed of. It's no different to visiting a doctor. I'd like to be of help."

"I haven't got any choice. I have to come." He glanced down quickly at his wristwatch. "I'm late. I have to go."

"Stay a little longer."

"I'm very late. I have to go now."

"I want you to come tomorrow night and every night for a few days. Just for a little while I'd like to see you daily. Will that be possible?" Weizmann nodded once quickly. Yudel scratched in a drawer and brought out a little bottle of valium. "I want you to take two of these every morning and two every evening for a few days. I'll tell you when to stop." He reached out to pass the bottle to Weizmann, but the other man made no move to take it from him. Yudel remembered the hands. He put the bottle down on the edge of the desk.

One of Weizmann's strangely gloved hands darted out and gathered it up. "What does it do?" he asked.

"It's just to help you relax. You're tense because of all the breaking in at your shop. Anyone would be. If you take them you will feel more relaxed. You'll feel happier. Will you take them?"

"I'll take them," Weizmann said. He seemed to look quickly round the room as if searching for something. "I want you to understand," he said. "I never look for trouble. I can handle myself, but I never look for trouble. I try to help people. I came out of my shop once and six blacks were attacking a man who was getting into his car. I ran and got my gun. Nobody else would help. I frightened them off. I help people." He was still not looking at Yudel, but Yudel could see that it was important to Weizmann that he should believe him. He wanted very badly that Yudel should understand that he was not a bad man. "I

24

sometimes help destitute blacks. My wife gives parties for kids. Five old-age pensioners come to my shop every day for a free meal. I don't charge them a cent. Once I found some blacks stripping an old man and taking all his things. I chased them . . ." The recitation of his good deeds came out in mechanical fashion. Like the condemnation of the youths and the blacks it was something that had been repeated many times in the past and was being held in reserve to use again often in future.

Yudel heard him out, trying to calm the most turbulent areas until he could deal with them properly, urging Weizmann to use the pills he had given him and to be sure that he returned the next evening. After the shopkeeper had left Yudel went to the front of the house to watch him walk down the path and across the road to his car parked on the other side. He was surprised at the old man's awkward hobbled walk, the legs held stiffly and the stride short and choppy. From a distance his bearing showed no sign of the failure and defeat Yudel had seen in his eyes. He held himself as rigidly upright as he had when sitting opposite Yudel.

Yudel waited until the car had disappeared from his sight down the quiet suburban street. Then he went to the telephone in the hall and dialled the home of Freek Jordaan, the man who had sent Weizmann to him and his own friend of many years. He heard the sound of the telephone being picked up and Freek's voice on the other end of the connection. "Jordaan."

"All right, Freek, who is he?"

Freek had been expecting the call. "He's a nice old uncle who kills people," he said.

TWO

THE PREACHER WAS young and earnest and believed every
word he was saying. Yudel doubted that he had ever before had
quite such a congregation though. The prisoners were assembled
in the quadrangle in the centre of the cell block and seated on
long wooden benches without backrests.

"You have become enmeshed in sin," the preacher was saying.
"Look at where your wild ways have led you. You have tasted
the very dregs . . ."

Convention demanded that Yudel sit on the low platform next
to the preacher. "What's it got to do with me?" he had asked the
head warder the first time it had come up.

"You're the psychologist," the head warder had said.

"You're the head warder," Yudel had said.

"It's the field of the psychologist," the head warder had said.
And that was the way it had stayed—the field of the psychologist.

"You have sinned," the preacher told his captive audience.
Yudel reflected that this was not the first time that fact had been
explained to them. "You have sinned and come short of the
glory of God. When you reached the bottom, when life had
become without meaning, when society itself had turned its back
on you, had turned its back on you with much justification I
might add . . ."

Yudel knew almost every member of the congregation. Even
the more recent recruits had visited him at least once, and in
one visit Yudel normally learnt a lot about a patient. He knew
them all, from white-collar criminals, some of whom would come
out of jail to live off the proceeds of their crimes, to old
recidivists who felt at home only in jail and would be back again
and again for as long as they lived. He had listened to them all
at length, hearing their justifications, confessions and accusations.

He had achieved real successes with some, who when their sentences were over would never come back, and had had no effect at all on others. They were in every way a typical prison community.

In the back row, seated right on the end of one of the benches was old Willem Roelofse, who must have been back a dozen times in the last twenty years. His speciality was burglary and whenever he had been too successful, with perhaps six or seven jobs behind him in which he had got away without a trace, he would start feeling lonely for the comradeship and security of prison life. He always assured Yudel that while he was on the outside he missed his talks with him too. At such times of success and loneliness—and Willem never kept a woman for long—he would always do something stupid at a job that would lead the CID straight to him. He had often told Yudel that these slips were unintentional, but conscious or not there was no doubt that they grew out of Willem's need to return to the only place that was home to him.

Yudel could see that Willem was chewing something—a single jaw movement every twenty or thirty seconds so as not to make it obvious. Willem was from a very old school and Yudel wondered where the chewing tobacco had come from. He hoped Willem was not going to spit on the floor and cause a disturbance. "Hell and damnation are staring you in the face," the preacher was telling them. He paused significantly to let this awesome fact sink in. "The wrath of God . . ."

Willem's bored half-closed eyes closed altogether and Yudel heard his hoarse voice sing out, "Amen, brother." The sudden emission of air caused a wave of tobacco juice to spill over his lower lip and down his chin. He quickly sucked in as much of it as he could, wiping away the rest with the sleeve of his tunic.

"The Lord has shown there will be no mercy for the unrepentant. The ungodly shall perish."

"Amen," Willem sang out, wiping his chin with his sleeve again.

In the third row Yudel could see Solly Abromowitz, glancing up and down the row, making furtive hand signals to some of his colleagues. Solly had been convicted of raising money for a fictitious Israeli kibbutz. He had invested the money in three racehorses that he had named Ben Gurion, Meir and Dayan. Out

27

of respect, he had told Yudel. The horses had won nothing and one of the fund's sponsors had tried to visit the kibbutz while travelling in Israel.

At the present time Solly was taking bets on whether the preacher would realise before the sermon was over that his pockets had been emptied. The preacher had made the mistake of asking to be introduced to each of the prisoners in turn as they came in. Yudel had watched Solly clean him out while Wally Price diverted his attention by an extra-hearty handshake. While Solly was taking the bets, which by now were probably running at about twenty to one against, Wally was selling the proceeds. He seemed to have already found a buyer for a watch with a broken strap and as far as Yudel could see was still negotiating a price for the wallet. Yudel imagined that he should have done something to stop it, but what the hell, maybe the preacher would stay away next time.

"I am offering you . . ." It was the grand climax. "Jesus is offering you . . ." Yudel wondered what offers Wally was getting on the watch. "God is offering you . . ." Were the offers being made in order of importance?

"Praise the Lord," Willem sang out. His eyes had not opened since his first "Amen, brother" and his head was nodding perceptibly.

"Which of you today, at this minute, is prepared to turn your back on your life of crime, of wickedness and sin, of evil and corruption, of vileness in the eyes of God and man: which of you is prepared to stand up . . ."

Willem was on his feet. "Yit, ou Willem," somebody shouted. It had the intonation of a cheer. Everyone always waited for Willem to stand up first or raise his hand or do whatever it was the preacher required of them.

". . . to stand up and be counted for Jesus . . ." The preacher's voice hesitated a moment, showing his uncertainty. He had not expected quite such a quick response. "Come now out of the dark and despair," he went on, trying to regain a little of his lost momentum, ". . . out of the sin and ignorance . . ." His voice trailed off into silence. He had not even come to the part about Jesus offering salvation, free and forever, and they were getting to their feet all over the quadrangle. Could this be the work of the Spirit? He had never known the Spirit to work in the

28

spontaneous way as recounted in the Acts of the Apostles, but this was something different. He was not even having the opportunity of issuing the Lord's invitation properly and look at them —hardened criminals, the very dregs of humanity, the lowest of the low, the transgressors of every commandment held dear by God and man, all jumping to their feet to accept Jesus.

"Amen. Praise the Lord." Willem's voice was deep and emotionless. Praise the Lords were echoing from all sides of the quadrangle now with Willem setting the pace. He was the acknowledged leader in all social activities and none of the others, excepting perhaps a new boy who did not yet understand prison protocol, would dream of shouting more Praise the Lords than Willem. It was his right the same way it was Yudel's right to ask them all sorts of questions about their fathers and mothers and wives and girlfriends and dreams and ambitions and the crimes of which the authorities had mistakenly accused them.

Yudel viewed the whole scene with an expression of bored amusement. He had seen it all before. The authorities allowed a visiting preacher every six months and, at all the many meetings that Yudel had attended, not one of them had ever been able to resist calling for a show of hands or something of the sort, some measure by which to test their ministry to these hardened criminals. In no case had there been less than a one hundred per cent response. The preachers had all gone home happy and the prisoners had gone back to their cells hoping that the authorities had taken note of their changes of heart, with special reference to reductions in sentences and other matters of that nature. Yudel caught Willem's eye and the old convict winked at him. "Amen," the hoarse deep voice sang out.

"Now all those who truly accept the Lord Jesus as saviour will walk up . . ."

Yudel had hold of the back of the preacher's jacket and tugged it hard. "They have to stay where they are."

The guards along the walls on either side, looking stricken at the idea of the preacher being swallowed up in that throng, had all taken a step forward. Those behind Yudel and the preacher had come right up to the edge of the platform. Yudel remembered the case well, when after just such a meeting a few years previously and all the prisoners had been converted, one lifer had stabbed another to death over a matter of prison territory

29

as they were leaving the hall. It was not likely that anything would happen to the preacher, but it was not sensible to take the chance.

"The Lord is working, brother. You have nothing to fear," the preacher said softly, almost affectionately, trying to explain it to Yudel.

"I was thinking about you, not me. If you call them up we're taking you out immediately."

"I assure you, brother . . ."

"That's final," Yudel said. The conversation that had been whispered had been almost drowned by the ecstatic cries of the congregation. Although they all understood what the preacher had been about to ask them none of them had moved. They understood the rules too.

The preacher looked sadly at them. "Let us pray," he suggested.

"Amen, brother," Yudel said.

"Did you enjoy the meeting, Willem?" Yudel asked.

Willem Roelofse was sitting on the bunk in his cell, leaning back on his elbows with his shoulders against the wall. "It's something to do, Mister Gordon." Willem was in his middle fifties. Even in prison his hair was carefully combed, slicked back across the top of his head, shining and immaculate. His eyes were always moving. The expression in them was bitter and he rarely looked directly at Yudel. He was totally anti-social, thoroughly untrustworthy, but of a charming easy-going personality and Yudel liked him very much. He sat down next to Willem.

"You seemed to enjoy it."

"You know me, Mister Gordon."

"That's true. And you know me. I need some information."

"Come on, Mister Gordon. You know better than to come asking me."

"I think you might be willing to help me on this one."

"You know me, Mister Gordon. I don't give trouble and I don't talk. When I get caught I do my time quietly, but don't ask me for information."

"Listen to what I want first." It was clear to Willem that he would at least have to listen to what Yudel wanted. He looked disappointed, as if he expected better than this of the psychologist. "You've worked a lot in Hillbrow, Braamfontein, Joubert Park—you know the area well, I think." Willem made no effort to confirm what Yudel was saying. "I want you to tell me what you know about Johnny Weizmann."

Willem turned quickly towards Yudel, trying to read in his face what this meant. "Christ, Mister Gordon, I never had nothing to do with that old man. What's this about?"

"What do you know about him?"

"Nothing. The same as everybody else. What is this?"

"Take it easy, Willem. I just want to know anything you know about him."

The old prisoner drew slightly away from him, his eyes continually flicking towards Yudel's. He could not sustain looking into the other man's eyes, but he was troubled by being connected to Weizmann and was trying to read the answer in Yudel's face. "Christ, Mister Gordon, I don't want you mixing me up with that old man. I never even met him. I seen him once when I was in his shop, but that's all. I never been near him otherwise."

"Relax, Willem. Nobody is mixing you up with him. I want to find out about Weizmann. That's all."

"That old man is bad news, Mister Gordon. That's all I know. I only seen him once in my life an' I don't know nothing about him."

"What about the people he's shot? Were they professionals?"

"What you talking about, Mister Gordon? They a buncha kids, drunk coons and dagga smokers. No pro would want to know anything about Weizmann's place."

"Why not?"

"Look, Mister Gordon. You know better than to ask me all this. There's no money in the till of a fish an' chip shop, not the sort a man is looking for if he makes a living from it. An' there's nothing else to steal there."

"All amateurs then?"

"Every one."

"Why do you suppose old Weizmann has all the trouble? I don't think the other shops around there have so much trouble."

"I don't know nothing myself, Mister Gordon, so I can't say for sure, but the word is that he leaves his storeroom door open at night."

"He leaves it open?"

31

"It opens onto the pavement. You know Jimmy Verwey?"

"The one in Leeukop for armed robbery?"

"Him. He told me he went past there one night and all the lights were out and the side door was open. He knew about Weizmann so he stayed away from the place. I don't want you mixing me up with that old bastard, Mister Gordon. He's bad news."

Yudel went to fetch the preacher in the head warder's office where he had been invited to tea. The head warder had been listening politely to his enthusiastic recounting of the way the Spirit had worked in the hearts of the dregs of society and how he, the preacher, had made things much easier for him, the head warder, because from now on all the prisoners were going to be very well behaved, having had the Spirit work in their hearts. By the time Yudel entered the office the head warder had a glazed look about his eyes from the verbal battering he had been receiving. His eyes seemed to brighten at the sight of Yudel. "Here's Mister Gordon," he said.

Yudel had never heard the head warder sound so pleased to see him. Old buck-passer, Yudel thought. You only had the tea party. I had the meeting. "You ready?" he asked the preacher.

The head warder got to his feet, rubbing his hands together in a way that indicated satisfaction or at least relief on his part. "Mister Gordon's taking you back to Johannesburg, is he?" he said warmly to the preacher.

You old bugger, Yudel thought.

"He has been kind enough to offer," the preacher said.

"I have other business there as well," Yudel said grimly.

When they were alone in the car on the road to Johannesburg the preacher directed the full blast of his joyful exuberance at Yudel. "Wasn't it remarkable, Mister Gordon?" he asked.

"Very interesting," Yudel said.

"It was something of great wonder to me, an event of great spiritual significance. I think I shall remember it as long as I live. It was without parallel, wouldn't you say?"

"Not quite without parallel."

The preacher turned uncertainly towards him. "What do you mean? I shouldn't think you've ever had anything like that before?" What he was asking was—I'm sure that the Methodists

32

or the Baptists or the Catholics or any of those other unfortunate types of so-called Christians with their diluted doctrines—I'm sure that none of them could manage what I managed today?

"Well, six months ago they were all converted by the Presbyterians."

"Oh."

Yudel took his eyes off the road long enough to glance at his passenger. The young preacher's face wore a thoughtful expression. "A year ago it was a Dutch Reformed minister that did it."

"All of them?" The voice was subdued, a prospector who had just realised that the diamonds on his claim were glass.

An inner kinder part of Yudel told him that he should leave the man with at least a part of his illusion. But he had sat through the meeting and the kinder part was quickly overwhelmed. "I'm afraid so," he said truthfully.

For a while the preacher thought about what Yudel had told him. When he spoke his voice was decisive. "They are not trustworthy," he said. It sounded as if he had made a discovery.

"I'm afraid not," Yudel said. "That's why they are where they are."

In the first moment after Yudel entered Freek's office it seemed that the room was empty. Then he heard a female groan from behind the desk, followed by a soft thump on the floor. "Freek?" he asked.

Freek's head came up behind the desk. "Hullo, Yudel."

"Can I come in?"

"Why not?" The police colonel's head disappeared again.

Immediately there was a second thump and the voice of Mimi, a lady constable Freek used as his private secretary, protesting in Afrikaans. "That's too hard. You're hurting."

Yudel took half a step into the office. "Are you sure I may come in?"

"Of course I'm sure." This time his head did not appear.

Mimi's voice shattered into a cascade of giggles. "Please come in, Mister Gordon. You're just in time to save my life."

"I'm the one who's saving your life," Freek's voice said.

Yudel advanced slowly to the front of the desk and leaned over it to see what was happening on the far side. What he saw was Mimi face-downwards on the carpeted floor with Freek

33

straddling her, seated on her buttocks and massaging the lower part of her back. "Look at Mister Gordon." Mimi's voice broke up into giggles again. "Look at his face." Freek turned to look at Yudel and chuckled softly. "What did you think we were doing, Mister Gordon?"

"Don't ask Mister Gordon things like that, Mimi," Freek said. "You'll embarrass him. At heart he's a puritan."

Yudel sat down on the edge of the desk. "I'm not a puritan. What are you doing?"

"Taking out Mimi's kinks." Mimi was twenty-four years old, pretty in a warm chubby way and with a figure that was good, but in a similarly warm and chubby way. She was married to a fellow constable and was of the opinion that everything done by the police, especially Uncle Freek, as she called him, was right and just and beyond reasonable criticism. Now Freek was massaging her shoulder blades and up towards the base of her neck. "She has back trouble," Freek said by way of explanation. "Once a week I've got to fix her up."

Mimi's shoulders shook as she started giggling again. "Don't look like that, Mister Gordon. This is as far as he ever gets."

"I thought that you two were sent here because they were so understaffed in Johannesburg. I thought you were terribly overworked."

"We are," Freek said. "We only take a break once a week for the kinks."

Standing erect, Freek was a man of above average height. He was broad in the shoulders, deep in the chest, with solid sturdy limbs and broad powerful hands, in each of which at the present time he had one of Mimi's shoulders and seemed to be trying to compress them into each other. Mimi groaned again. "Not so hard, Uncle Freek."

"Are you sure you know what . . ."

"I'm an expert," Freek said modestly. "Ask Mimi."

Yudel obliged. "Is that right?" he asked Mimi.

"I always feel better afterwards," she grunted. " Not so hard, Uncle Freek."

"That you feel better is simply the relief at having him stop." Freek ignored Yudel's wisdom and Mimi was too preoccupied with the discomfort of his attentions to say anything. Conversations between Mimi, Freek and Yudel were always conducted in both English and Afrikaans. Mimi spoke little English and always spoke Afrikaans to Yudel. Freek spoke English to Yudel because he had little other opportunity to exercise his good knowledge of that language and Yudel was caught between the two, addressing Mimi in one language and Freek in the other.

"So you met our Mister Weizmann last night," Freek said.

"What's it all about, Freek?"

"Just an old man that needs your attention the way Mimi needs mine."

"You also work him over like this?" Mimi giggled between the grunts.

"The technique is different," Yudel said. "The object is also to take out kinks."

"Johnny Weizmann has shot eight people dead in the last ten years," Freek told him, "all except one having been black. All of them have apparently been breaking into his shop." He pointed to a pile of files on a corner of his desk. "Mimi has prepared these for you. They cover all the cases. The inquest on the death of the most recent victim is due next Friday, eight days away."

"And you sent him to me?"

Freek stopped what he was doing and looked straight at Yudel. "What's wrong with that?"

"What if he has to stand trial for murder? He might want me to testify in his defence. I am employed by the state, Freek, for Christ's sake."

Freek went back to his manipulations. "I thought of that. But I doubt they'll put him on trial. They never have in the past."

"Why not?"

Freek had Mimi's torso pinned to the carpet with one hand while he lifted her arms, one at a time, high behind her with the other. He was growing flushed from the effort he was making. "It's a question of law. The Criminal Procedure Act. It says you may use reasonable force to defend yourself and your property."

"Killing people is reasonable?"

"It's always been late at night and most of the time in the storeroom of his shop. Only in a few cases have there been witnesses. If the other person is trying to kill you, it becomes reasonable to kill him."

"And were they all trying to kill him?"

Freek had finished his treatment of Mimi and he turned to

35

face Yudel, still seated on her buttocks, but no longer straddling her. He seemed to have forgotten where she was or what he was sitting on. "He says so. The latest was a coloured kid of fourteen or fifteen or so. When the Flying Squad got there she was holding a hammer in one hand. Weizmann said in his statement that she had tried to hit him over the head. It was Weizmann's hammer that she had apparently picked up in the storeroom."

"Uncle Freek." Mimi's voice held a small measure of panic.

"Ah Mimi. Almost I forgot you." Freek pressed down on her back with one hand as he levered himself up, then he took her firmly above one elbow and lifted her to her feet. "There we are. Fine again." Mimi stood still for a moment, stretching her arms and wriggling her fingers. "Feel well?" Freek asked her.

"Perfect," she said.

"I love loyal people," Yudel said.

After Mimi had left the office, attending to some of Freek's other business, and Freek had invited Yudel to sit down, he went on telling about Weizmann. "There's something else. If you make a citizen's arrest and the person tries to flee you are entitled to use force to stop them, and that includes shooting them. For that reason any burglar shot dead by the owner of the property is unlikely to result in a conviction—I've never heard of a case— and most often the matter will not even reach a court. The only white Weizmann ever killed was a twenty-five-year-old railway stoker and Weizmann shot him from behind. His defence was that he had made a citizen's arrest and it worked."

"It's sick, Freek."

A quick expression of annoyance passed over Freek's face. "Don't tell me it's sick. It's the way things work. It's the law. It is that way and that's all there is to it. At least it protects law-abiding people."

Yudel saw no point in debating the matter. "Where is his place?"

The expression remained for only a moment, leaving a vague shadow on his face. "Myburgh Street, corner of Hayes. It's near that corner where the whores are."

"Whores?"

"Prostitutes, Yudel, ladies of the night, bad women, street-walkers," Freek explained.

"I know what whores are." Yudel felt hurt.

36

"It didn't seem like it. The corner they operate from is just across the road from Weizmann's place."

"I thought prostitution is illegal."

"Which are you more interested in—the whores or Weizmann?"

"That's a helluva thing to ask," Yudel said.

"I'm not in the Vice Squad, Yudel, and I won't take a transfer there. I don't give a damn about the whores."

"Okay. Let's talk about Weizmann. What's wrong with his hands?"

"Apparently there's something wrong with his circulation and he has gangrene at all the extremities. I understand his feet are also bandaged all the time. Every few months or years he loses a joint of a finger or a toe."

"Dear Christ," Yudel said, "how bloody awful."

"It is. You could say they are amputating him inch by inch. It's only a matter of time before he can no longer hold a gun. Already the forefinger is down to a stump on his right hand. He pulls the trigger with his middle finger. He must have practised a lot because he still hits what he aims at."

"How long has this been going on?"

"About ten years."

"More or less since the killings began."

Freek nodded in agreement. He looked away from Yudel, moved uncomfortably in his seat and tried to make his expression of face as stern as possible. Yudel knew the ritual as one that preceded Freek making one of his rare confessions of uncertainty. "I tried to interest the Department of Justice in doing something more positive about him, but I don't get anywhere. My own bosses tell me I'm in Johannesburg to help out, not to tell them how to run things. I'll soon be going back to Pretoria and they like to remind me of it. The only one who ever tried to do anything about Weizmann was the widow of Malherbe, the stoker. She sued him for the loss of her husband. I think some liberal outfit gave her the money. But she lost. Even on appeal Weizmann won."

"One thing I never learnt last night—is he married?"

"To a niece of Jan Moolman, ex-president of the Senate. The relationship is not close though. I think old Moolman is probably barely aware of her existence. Weizmann's a strange animal, Yudel. He was born and bred Jewish, but he lives as an

37

Afrikaner with Afrikaners now. Not the best sort of Afrikaners, I'm afraid." This was not the way Freek liked to talk about his people. No man loved the Afrikaner more than Freek, but he was not blind to their weaknesses, even if he did not always readily admit to them.

"I'll have to see her," Yudel said. "One more thing. He said you forced him to come and see me."

"In a previous hearing, when he was acquitted, the court ordered him to see a psychiatrist. It was years ago, in '74. And he ignored it. Of course nobody bothered about it, even with more killings since then. Until this latest thing. I told him I'd have him behind bars in twenty-four hours unless he came to you."

Freek stopped speaking suddenly and in the silence each could almost feel the other's thoughts. "What are we going to do?" Yudel asked at last.

"There's only one thing. You have to cure him so he won't do it any more."

THREE

FOUR HOURS AFTER Yudel left Freek's Johannesburg office he was in his study and Johnny Weizmann was seated opposite him. As on the previous evening he was holding his back straight and his head carefully erect. His face also held the initial look of calm and dignity that Yudel had seen there before and, again, it was in the other man's eyes that he could see that it was not real.

"How are you today?"

"Very well. Very well." He raised both hands in a brief gesture of gratitude, immediately returning them to his lap. "I thank the Lord that he spared us all to see this day."

The moist almost pleading eyes held Yudel's attention. He wondered to which Lord the other man was referring—the Jewish one of his beginnings or a possible later affection. If he was to know and understand the whole man, such shades of meaning would be important to Yudel. "Yes, he spared us all," Yudel said. He was interested in who Weizmann included in "us all", but he would have preferred to find out without asking him.

"I told my wife this morning how wonderful it is that the Lord has spared us all. We have much to be thankful for."

"You have children?"

"Two beautiful girls, twins. They are both married now. And we've all been spared, the girls and their husbands, the grand-children and me and my wife."

"No one has been sick?" Yudel asked. He wondered why it was so surprising that the Lord had spared them all.

"No one. None of us has ever been sick. We have so much to be thankful for." Yudel thought he saw a softness in the sad defeated eyes that had not been there the day before. There was also something in the nature of his gratitude at having been spared that gave Yudel cause to think he had been drinking to strengthen himself for this meeting. Weizmann had probably needed a few shots of something odourless to get him through Yudel's questioning. "I thank the Lord every day for sparing us."

"If no one has been sick," Yudel said, "it seems normal that you were all spared."

"I'm very thankful to the Lord."

"I understand that, but no one has been sick."

"I am very thankful for that. We have all been spared to see this day." Weizmann was smiling at Yudel, his eyes soft and pleading and hopeless, asking him, Be glad with me. Don't dig into my soul for things I would rather leave buried. Just be glad with me.

But, for Yudel, that was not possible. "Your brother was not spared," he said.

Weizmann drew slightly back in the chair, putting a little more distance between himself and Yudel. "They killed my brother," he said. "I saw his body. They beat him to death."

"He did not live with you?"

"No. If he lived with me it would never have happened. He had a flat near to my shop. They came in the night and broke into his flat and beat him to death. All for three hundred rands. He should have stayed with me. I protect what is mine. I look after my wife and my girls. Those little grandchildren of mine— no one will get near them. I'll see that they're well looked after. I tell them the child must not throw away the father and the father must not throw away the child. We must look after each other. The Lord says so. Look what happened to my brother."

Yudel was beginning to understand. He was beginning to grasp the fear with which his patient lived and he was beginning to see that the fear was not for himself alone. "Where does the danger come from? From the streets?"

"You walk out of the door and you are alone." Weizmann could no longer look at him and the softness had left his eyes. He looked quickly round the room, searching for a way to escape, as if he was on those lonely night streets now among the hostile ones that he knew to be waiting for him. "No one cares about you. No one does anything. No one will come to help you. You are all alone. I have seen kaffirs attacking old people and no one goes to help. I am the only one. I always try to help other people. And I look after my own. I watch over them. If I have to go out and my wife or the girls or the grandchildren are there, I see that the son-in-laws are there as well. I never leave them alone. I never let them go out in the street alone at night." He paused for a moment, seeming to be searching for words, looking for some way to make Yudel understand how great the dangers were. "We help other people. And we help the police. We check kaffirs in the streets to see if they've got passes. And if they haven't we take them to the police station."

"Who helps you in this?"

"My son-in-laws. And I've also got friends. I've got good friends. Some are policemen. We stick together."

"Then you are not alone."

"At night you are alone. There is nobody else there." Weizmann was anxious, almost frantic to persuade Yudel. "My friends are at home. And there is nobody else. The streets are full of kaffirs. They want everything, but they don't do nothing. They want everything for nothing."

"But the police are there to protect you."

"I attend to my own business. Most of the time the police are not there. They are not there when you need them."

"Is it just the blacks then?"

"No. White youths too. Mostly it is the blacks loafing on the streets, but white youths too. They have been falling in with the wrong company. They didn't grow up hard like I did. I grew up hard. It's good for you. I had to learn the hard way. You can ask my sister, Mrs Sammel . . ."

"Mrs Sammel? Does she also live in Johannesburg?"

"Yes. She lives in Malvern. You can ask her. We grew up hard. But it's good for you. You learn to walk a straight path." Weizmann held both hands in front of him, one above the other, pointing straight ahead. "I learnt to walk a straight path. I like a man who doesn't go to the one side or the other. A man must walk straight." Then as always he became aware of his hands and dropped them quickly, almost wincing as he did it. "These youngsters don't walk straight. They never grew up hard. They had a soft life. That's what's wrong with them. That's why they don't walk a straight path."

"Is it very important to you that a man must live correctly?" Yudel framed the question as carefully as he knew how.

Weizmann's manner was becoming more forceful. It seemed that this strange little man to whom the police had sent him was

41

at last understanding him, perhaps understanding how difficult life was for him. He tried to push home his imagined advantage. "A man must live the right way. He must not wander off to the right or to the left. He must walk a straight path." His shoulders moved as he almost raised his hands to gesticulate, but this time he was able to restrain them. "If a man grows up hard he learns to live the right way."

"Your daughters—did they grow up hard?"

"I look after my daughters." For a moment Weizmann's face was shocked. "I look after my daughters," he repeated.

"Your father?" Yudel asked. "Did you grow up in your father's home?"

"Yes. My father was a good man. You have to do what your father tells you." It was said without thinking, an almost unconscious reaction.

"You always did what your father told you?"

"Always. You have to obey your father. You can't throw your father away."

"Of course you can't," Yudel said. "I want you to know that you can afford to feel safe here though. We never have any trouble here."

"Here it is different. This is Pretoria. I would have no trouble if I lived in Pretoria. In Johannesburg it's bad. Most of all in Hillbrow where I stay."

"But it's safe here," Yudel assured him.

"I know. Here it's safe."

Yudel had a problem. Under any normal sort of conditions he would have taken a long time over Weizmann. There would be many visits. He would try over many months to help this sad tortured man reach some measure of wholeness. But now he did not know how much time he had. He might have years. Or the shopkeeper might kill again next month. Next week. Tonight. Yudel knew that he would have to try a short cut. And he had no guarantee of success. "It is very safe here," Yudel repeated, "You are with friends. We are all friends here. I grew up as you did. And we are safe here." He waited, trying not to rush things, trying to let his words, spoken softly and smoothly, sink through, deep into Weizmann's mind. "We are safe here, very safe here. And we are friends. And, because we are friends and because we trust each other, I want you to put yourself into

42

my hands for a short time." Yudel was naturally a very talented hypnotist. It was not only what he said that was effective, but also the way it was said, and the way he changed his tactics and manner for each particular subject. Also he did not limit himself to a particular method for an individual subject. He fitted his induction method to the needs of the subject at that moment.

For a short while he continued to reassure Weizmann, telling him that he was among friends, that all would be well, there was nothing to worry about, keeping the tone of his voice smooth and even, allowing his eyes to half close so that Weizmann, looking at him, would be lulled even further. Yudel had doubted that the shopkeeper in his present state would yield easily to hypnosis. Weizmann seemed too suspicious of everyone, including Yudel, and too fearful, to allow his mind to slide that easily into Yudel's care. But he was a tired man, sick at heart of all that was closing in upon him, of the dangers in the streets, the threats to himself and his family that only he could discern. The warmth and relaxation that flooded upwards through his body was an immediate relief and he yielded to it without resistance. Yudel told him to be aware of his feet, of the tingling in them as they relaxed, to feel the warmth from his feet flow gently upward. He allowed Yudel more control than had seemed possible, for a short while forgetting all his problems and letting the other man's voice coax the warm relaxing sensation up from his feet until it filled his whole body, his head, his brain . . . And Yudel slid him deep into unconsciousness, far below normal levels of awareness. It was something he would normally have waited far longer before trying, but intuitively Yudel knew that he had only a little time and he must use it well. Somewhere deep below the levels of daily thought were the roots of Weizmann's personality defects and Yudel already had some idea of where he might find them.

"You are going back into your past life," he told Weizmann. The other man's face was very calm now, his eyes closed and his chest moving regularly as if he was asleep. For the first time in Yudel's company he seemed relaxed. "Back, back, back," Yudel instructed him, "back to the time when you were twenty years old. Right back through your life and you are twenty years old again. You are at home now. I want you to tell me what you see."

The calmness was falling away from Weizmann's face. He had straightened his back in his usual way and was holding his head upright, again manufacturing that false impression of dignity and worth. His eyes opened and he looked straight at Yudel. For a moment Yudel thought that he had come out of the hypnosis, but his eyes were completely dry as Yudel had never seen them before. "What do you see?" Yudel asked.

"I must go," Weizmann told someone, but he was not talking to Yudel. "I must go. If he wants me, I can't throw him away . . ." The last word slurred off and something else seemed to follow, but Yudel could not catch the words.

"Who wants you?" Yudel asked him.

"I must go," Weizmann repeated. "I have to."

It had come so suddenly that Yudel was surprised, but already he felt himself near to what he was seeking. "Why must you go?" he asked Weizmann.

But the other man was no longer staring at him. He seemed to be sliding back into the relaxed state, the vision fading.

"I want you to go back," Yudel said. "I want you to go back to the age of seventeen. You are seventeen now. You are at home. Look around you. Tell me what you see."

Again Weizmann sat stiffly upright and opened his eyes. You learnt your methods of self-protection very young, Yudel thought, much too young for your own good. When Weizmann spoke this time his voice sounded young. The hoarseness of his adult voice was still present, but in a far softer form. "I see Mama. She is working on the tobacco. She is classifying the leaves. She is very tired. There is a light in the shed and a little bit of smoke coming from it. Dan is also there. He is also classifying. Their fingers are dirty, very dirty. They are black on the insides and under the nails is all black."

"What are you doing?" Yudel asked him.

"I am in the shed." He stopped speaking as if he had answered the question.

"But what are you doing?"

"I am in the shed where Mama and Dan are classifying."

"Have they been busy a long time?"

"They are very tired. Dan is nearly falling asleep."

"Is your mother also tired?"

"She is very tired. There are cracks in her hands."

"And what are you doing?"

"I am in the shed with the others."

"Are your hands dirty too?"

"My hands are very dirty."

"Are you also classifying the tobacco?"

"I am in the shed." Suddenly Weizmann drew himself up even more rigidly than before and the eyes he focussed on Yudel were filled with fear. "I have done my share," he said. "I am tired. I have done my share. I am finished now. I don't care. I am tired."

"Who are you talking to?"

"I've done my share. I'm tired." Weizmann did not seem to have heard Yudel's question. "I'm tired now. I'm tired." Before Yudel could question him further he had slipped away from the picture in his mind, his body again relaxing, his eyes closing.

"We are going further back," Yudel told him. "We are going back until we reach the time when you were eight years old. You are eight now. You are eight and you are at home." Yudel felt that he needed to take the image a step closer to what he wanted. "You are with your father. You are in your home and you are with your father."

Without warning Weizmann rose to his feet. The tense erectness of his posture was even more pronounced with him standing. His eyes were staring at a point above Yudel's head. It was an unbelievable way for a boy of eight to hold himself in the presence of his father. "Tell me what you see." But Weizmann made no answer. He did nothing but stand stiffly at a sort of attention and stare at the point above Yudel's head. "What do you see?" Still there was no answer. Yudel decided to provide the answer himself. "Your father is coming towards you. He is walking very slowly. He is coming towards you." Weizmann's eyes remained fixed on the same point, but he seemed to draw his head into his shoulders and drop it forward a little. "He is still coming towards you," Yudel told him. "He is only a few steps away and he is approaching you." Weizmann's head dropped further, his shoulders hunching up on either side, an eight-year-old expecting to be struck on the head. "He is reaching out," Yudel said. "He is reaching out with one hand." Weizmann was bending slightly at the knees and he seemed to

45

be shivering. Out of the corners of his eyes he was glancing quickly from side to side. Despite the crouching position some small vestige of the determinedly erect posture remained, no more than a vague shadow of a dignity to which he aspired, but that was normally denied him. "He is laying his hand on your head now. You can feel it touch your head." Weizmann ducked low, his body strangely supple, and turned as if to run for the door. The room was suddenly filled with the smell of urine and Yudel could see the darkening of his patient's trousers as the liquid flowed down the inside of them. "Your father has withdrawn his hand," Yudel told him. "He has withdrawn his hand and he is turning away. He is going away now." Holding onto the arms of the chair to steady himself, Weizmann slipped into it and fell heavily against the backrest. His whole body relaxed and his eyelids closed. "We are returning to the present time. You are returning to your normal age. The year is 1978. I am going to wake you up now and you will have forgotten everything that happened while you were in this condition." Yudel was very anxious that Weizmann should remember no part of his experience so he repeated himself, using different words to reinforce the original instruction. "You will forget everything that happened while you were under," he said. "You will remember no part of it at all." He paused a moment, allowing his words to sink through to the deep areas of the other man's thought processes. "And now you are going to wake up. When I count to three you are going to wake up refreshed and you will remember nothing that took place within the last ten minutes. One, two, three."

Weizmann opened his eyes and immediately the clearness and sureness of his young man's eyes were gone and replaced by the watery defeated eyes Yudel had got to know. "We had a little accident," he said gently, "but it's not important."

Something had changed in the other man and Yudel could see it. The pretence of dignity and the careful posture: both were gone. Weizmann was sinking back in the chair, seeming to draw away from Yudel. In reply to Yudel he could manage no more than a quick nodding of his head. Yudel interpreted it to mean, I am fine. I need nothing.

"I'll take you to the bathroom where you can clean yourself up. I'll lend you a pair of clean trousers." Yudel had come round the desk and was reaching out to take Weizmann by the arm.

The other man drew his arm away, partly turning in his seat to avoid the touch. "I've got to go," he mumbled. "I'm dirty."

"I'll take you to the bathroom. You can clean up here. I'd like you to stay a little longer tonight." But Weizmann was getting up, not moving forward out of the chair, but slipping over the armrest to the side, not getting any closer to Yudel than was necessary. Part of Yudel had been expecting Weizmann to flee and he had him by the arm before he was half way to the door. "Don't go yet. Stay a little longer," he said.

"I've got to go. I'm late." The older man was standing quite still as if it would not be possible for him to break Yudel's grip on his arm and that even to try would be unthinkable, but he was facing the door and had turned right away from Yudel.

"Don't you want to clean up first?"

"I'm late. I've got to go."

"But don't you want to clean up?"

"I've got to go. My wife is waiting."

"It won't take long to clean up. You'll feel better for it. I think you should."

"I'm late. I can't stay any longer."

"You should still have some of the pills I gave you. Do you still have some?"

Weizmann nodded. His head was bowed and he was looking at Yudel out of the top of his eyes. From one of his pockets he brought the bottle, still three-quarters full, held it up for Yudel to see and quickly replaced it.

"That's fine. Have you taken them as I told you?"

He nodded quickly again. "Will you come back tomorrow evening at the same time?" There was no answer and Weizmann was being very careful not to look at him. "I have to see you again tomorrow evening. Will you come?"

Weizmann nodded a third time, but Yudel knew that the gesture was a lie. The shopkeeper would not willingly be coming on the next evening or ever again. "Will you take the pills the way I told you to?" Again the quick nodding and Yudel was not sure whether he would or would not take them. "I want you to understand how important it is for you to come again tomorrow. If you aren't able to come to me, I'll certainly come to you."

Weizmann pulled towards the door. "I've got to go. I'm late."

There was no law that allowed psychologists to restrain their patients physically without first going through complicated legal wrangles and had such a law existed Yudel would have had no faith in his ability to make use of it. He released the other man's arm, but followed him as he went through the house to the front door. "It is really very important for me to see you tomorrow night," Yudel told the retreating back. "We are very close to ending your problems." As he reached the front door Yudel took hold of his arm again. "Do you understand?" he asked. But some desperate knowledge within Weizmann would not allow him to stop. He shook himself free.

Yudel stood in the open door and watched Weizmann walk down the path with his peculiar hobbled walk—the result of missing toes, eaten away by the encroaching gangrene. Crossing the road to his parked car, he seemed to try consciously to regain something of his erect posture. His hands were plunged deep into the pockets of his jacket where no one would see them and only he would know of them.

FOUR

"IS THAT SAD-LOOKING man gone?" Rosa asked. She was already seated at the dinner table.

Yudel sat down opposite her. "Yes, he's gone."

"What's wrong with his hands?"

Yudel told her.

"That's awful." But before her sympathy could become something believable she was talking again. "He's one of the patients you like, isn't he?" Rosa's voice sounded bored and the expression of her face indicated only the most casual interest.

Her manner was too uninterested to be true, Yudel decided. "What's that supposed to mean?" he asked.

"There are some patients you like and some that you don't like and he is one that you like. Isn't that true?"

Yudel could see the direction in which Rosa was trying to steer the conversation and he tried to slide out of it. "My conduct is always guided by professional considerations," he said, wishing that he could sound less pompous while saying it.

Rosa was not to be avoided that easily. "But it's true, isn't it?"

Yudel sighed. "It is true that I find some cases more interesting than others. That's not unusual, I shouldn't think."

"Yudel, you don't just find some cases more interesting than others. Some cases become a grand passion and some you just chase away or ignore."

Yudel shrugged. "Perhaps."

Rosa was getting into her stride. Her voice was growing in volume and decisiveness and she was dishing up the cottage pie with brisk agitated little movements. "Perhaps? What about Mrs Rosenkowitz, Mrs White and Mrs Atkins last night?"

Yudel took his plate from Rosa and started eating. It was not a bad cottage pie at all. That was something he had to grant Rosa. She was a much-better-than-average cook. "Nothing wrong with them," he mumbled through a mouth three-quarters filled with cottage pie.

"Nothing wrong with them? Their doctors referred them to you. They had reason to think that there was something wrong with them." She was leaning across the table, pointing her fork at Yudel in a menacing manner and waggling it up and down for effect as she talked. As she stopped speaking a piece of mashed potato detached itself from the prongs of her fork and flew into Yudel's plate. He looked down at the erring piece of potato and then into Rosa's face as if wondering whether the incident was significant in any way. "Sorry," she said.

"Rosa." Yudel said her name slowly, almost thoughtfully. "Rosa, there is nothing wrong with those women that a kick in the jack wouldn't fix. Their problem is that they are bored." He was explaining the matter carefully to her. "They sit at home, conducting tea parties, without any form of employment. They are overrun by servants who do all the work around the house. They have nothing to do except discover all sorts of ailments within themselves. They are leeches on the backside of humanity. They should be called up for military service or something."

Rosa drew herself up as far as was possible in a sitting position. "That's ridiculous," she said. "In any event, they pay."

"This preoccupation of yours with money is a pocket of immaturity in your make-up," Yudel said. He was being a very superior person.

"Immaturity." Rosa seemed likely to explode. For a moment Yudel thought that she was going to throw her fork at him, not just the bit of mashed potato. "A pocket of immaturity? You sit in your study with a fast asleep patient for hours on end, letting the living-room fill up with other patients and then you ignore them . . ."

"I was busy," Yudel said.

". . . You ignore them flat—and I have a pocket of immaturity?"

"Rosa, you are not being fair. I am not a lazy man. I could not see private patients when we had the flat. Now that we have a house I am trying to make us some extra money by seeing patients. I don't think you are being fair. I work long hours."

Rosa ignored Yudel's defence. "Immaturity," she said slowly, her mind considering the meaning of the word, exploring any

50

hidden connotations it might have. "I am trying to be fair, Yudel. And I am trying to be patient. I am willing to forget about this immaturity business, but I can't ignore the fact that if you don't fancy a patient you just push them aside."

"I saw quite a lot of patients last month. I don't think you are being fair." Yudel was on the defensive, but this was not unusual in his dealings with his wife. If it had been any other way he would probably have been too surprised to make use of the advantage.

"Don't talk about last month," Rosa said. "Remember what happened to last month's accounts."

"It was an accident, Rosa. It could have happened to anyone. They got mislaid on my desk. That's all."

"That's all. The condition of that desk denotes a pocket of immaturity."

Yudel did not answer. Instead he gave the cottage pie his full attention. After a while he glanced at Rosa. She was looking fixedly at her plate and was eating with the sense of purpose of the truly frustrated. Yudel reflected that it was a rather sad end to a rather sad conversation. So many of their conversations ended in a similar sort of way. It was no way to live. "Rosa," he said at last, "we've got to do a little better than this."

"That's what I feel, Yudel," Rosa said, not unkindly. "We've got to get the accounts out on time and you've got to look after your patients. That's very important. I'm glad you're getting to see that."

Oh what the hell, Yudel thought.

Rosa looked curiously at him. "That is what you meant, isn't it?"

Yudel nodded vaguely at her and finished the cottage pie. For company Rosa's cottage pie beat her hands down any day of the week.

They had finished the meal and were having coffee when the front door bell rang. Rosa got up to answer it, walking purposefully across the room—her goose step, as Yudel thought of it. He heard her say, "Good evening," and then, "Yes, he's here. Shall I call him?" her voice sounding troubled and hesitant, and finally, "All right. Come inside."

Two men followed Rosa into the room. One of them looked to be in his middle forties and the other about twenty years younger. They were both wearing conservative suits, plain white shirts and rather dark colourless ties. They were definitely not dressed to attract attention and their clothing could have come out of the same wardrobe. The senior of the two reached out his right hand towards Yudel. "Mister Gordon? I am Captain Dippenaar. This is Warrant Officer Marais. I wonder if you could spare us a moment." He spoke English carefully and with a strong Afrikaans accent.

Yudel had risen to his feet and he shook hands with the man called Dippenaar, then with the other man. "Police?" he asked.

"Yes. We wondered if you could spare us a moment." It was a friendly request. Dippenaar was smiling at him. His eyes were wide-set and soft brown, but he did not look directly into Yudel's eyes when talking to him.

"Of course," Yudel said. "What can I do for you?"

"We think that you might be able to help us. Do you think you could?"

It was an unusual question. Yudel was a prison psychologist. His work consisted of helping the police. It was not normally necessary for them to request it. Yudel looked from one bland smiling face to the other. "Of course, gentlemen. I often work with the police. If you know who I am you'll know that."

"Yes, we know that." The statement was left hanging, possibly suggesting that what Yudel had said was of some interest, but did not resolve anything.

"Would you like some coffee?" Rosa asked.

"Thank you very much. We'd like that," Dippenaar told her, smiling warmly in her direction if not directly at her.

"Sit down," Yudel said. He followed his own instruction, sitting down at the dining table, and watched the two policemen sit down opposite him.

For the first time the younger policeman spoke. He was a thick-set man with a pudgy formless face. To Yudel he looked brutalised, a man who might have seen much ugliness and participated in most of it. He glanced at a bookshelf, closely-packed with psychology textbooks and paperback novels, and seemed to direct what he said more at Dippenaar than at Yudel. "Just like the communists' houses—books everywhere." Then he looked at Yudel and grinned at him, as if trying to tell him, It's all right, old chap. I know you aren't a communist.

Yudel looked at the younger policeman, then curiously at the bookshelf, wondering if there might be something wrong with it. The word "communist" was a feared one in the society in which they lived. Associated with it were 90 and 180 day periods of detention without any trial whatsoever, restriction orders imposed entirely at the will of the political police, house arrest orders confining the victim to his house or apartment, prison sentences . . . It was not a description many South Africans wanted to have linked to themselves.

But the two policemen were both smiling broadly, apparently eager to show Yudel their friendly intentions. "I wonder if they read them all," Dippenaar said to Yudel.

"Did you come here to borrow a book?" Yudel asked. From where he was sitting he could see that Rosa was standing close behind the kitchen door, ostensibly waiting for the coffee to boil, but in fact listening to the conversation.

Dippenaar smiled at Yudel, then turned and smiled at Marais. "No. We thought you might be able to help us."

"Of course," Yudel assured him. "As I said just now I am willing to help you." He looked intently at Dippenaar. The policeman seemed in no hurry to continue. Dippenaar looked at Yudel with his soft eyes, then at Marais, then half-turned in the direction of the kitchen as if wondering where the coffee was, deliberately prolonging the moment. Eventually he turned towards Yudel again, a little smile around his mouth, still assuring Yudel of his favourable intentions, but still not looking directly into Yudel's eyes. Even then he waited before asking the question that had brought him there. "I believe Mister Johnny Weizmann has come to you for . . . er . . . treatment. Is that true?"

Yudel was aware that some sort of game was being played with him. He was also aware that its probable object was to ensure that they got what they wanted from him. And now it was his opportunity to join the game. He looked inquisitively at Dippenaar, trying to imitate the policeman's own expression, turned to look briefly at Marais, then back at Dippenaar and, in the same way as the policeman, he waited before answering. "Why?" he asked.

The smile remained on Dippenaar's lips and the voice was gentle and polite. "That's not important, Mister Gordon," he said.

53

Yudel tried to keep the inquisitive look on his face and said nothing.

Dippenaar moved in his chair as if the position he was in was no longer as comfortable as it had been. There was the smallest hint of chagrin in his expression. Glancing down at the ground, he asked, "Is Johnny Weizmann a patient of yours?"

"Are you involved in the inquest?"

Out of the corners of his eyes Yudel could see Marais turn quickly to his senior officer, then glance back at Yudel. Clearly the way this question and answer session was going, was a new experience for him. It was not easy for Dippenaar to keep smiling and to sound casual when he spoke again. "Please, Mister Gordon, it will help if you answer my question."

"It would help if you answered mine."

"We aren't getting anywhere, are we?" The smile was still on his face and the voice was still polite, but the constraint that kept them that way was obvious to Yudel.

"I'm afraid we aren't. Psychologists don't give out information about their patients."

Dippenaar made a quick impatient gesture with one hand. "I only asked if he was a patient."

"That's the part I can't answer."

The policeman's smile grew broader. He seemed to feel that he had won a point. "Then I can assume that he is your patient."

Yudel said nothing. He continued looking at the policeman in the same inquisitive way. The second policeman gave a short unexpected chuckle. "This reminds me of the Muntu Majola case," he said. Yudel looked at his face and then at Dippenaar's. Now both of them were staring keenly at him. Without turning to look at her, he could see that Rosa was still in the kitchen doorway, watching and listening. He raised his eyebrows still further and gave Dippenaar the full benefit of his curious attention.

"Then you won't say any more than that?" Dippenaar asked at length.

Suddenly Yudel smiled his broadest most friendly smile (Rosa would have called it a grin). "It's a question of professional ethics, gentlemen," he said. "I'm sure you understand."

"It can be that sometimes other things are more important," the second policeman, Marais, said.

Yudel ignored the remark and smiled at Dippenaar. "I'm sure you understand," he repeated.

Dippenaar got to his feet with Marais following. "If you're not willing to help us we might as well go, I suppose."

Yudel got quickly to his feet, raising his hands in a friendly helpless gesture. "Any time I can help you any other way you only need to call."

The policemen showed themselves out and Yudel watched through the living-room window as they went down the path to their car. He turned away from the window and went straight to the telephone, brushing past Rosa on the way. "They didn't wait for their coffee . . . Yudel?"

"Just a moment, Rosa." He was dialling Freek's number.

"The Jordaan home." One of Freek's daughters answered the phone.

"Bapsie, is your father in?" Yudel asked in Afrikaans.

"It's Bettie, Uncle Yudel."

Yudel waited for her to call her father. After a few seconds he became aware that he was listening to the child's breathing on the other end of the connection. "Aren't you going to call your father?" he asked.

"It's Bettie, Uncle Yudel," the child said again.

Yudel sighed. "Hello, Bettie. May I speak to your father?"

"Yes, Uncle Yudel." He heard her running away from the phone and her voice in the distance. "Pappie. Pappie. Uncle Yudel is on the phone."

"Yes, Yudel," Freek said. He sounded a little sleepy, a pleasant after-dinner condition.

"I've had a couple of your colleagues round. They want to know if I'm treating Weizmann."

"Really?" The sleepy sound of his voice was gone.

"What are they? Members of your team?"

"No . . ." Freek considered what Yudel had told him.

"They wouldn't tell me if they are working on evidence for the inquest. In fact they wouldn't tell me anything."

"Don't worry about it." Yudel heard the sound of Freek yawning on the other end of the connection. "I wouldn't worry about it. Some routine thing." The entire tone of Freek's voice had changed. The brief interest Yudel had heard in it had gone as quickly as it had arrived.

55

"But why wouldn't they answer my questions?"

"Policemen normally expect to ask questions, not answer them." Freek yawned again. "Listen, Yudel, I'm watching a good programme on earthquakes. You can tell me about it some other time. You and Rosa are coming for dinner next week . . ."

"Next week? Listen, Freek . . ."

"Ah, come on, Yudel. I'm missing my programme. See you next week."

Yudel heard the click as Freek hung up. Rosa was standing close enough to him to listen to most of the conversation. "He hung up," Yudel told her.

"What's been going on, Yudel?" she asked. "Who are those people?"

"They came to find out whether I'm treating Weizmann."

"I heard that. But why? Who are they?"

"I don't know—policemen."

"They are security policemen, Yudel."

"Nonsense."

"I don't think it's nonsense—the way they talk about communists . . ."

Yudel's dealings with the police and prison authorities had covered a wide field in the past, but he had never had dealings with the Special Branch. He had no experience by which to judge the accuracy of Rosa's guess, but he also wanted to set her mind at rest. "I don't think they are security policemen. They're probably CID."

"If they were CID Freek would have known about them." Rosa paused a moment, looking intently at Yudel, possibly studying him for potentialities that had so far gone unnoticed. "You haven't been up to something, have you, Yudel?" She shook her head as if to rid it of the thought. "No, you haven't," she decided. "You aren't built that way."

"Well. There's nothing to worry about," Yudel said. He was speaking for Rosa's benefit. "We've done nothing wrong, so there's nothing to worry about."

"I don't know . . ."

"No one can do anything to us, Rosa," Yudel assured her. He was steering her into the living-room and towards her favourite chair in front of the television set. "We're quite safe. There's nothing to be worried about."

56

"But, Yudel . . ."

"We're all right," Yudel recited. He was not listening to his wife's protestations. "We've done nothing wrong." He was barely even listening to himself. His mind was filled with the events of the last two evenings and Rosa was only a distraction. "There's nothing to worry about." He had led Rosa to her chair and she sat down. She was still looking at Yudel so he grinned at her and nodded in the direction of the television tube. Then he drifted out of the room and into his study, giving her a little wave of the hand as he went.

Much had happened since the previous evening and, as he so often did when trying to straighten out his thinking, Yudel sat at his desk in the darkness, allowing his brain to work over all he had learnt about Weizmann and all he had not learnt about his most recent visitors. One question dominated all others in his thinking—who are they? Rosa's guess was disturbing to him. She was right as far as the remark about communists' houses was concerned. Ordinary policemen, not having the same sort of experience, would not be likely to make that remark. And she was also right that Freek should have known them. And if they were Special Branch, what was their interest in Weizmann? Perhaps they were not police at all. He should have insisted on seeing their identification.

But, more important than them, was Weizmann himself. The old shopkeeper, so isolated and vulnerable, the victim of his tortured state of mind and gangrenous body: when would his fear drive him to kill again? What was it that had twisted the most natural of instincts, defence of the territory, the nest, the home: what had subverted that basic drive until it reached its present distorted condition? Yudel wondered if he would be back the next day to keep his appointment.

He had been sitting at his desk for no more than five minutes, unaware of the sounds coming from the television set in the lounge, when he heard a muttered oath from the garden, "God damn it," immediately followed by the sound of a body breaking through shrubbery. He got quickly to his feet, armed himself with a can of anti-burglar spray, guaranteed to cover the intruder with red paint and disable him for long enough for you to phone the police and get out of the house to call the neighbours, should they feel inclined to assist—armed with this can he switched on the outside light, drew open the curtain a fraction and peered out. Freek was stumbling through one of Rosa's flowerbeds and cursing to himself.

Yudel opened the sliding door to let him in. "Switch out the light," Freek said. He looked irritable, as if he may have been sleeping and was not fully awake yet.

"What are you up to?" Yudel began.

"You better tell me about them," Freek said.

"I wanted to tell you on the phone."

"When dealing with certain people it's wisest not to use the telephone. That's also the reason I came in through the garden. I didn't want to park in front." Freek took Yudel's shoulder in one hand, holding it firmly. At such times with Freek's strong fingers clamped onto his shoulder, seeming to steady him, Yudel always felt like a child. Freek seemed to think that he needed protection. "Now tell me all about it."

Yudel told him.

When he had finished Freek was silent for a while. At length he released Yudel's shoulder and sat down on the edge of the desk. "Did you ask to see their identification?"

"No," Yudel said. "I should have, I suppose."

"A man of your experience, Yudel—of course you should have. It doesn't matter though. I'm almost sure there is a Captain Dippenaar in Security. I'm not so sure about Marais."

"Freek, there is one thing," Yudel remembered. "They dropped a name while they were here. It had nothing to do with the conversation. They slipped it in neatly and then both of them sat back to watch for my reaction."

"What was the name?"

"Muntu Majola. Do you know him?"

Freek looked deeply puzzled. "I think I've heard of him. If I remember right Security is looking for him. I think the story is that he has killed a couple of their men."

"Is that all you know?"

"I don't pay much attention to Security's things. To me they're like the Vice Squad. Somebody else can do it."

"What could this man have to do with Johnny Weizmann or me?" Yudel asked. The two men looked at each other for a long time before Freek shrugged with the smallest, but most doubtful movement of his shoulders. He did not know either.

FIVE

IT HAD HAPPENED because of all the important things currently filling his mind, Yudel told himself. He had reversed the car just the way he always did, having first brought it forward into the bay opposite, then driven it straight back. But this time the concrete pillar had been obstructing his path. He had broken the left tail light and dented the bumper.

"This one in duplicate," the clerk said. "This one in triplicate. I'll give you three copies so you won't make a mistake. Just one copy of this one. Then you have to give this one to Doctor Williamson to fill in. That's the disciplinary one. On that one Doctor Williamson has to say whether he wants any action taken against you or whether you've learnt your lesson and won't do it again."

"Thanks," Yudel said.

"There also has to be a diagram in duplicate, showing the positions of all the vehicles involved . . ."

"There was just mine."

"Then you have to show its position and the position of the stationary object that you struck. You have to mark the point of contact on both copies with a cross in red—it must be in red. Have you reported it to the police?"

"No. It didn't happen on a public road. It happened in our parking garage."

"That's a good one," the clerk said.

"Isn't it? Is this everything now?"

The clerk looked thoughtfully at the little pile of paper between them. "I think so." Yudel gathered up the papers and was about to leave when the clerk spoke again. "Mister Gordon, I wish you would have a word with Doctor Williamson."

"About what?" Yudel asked.

"This morning he came in here and asked me if I didn't know my job. He had some subsistence claims that he thought I'd filled

59

in wrong. There were some damn fool junior clerks in the office too. I just don't think you should speak to a SACO that way in front of junior clerks. It's not right." The clerk had been promoted recently and was more than a little touchy about the dignity of his rank. "And he wasn't even right. I was right." Yudel made a sympathetic clucking sound and started edging towards the door. "Perhaps you could speak to him. It's difficult for me." Yudel made his clucking sound again. He was more than half way to the door and still moving steadily. "I'm not cross about it, but I'll be glad if you could mention it to him. It just isn't right to speak to a SACO that way in front of a bunch of damn fool junior clerks."

Yudel had reached the door. "I'll speak to him," he promised, gave the clerk a reassuring wave of his free hand and had forgotten about the status problems of Senior Assistant Control Officers before he had reached his office at the far end of the passage. He sat down at his desk, put the little pile of papers aside and started drawing the diagram that was to illustrate how he had hit the pillar. Yudel was no draughtsman. At his first attempt the car, shown from above, was a strange narrow trapezium instead of a rectangle. Yudel could not believe that anyone would recognise it or be able to understand the diagram. At his second attempt the car was larger than the parking bay it was trying to enter. Half way through the third attempt Yudel remembered that he had brought the Weizmann files with him. He pushed away the ill-fated diagrams and opened his briefcase.

Mimi had grouped the various documents under the cases to which they were related and gathered them into cardboard files. The first one that Yudel withdrew was marked "Cissy Abrahamse. 6 June 1978." Yudel looked at the calendar on his desk. Today was Friday. The 6th had been the previous Wednesday, only nine days before. He went quickly through the papers in the file, not finding it necessary to read every word, his practised eye picking out the points that would be important. The file contained a statement by Weizmann, telling how he had come downstairs after hearing a sound in the storeroom of his shop and how he had fired in self-defence when a young woman armed with a hammer charged at him out of the darkness; a statement by the investigating officer, telling how he found the body of the girl shot twice through the abdomen and describing her wounds, how she had been holding a two-pound hammer in one hand; a note in Freek's handwriting that there would be an inquest on Friday the 22nd, in a week's time, and a statement by a Mrs Sinclair who lived in a flat across the road, saying that she had been looking out from her balcony and had seen a Bantu man passing the side door of Weizmann's shop. The man had started running at the sound of shots coming from inside. She had called the police. And finally a social worker's report on Billy, the girl's brother. It had taken her three days to find anyone who knew who the boy was and that person had been the landlady who let Cissy's mother the room in which they had lived. The social worker had reported her as saying, "That lot were always drunk. I'm not surprised."

Yudel dropped the file into his briefcase and withdrew a second one. Neatly printed across the front page was the name, Isaiah Zulu, and the date, 15 February 1978. Only four months previously. The file contained statements by Weizmann, his wife and a police sergeant. According to the contents of all three statements, Weizmann had been travelling through the silent streets of the Roodepoort industrial area late one night, having lost his way after visiting a friend in Krugersdorp, when a drunken Bantu, one Isaiah Zulu, dashed out of the shadow of a building in front of the car, leaving Weizmann no time to brake or take any other avoiding action. A note attached to the back of the file in Mimi's handwriting said that Zulu had died in hospital that night. He had suffered a rupture of the spleen and severe brain damage. Mimi's note also referred to the inquest, giving the date on which it had been held. The magistrate had decided that no one had been to blame for Zulu's death.

The phone on Yudel's desk chirped shrilly at him. He answered, "Gordon here," without pausing in his reading.

Through the barrier built up by the intensity of his interest in what he was reading Yudel heard Rosa's voice faintly. "Yudel?" All day Yudel had gone about his business mechanically while his thoughts had been filled with the Weizmann affair. Now that he was able to concentrate on it fully, it was no easy matter to break through to his attention. "Yudel-dear? Are you there?"

On the cover of the third file Mimi had printed, Jakobus

61

Malherbe. 16 December 1972. This file was very much thicker than the two Yudel had already been through. It started with Weizmann's statement to the police. All of them seemed to start with Weizmann's statement. "Yudel-dear? Is that you?" Rosa's voice was drawing closer, reaching to him through the mists caused by his concentration.

"Mmmm," Yudel said thoughtfully.

"I heard a sound in my shop," Weizmann had told the police. "My flat is directly above the shop. I fetched my revolver and went downstairs to investigate." He had started it almost identically to his statement after the killing of Cissy Abrahamse. "Two young white men were breaking into the door of the storeroom behind my shop."

"I heard you, Yudel. I know you're there." Rosa's voice finally broke through to him.

"Gordon here," Yudel said.

"I know it's you," Rosa said. "What's going on there?"

This time Yudel had listened to and recognised his wife's voice and comprehended what she was saying. "I'm reading," he said.

"Don't be late. Remember you have patients tonight."

"I won't be late."

"It's half-past three and you stop working at four on Fridays. Remember that."

"All right, Rosa. I'll be on time."

"I hope so, because Mrs Atkins is coming back this afternoon and we don't want the same thing to happen this time that happened last time. Do we?"

"No," Yudel assured her, "we don't. I won't be late. Goodbye, Rosa."

"Goodbye, Yudel. Only half an hour to knock-off time."

"All right, Rosa. Goodbye."

"Goodbye."

"I grabbed hold of one and tried to arrest him, but he pulled away and they split up," Yudel read. "One went up the road and one went down the road. I chased the one that went up the road towards Hillbrow, but he ran too fast for me. I then fired a warning shot. I tried to miss him by about six feet. The pavement is very dark in the shadow of the trees, so I lost sight of him. I found him two blocks further on near the corner of

Hayes and De Korte. He had a wound in his neck. I tried to take his pulse, but he seemed to be dead. The police came and they said he was dead."

It was that simple, Yudel thought. A warning shot had been fired and of all the places the bullet could have struck it had struck a young man and killed him and no one was guilty.

The second statement was by a Wynand van der Westhuizen who had been nineteen years old at the time and had been a close friend of Malherbe. According to van der Westhuizen they had been ". . . having a beer in the Victoria bar. We were both a little bit drunk when we passed Mister Weizmann's place. We started wrestling in front of his shop. I don't know why. We were not angry with each other. We were just playing. I think we bumped against the door of Mister Weizmann's shop. The next thing I knew the door was open and Mister Weizmann grabbed hold of Kosie. I don't know how the door got open. I broke away and ran down the road. I was round the corner already before I heard the sound of Mister Weizmann shooting . . ."

Yudel skimmed quickly through a statement by a police officer that added nothing to what he already knew, statements by the dead man's wife, mother and a clergyman, dealing with his unblemished character up to that point and one by a passer-by who had seen Weizmann fire a shot, but had not been able to tell at what he was aiming.

Towards the bottom of the file the state pathologist's report caught Yudel's attention. "Death was caused by a haemorrhage of the jugular due to the bullet wound . . . nature of the wound seems to be compatible with either a ricochet or the muzzle of the gun being held against the skin of the jaw . . ."

Immediately following the pathologist's report was a copy of the magistrate's finding. "Mister Weizmann was within his rights in firing a shot in the air. Under the circumstances he was fully entitled to fire a warning shot. The court finds that Malherbe's death was justifiable homicide." Which meant that the magistrate had decided that Malherbe was killed by a ricochet. Clearly no one fires a warning shot while holding the gun against someone's jaw. Yudel wondered how a shot fired into the air could ricochet. Off a streetlight fitting perhaps?

He was about to go on to the next file when he noticed that

it was a quarter to four. If he read another one he might be late and then there would be problems with Rosa. On the other hand he was not supposed to go home early. "We have to set an example to the non-professional staff," Doctor Williamson had told him on many occasions.

Yudel packed the files into his briefcase, left his office and strolled down the passage to Doctor Williamson's, stopped in the doorway to establish that Williamson was not in (probably slipped away early himself, Yudel thought), dashed back to his own office, scooped up his jacket and briefcase and made for the lift. As he reached out to press the calling button the lift doors opened and Doctor Williamson stepped out. Yudel saw the other man's face stiffen into a prim self-righteous expression as the pale blue eyes took him in, jacket, briefcase and all. "Have a nice weekend," Yudel said bravely as he stepped into the lift.

He saw Doctor Williamson make as if to glance at his watch, but restrain himself before he got that far. "Goodbye," he said.

"Mrs Atkins cancelled her appointment," Rosa said. "I'm not surprised. So there'll only be your Mister Weizmann. That should please you."

Yudel and Rosa were at the dining-room table, drinking coffee. "He should have been here more than an hour ago," he said.

"He can stay away as far as I am concerned, as long as he keeps those other people away too."

Yudel knew who she was talking about and he nodded slowly in agreement. That Weizmann was not going to come was something he had felt on the previous evening. He had come too close to the source of Weizmann's problem and he had done it too quickly. He knew how all human beings clung to their illusions and dishonesties, the strange distortions of reality that all need in order to go on living. Weizmann had felt the nearness to reality, the truth that he had never all his life been able to face. It was a truth that Yudel knew he had enclosed in a shell of fiction in order to protect himself against it, and now he had retreated before the prospect of having it revealed. Compounding matters, there was his urinating at their last meeting and the shame that had caused. Had Weizmann come Yudel would have been astonished.

He finished his coffee in silence, hardly hearing Rosa's few ineffectual attempts at conversation, then went into the study to phone Weizmann. He found the number of the Twin Sisters Restaurant in the Johannesburg directory. A woman with a shrill voice and a slovenly manner of speaking answered. "Hullo ja. Twin Sisters."

"Is Mister Weizmann in?" Yudel asked in Afrikaans.

"No. He's not here. Who's speaking?"

"Might he be in his flat? Has he got a telephone there?"

"There's no phone there, but he's not there. He's out. Who's speaking?"

"Thanks very much," Yudel said. "That's what I wanted to know."

"Who's speaking?"

Yudel hung up and went in search of Rosa. She was already settling herself in front of the television set. He looked speculatively at her and something in the nature of the look alerted her. "You're not going out?" What she meant and what Yudel knew she meant was—you're not going out and leaving me all alone on Friday evening after you've been away at work all week and I've hardly seen you : you aren't doing that?

"He's a dangerous man, Rosa. And at this stage he's my responsibility."

Rosa got quickly to her feet. "What if they come while you're away?" Her face was anxious and Yudel had no doubt to whom she was referring.

"They won't come back. There's no reason for them to come back."

"They might. I'm not staying here alone."

"This is your home, Rosa." The first uncertain beginnings of a personal hostility towards the security police were making themselves felt within Yudel. Who were these bastards to make his wife feel afraid in her own home?

"If you're going to Jo'burg you can drop me at Irena's place."

"I won't be able to come in though." Rosa's hugely obese sister and her sister's even more hugely successful husband were not among Yudel's favourite people.

65

"I just don't want to stay here alone tonight," Rosa said.

The Twin Sisters Restaurant was on the corner of Myburgh Street, a busy well-lit thoroughfare, and Hayes, a narrow tree-lined side street, dark at night because of the trees that cut out the light from the street lamps. The buildings in the area were a mixed bunch, some of them new—concrete, glass and steel, thirty or forty storeys high, housing the offices of large and affluent businesses—others were old, brick and plaster, rarely more than five or six storeys, having had their origins in an earlier, less prosperous period. The paintwork was often scarred and stained. Glass-panelled doors were perhaps not cleaned as often as had once been the case. Letter boxes with sagging hinges, dusty passages in cheap apartment buildings: all showed signs that there was not now as much money as there once had been.

By the time Yudel reached Weizmann's place it was already early evening. He stopped in the side street across the main thoroughfare from the shop, got out of the car and stood for a while in the shadow of a small struggling oak. The front of the shop and part of its side had plate glass windows through which he could see into it. The word Restaurant described it in large painted letters on one of the windows, but it was a generous description. Weizmann's place was what Yudel had known in his childhood as a fish-and-chip shop. Its front was divided into two sections. The section on the corner through which it was entered held a counter where you could buy sweets, cigarettes and cold drinks, and a second counter where you could get your fish, chips, sausages, meat balls, pigs' trotters or whatever took your fancy. Behind this counter Yudel could see the vats where the food was fried. Two women, one middle-aged and the other young, were behind the cigarette counter. He could see no one else in that section of the shop. The other section had wooden chairs and tables and a number of people were seated at them, eating and drinking. Down the side in deep shadow Yudel thought he could see the doorway that led into the storeroom at the back. Above the shop a few lights were on in the flat, but he could see no movement in any of them. Yudel waited for a break in the traffic, then crossed the road to enter the shop.

The two women turned to look at him as he came in. He

66

addressed himself to the older of the two. "Is Mister Weizmann in?" he asked her in Afrikaans.

The woman looked to be about Weizmann's age. She had very fair skin with few wrinkles, a flat ugly face and krinkly red hair. "Do you want him?"

Yudel recognised the voice as the one that had answered the telephone. "I would like to speak to him," he said.

"Can I give him a message?" She spoke in a quick abrupt, almost irritated way, her small green eyes fixed angrily on him as if he should have known better than to ask such a thing.

"Is it not possible for me to speak to him?"

"He's out." Again the quick manner of speech, the same hint of irritation. "Who can I say was seeking him?" And again the same curiosity as to his identity.

"Say Yudel Gordon came to see him. He missed our appointment this evening and I was concerned that something might have happened to him."

"Appointment?"

"Yes. He had an appointment to see me."

Suddenly the woman knew who Yudel was. He could see the moment of awareness in her face, but it was not an awareness that was filled or even tinged with pleasure. She smiled, but it did not happen naturally. The expression had to be forced into appearing. "Oh, you are . . ." She was looking for the word.

"That's right," Yudel assured her. "Is your husband in?"

"No, he's out. I don't know where he is."

There was only an archway between the room they were in and the store at the back. Yudel could see straight into it, but he could not see the stairs that connected it to the floor above. The light in the store was out and all that he could discern clearly was a set of steel shelves against the opposite wall. "I'd like to say how sorry I am about the trouble you've been having," he said. "Naturally your husband has told me about it."

The woman adopted an air of serenity. Yudel half expected her to clasp her hands before her in the manner of an angel in an Old Master. "I can only thank all the wonderful people who have stood by us," she said.

A black man in his late teens or early twenties, wearing an open-neck shirt and sports jacket, entered the shop and stopped a pace behind Yudel and to his left, waiting to be served.

Neither woman looked in his direction. "People have stood by you then?"

"All our friends have stood by us." Yudel glanced in the direction of the man who was waiting to be served and back at the woman, but she did not seem interested in his needs. "Shall I tell my husband you were seeking him?"

"Tell him I'll phone him."

"Good. I'll tell him and I'll tell him you came all the way from Pretoria to see him." She lingered over the word "all" as if emphasising the distance, possibly indicating to Yudel that she appreciated his effort. Yudel doubted that the appreciation was real.

Along the side windows there was a row of glass-fronted refrigerators, filled with cold drinks. "I think I'll have a drink," Yudel said. He went across to the nearest one, all the time conscious of Weizmann's wife watching him. He turned quickly to look at her. There was nothing in that pale hostile face to indicate that he was welcome. Yudel smiled and she turned quickly to her other customer. The man wanted cigarettes and he was served with a sort of efficient anger that seemed to say, here you can have the cigarettes and I'll take your money, but now move your black arse out of here. On the other hand, Yudel conceded, it may have been himself that brought on her anger, not the black man. He selected his cold drink slowly, managing to get a direct look at the younger woman. She was not unattractive, but slovenly, a grubby fawn-coloured sweater hanging loosely over a too-full bosom that did not seem to have the benefit of artificial support. There was no hostility at all in her face. Meeting Yudel's eyes, she smiled at him, her mouth opening wide, revealing large yellow teeth, bright pink gums and the remainder of a meal or many meals wedged into the crevices. Yudel withdrew his earlier impression that she was not unattractive. At a guess he made her one of the twin sisters. The attitude of the two women towards each other seemed like that of a mother and daughter.

His choice fell on apple juice. He brought it to the counter and put it down in front of Weizmann's wife. "Drink it here or take it away?" she asked.

"Could I drink it here?" He gestured towards the next room with his head.

For a matter of so little importance Mrs Weizmann spent a long time considering it. "You can go and sit down," she said at last. He paid her with a note and while she fetched the change from the cash register and opened the cold drink bottle, he looked quickly round the shop. Old caked fat had collected on outer ledges and in corners of the vats. Grease-spattered walls around them did not appear to have been washed in a long time. Dust and pieces of paper wrappings littered the corners of a seemingly seldom-swept passage behind the counters.

Yudel took the bottle and his change from Mrs Weizmann and started towards the other part of the shop. He stopped in the doorway long enough to see the daughter hurry into the store where the stairs that led to the floor above were situated. Going to tell the old man not to come downstairs, he thought.

The second part of the shop held perhaps a dozen cheap wooden tables, each with four chairs. A partly open doorway led into a dark yard. The only windows were the plate glass ones on the street side and they were without curtains, so that the people at the tables were in full view of those passing on the pavement outside. Three of the tables were standing upside-down on other tables and the floors were as dirty and unswept as in the front of the shop. In the centre of the narrow corridor between the chairs an old newspaper had been dropped on the floor to soak up a pool of liquid. As Yudel stepped over it the smell of urine reached him. He selected a table as far from the newspaper as possible.

Three of the other tables were occupied. At one of them a prematurely greying man, wearing a leather jacket and jeans, was reading a copy of *The Citizen*, a government-supporting newspaper the funding of which was soon to be the subject of a national scandal. At another table two buxom women with artificial-looking blonde hair were discussing the immoral behaviour of a friend in voices that reached Yudel clearly. The third was a tired-looking man in the uniform of a bus driver, drumming his fingers on the surface of the table and looking absently in front of him. These were the whites among Weizmann's customers, less privileged than the majority of their fellows, useful people who carried their share of society's load, but had grown to maturity in surroundings that had probably not encouraged achievement. They were also those who would

69

be threatened most immediately by black advancement. Yudel had often heard their poorly articulated arguments and he felt that he understood their fears.

"My oupa fought the kaffirs for this country," Yudel had heard them say. "Now don't tell me I have to sit next to them on the bus and on the train. And don't tell me my kids have to go to school with them. Don't tell me that.

"I don't mind giving them a chance. I'm not against the kaffirs, but if they can take any job they want where will my Jannie and my Hennie get jobs?

"The government gives them everything. They give them homelands. They give them schools. They give them everything and where have you heard of a kaffir paying tax?

"I don't care a hell. They just mustn't try to mix them in with us. They must just keep them over there on the other side, far from us. I don't care what they give them. They just mustn't come mixing them in with me.

"It's all right for those rich buggers. They want the kaffirs to catch our buses. Not one of them ever catches a bus. The gentlemen from Houghton want the kaffirs in our schools, but they send their kids to private schools. They want blacks to get our jobs, then they can pay them less than they pay us. It's all right for those rich buggers, but it's different with us."

Weizmann was part of all this. It seemed possible that his shop could even be a gathering place. And the fears of these people were Weizmann's fears also. But there was more. Not every man who feared for the future of his young and who struggled to hold onto an insecure position near the bottom of his society's structure—not every such man became a killer.

On a magazine rack against one of the walls the daily newspapers were advertised for sale. Yudel could see copies of the paper that the man in the leather jacket was reading and copies of the various Afrikaans dailies, all of which were government-supporting. The other relatively liberal English papers which had the bigger readership in Johannesburg were not for sale.

The door to the yard was nudged open gently and a large alsatian came into the room, trotted slowly towards the front of the shop, stopping for a moment to sniff the urine. Mrs Weizmann appeared in the archway leading to the front, scooped up an empty cold drink box from the floor and aimed a kick at the dog who tucked away his tail and scuttled in behind the counter. "Away with you," Yudel heard her tell the dog. "Your boss likes you. I don't. You piss on the floor all the time." She moved in behind the counter again where he could not see her. From somewhere in that section Yudel could now hear the sounds of children's voices, shrill and excited, the words poorly defined. The woman was scolding again. "Why do you let the children speak English," she was saying. "You should let them speak their own language."

Yudel drank his cold drink and left. It seemed that Weizmann's problems were multiple.

"I don't know," the Greek said. "I keep no gun. I have no problems."

"No burglaries?" Yudel asked.

"I had one five years ago, then I put in burglar guards and I put in an alarm. Since then—no trouble."

"What about the other shops around here?"

"Some got guns. Some got nothing, like me. Hardly any problems. Mister Weizmann is the only one who has problems."

"Thanks," Yudel said.

There was a lot of the evening left and Yudel started down the hill in the direction of the city centre. A few blocks from Weizmann's place he reached the network of tracks from the west that streamed into Johannesburg station some thirty feet below street level. The broad stretch of tracks was crossed by a series of bridges that joined the main business area to the north side of the town, carrying the incessant streams of traffic back and forth on their daily rounds. Johannesburg was a busy city. A lot of people were getting rich and a lot were going broke. Others thought they were going to get rich, but were never going to make it. The blacks were rising faster in the scheme of things than in any other South African city and when they rioted they did it with greater anger here than anywhere else. It was a place of contrasts and extremes. There were the super-liberals who almost felt ashamed to be white. There were the most violent and desperate racialists who would willingly kill to protect a position of privilege. There were artists and railway stokers, Jews and anti-semites, nuns and whores, millionaires and the dispossessed . . . Yudel loved it all. The whole vast catalogue of human experience and motivation was there for him to observe and try to comprehend. Without this immense diversity he would have found life a dull affair.

The night was cold, but without the intensity that the Highveld's winter nights could bring. He crossed the tracks, in his mind following the likely path from which Weizmann's intruders would have come. Where he came off the bridge he turned to his right, zig-zagging his way slowly westward, among narrow streets of small Indian-owned shops: tailors, grocers, herbalists, shoe-repairers . . . The people that filled the streets, often just standing in groups and talking, were almost all members of the various and complex groupings that in South Africa fell under the general heading of "blacks".

Above the shops were the sort of flats where Cissy Abrahamse might have shared a room with her prostitute mother and little brother. They were tiny and filthy with the sort of deep reinforced dirt that would now be impossible to eradicate. It was not the griminess or the down-at-the-heel weariness of the buildings around Weizmann's shop. It was an entrenched condition that could not be eradicated by painting the old and crumbling buildings. The ancient splintering floors, the cockroach hordes, the putrefaction in the yards where no one had cleaned the overflow from the rubbish bins would all still be there tomorrow and on all the tomorrows. Along the balconies there was often washing hanging out to dry, washing that probably had to be done daily because the wearers only had one set of clothing.

It was the sort of area you can find in large cities everywhere. People whose talents are inadequate or ill-adapted to the needs of the societies in which they live, crowding together into old and cramped apartments to keep the rent low: women without other talents turning to the one talent that is easiest to learn, a surefire seller at all times and in all communities: and men, hiding the formless future from themselves, keeping going somehow, getting through each day . . .

It was the slow illimitable rise of these people that was feared by those like Johnny Weizmann and his customers. Every young man or woman who succeeded somehow in breaking with this depressed and stultifying life was a threat to the people sitting at the tables in the Twin Sisters Restaurant and to their children.

Yudel turned into a narrow alley, lined on either side by small stalls that were occupied by Indian greengrocers. The alley was packed with the people of the neighbourhood, mostly women doing the shopping for their families, making the small careful purchases that would please the kids and hopefully satisfy the husbands. In an empty stall a young African woman, dressed in a thin woollen dress and cracking patent leather shoes, with a little girl of three or four staying close to her side, was grilling mealies over a brazier. She had four on a wire grill over the coals and another ten or twelve in a fruit box next to the brazier. "Are you selling them?" Yudel asked.

"Twenty cents." She was lean and her features were good, her skin almost oriental in colour. She would have been pretty if it had not been for the weariness in her face.

"May I have one?" Yudel asked her.

"Yes, sir." She dropped her eyes while speaking to him.

Yudel stood close to the brazier, warming himself while he waited for his mealie to be grilled. The child was also close to the warmth, holding out tiny hands to the coals, the fingers spread wide. Among the people in the alley Yudel could see some who did not appear to be shopping. They seemed only to want to be in some place where there was human warmth and talk, and perhaps at the end of the evening the hawkers might give them very cheap the produce that was left and would not be good on the next day. Most of them were poorly dressed and Yudel could see that they had been that way for a long time. Were these the ones that eventually found their way into Johnny Weizmann's store? Were they the ones who, having been unable to survive the pressure of the city and without other hope, would not be able to resist the tempting opening of a storeroom door?

Yudel knew that theft was a great crime to those who possessed much. He also knew that it was a far lesser crime to those who possessed little and that it was no crime at all for those who were hungry and owned nothing. They had come to Weizmann's place in the past. Late at night when no hope had remained they had come upon the partly open door in the dark side street. They would come again in future. Of that Yudel had no doubt at all.

73

SIX

YUDEL PICKED UP the unposted letter in Rosa's handwriting as an alien object in the confusion of his desk. He took it and his brief-case with the Weizmann files to the living-room, making a detour through the kitchen to fetch a cup of coffee he had already poured, and sat down before the lifeless television set. Rosa had gone to bed as soon as they had got back from Johannesburg, at the same time instructing him not to stay up too late.

The letter occupied only one sheet of paper and was not in an envelope. Yudel sighed and looked fleetingly up at the ceiling as if assistance might be available from that direction before concentrating his attention on it. It was not addressed to him. That was something at any rate. Yudel read:

The Editor,
The Rand Daily Mail.

Dear Sir,

It is high time that your newspaper took a definite stance against the cruel and barbaric sport of bullfighting. Every year thousands of horses and bulls are inhumanly slaughtered for the entertainment of a few greedy blood-lusting human beings. Innocent young men are tricked into taking part in this dangerous pastime with promises of fame and riches and they get nothing out of it except perhaps an early death. Unless newspapers like yours wake up to the evil of bullfighting and decide to do something about it mankind is doomed to be plagued by this wickedness for all time.

Yours very sincerely,
Rosa Gordon

74

Yudel sighed again, folded the letter and put it in his shirt pocket. The fact that there was no place within six thousand miles where bullfighting was practised touched fleetingly on his thinking. When Rosa started campaigning against bullfighting it was a sure sign that she was reaching the end of her patience with him. In Yudel's profession it was termed redirected aggression. He made a mental note that he should do something about appeasing Rosa and filed it deep in the back of his mind.

Yudel arranged the files like a hand of cards in front of him on the coffee table, took a mouthful of coffee, filing another mental note that he should drink less of it, and selected a file marked John Nkabinde, 5 May 1968. The handwriting was Mimi's again. It was another name and another date on which a human being had died, this time ten years before.

The state pathologist's report was on top and according to it Nkabinde had died of a wound caused by a single bullet in the shoulder just above the heart. There were no burn marks on the skin.

The statement by the police officer was of no value, saying only that Nkabinde was found dead on the floor in Weizmann's shop. One of the plate glass windows was broken and an iron bar was found next to him.

Yudel read Weizmann's own statement with more care than he had read the others, some of the shopkeeper's phrases sticking in his mind. "I heard the sound of glass falling and went down to my shop to investigate . . . he was holding an iron bar . . . one of my windows was broken . . . I only pulled out my gun after he threatened me . . ."

The magistrate had decided that no one was to blame for Nkabinde's death.

The files told Yudel little that he did not already know. He went through them quickly, searching for some little thing that would make everything more clear and would give him a lead as to the direction he should take. Jonathan Qumbisa had died on the 21st of October 1972. According to the contents of his file he and a friend had tried to steal a van that had been parked near Weizmann's place. Weizmann had interrupted them at work and Qumbisa had died with the first bullet. The incident had taken place in Hayes Street. The second man had got away and the police had been unable to trace him. "I like helping the police," Weizmann had said in his statement. No one had been found guilty of the man's death.

Henderson Mhlope had died on the 28th of January 1968. He had been one of two robbers cornered in the store behind Weizmann's shop. He had bled to death after a bullet severed the aorta. His colleague was found guilty of breaking and entering and sentenced to a year in prison. He had not been harmed. No one was to blame for Mhlope's death.

In the early morning hours of the 9th of February 1973 Oscar Mbhele had died of multiple gunshot wounds, also in the store behind Weizmann's shop. He had been alone and had threatened Weizmann with a knife. No one could be considered responsible . . .

Feeling a growing sense of disgust inside him, Yudel pushed aside the files. In no case had any real evidence been offered. He had read only Weizmann's self-excusing explanations of what had happened in each case. And Weizmann had not kept his appointment of that evening. Yudel knew that if he refused to come for treatment something else would have to be attempted. But here the possibilities were limited and he shrank from all of them.

He would have preferred to stop reading, but the whole thing was developing the aspect of a compulsion in his mind. He snatched a new file from the coffee table.

Yudel read that after a short chase in Hayes Street one of three robbers had been shot dead. The other two had got away. The dead man had been identified as one Rakabaele Sono, seventeen years of age. It had happened at 2300 on the 18th of September 1967. A photograph of the body showed that he had been wearing only shorts and a shirt. His arms and legs had the appearance of being unusually long, but Yudel could see that this was only because of their emaciated condition. No one was guilty . . .

Mimi had done her job thoroughly. Among the others there was a file marked Daniel Weizmann, 17 December 1977. According to the police Daniel had been alone in his flat at the time he died. The district surgeon found that he had died of a heart attack. For some unexplained reason the police had taken a statement from his brother. "Often at night there were youths and blacks hanging around the flats where my brother lived. Some of them had threatened him . . ."

One line from the report by police sergeant Wolmarans alerted him. "There were no signs of violence. The body was unmarked."

Yudel remembered what Weizmann had told him. "The police took me there and he was unrecognisable. I couldn't recognise my own brother, they beat him up so much." But the police report said that the body was unmarked and the district surgeon said that Daniel had died of a heart attack. The conflict between the two versions could only mean that either the authorities had concealed the nature of Daniel Weizmann's death or that in the months since then his brother's mind had succeeded in transforming an ordinary death into a killing. Knowing Weizmann as he already did Yudel had no doubt that the authorities were not guilty on this score.

Yudel had been counting the killings and he had reached eight, the number that Freek had given him, but there were still two files left. He opened one marked Barney Tsatse, 25 December 1977. Tsatse had lived to make a statement. "I went to Mister Weizmann's shop at about ten o'clock in the morning . . . asked for a cold drink. . . . Mister Weizmann would not give me change . . . I told him, I will not go until I get change. . . . He threw a lot of pennies on the ground. While I was picking them up he hit me on the head with a bottle. . . . I stabbed him in the arm with my knife and he hit me again. . . . I do not remember . . ."

Weizmann had told a different story. "He said I owed him change. He came in there to make trouble for me. He knew I had trouble in the past so he wanted to make trouble for me. He pulled out a knife and I had to defend myself . . ."

There was also a statement by a Connie Morudu. "I tried to go into the shop and Mister Weizmann pushed me out and locked the door. Through the glass I saw Mister Tsatse on the floor. I saw Mister Weizmann hitting him with a bottle. We tried to break open the door. We thought he was killing Mister Tsatse . . ."

A note in Freek's handwriting said that no charges had been laid.

Yudel left the last file and returned to the kitchen to make himself yet another cup of coffee. By the clock there he saw that it was after one. At least I'll be able to sleep late tomorrow, he told himself. Freek's Weizmann files were a little beyond Yudel's normal terms of reference. He could not see how this man could have gone on killing all this time without anything being done. Each incident seemed to have been followed by immaculate legal proceedings, but nothing had happened. So far as Yudel could see he had never even been reprimanded. Freek had threatened him it was true, but it had taken eleven years and eight killings to reach even that point. The whole thing was beyond the understanding of any reasonable man.

And yet in another sense it was not that hard to understand. It was an unwritten fact of the South African legal code that the housebreaker, the intruder into the sanctity of the home, could be shot dead. No court ever found against the armed defender of the home and in favour of the unarmed intruder. In a society where all the goods worth stealing were in the homes of those who made the laws and were the only ones allowed, under those laws, to go armed: where almost all burglars came from among those who did not have anything worth stealing and who were not allowed to carry arms: in this society the killing of a burglar was a small matter. The legal proceedings that followed were most often little more than a formality.

While Yudel waited for the kettle to boil he allowed his mind to wander among the disjointed bits of information he had come upon so far. Perhaps Weizmann's anger was satisfied for the moment, perhaps there would now be a pause that would allow him the time that he needed. But he seemed to remember that some of the dates on the files were very close together and from his conversations with Weizmann he doubted that the danger was past, even temporarily. He remembered too clearly the weak tearful eyes, the desperation in the old man's voice ". . . At night, you are alone. There is no one else . . . The kaffirs are on the streets . . ."

Then there was the open door, an invitation to the hungry. "I'm a light sleeper," Weizmann had said. "I'm a very light sleeper." Was it as simple as that? The door left open and he was such a light sleeper that he always woke? And what about the broken window in the Nkabinde case? What need was there

78

to break a window if the door was open, or had the window been broken afterwards to convince the court? And if it had surely someone would have heard the glass breaking after the shots were fired and would have offered such evidence? Or would they?

And Weizmann's wife? To what extent was she a partner in it all? The history of homicide had a fair representation of partners: couples neither of whom would have killed if it had not been for their relationships with each other. Yudel wondered if this could be such a case and if the woman could have been the trigger to the racial aspect of it. He recalled the way she had dealt with the black customer while he had been in the shop. He remembered the quick impatient gestures. He remembered her scolding the children for speaking English. It might be nothing, Yudel told himself. But he remembered the absence of the more liberal newspapers and he remembered the contrived serenity as she had said, "I can only thank all the wonderful people who stood by us."

The water boiled. Yudel made his coffee slowly, going through the actions almost unconsciously. One fact was a special problem to him. Weizmann had not come for his appointment of the evening. Yudel wondered how much he would be able to do for a patient with whom he had no contact. Ever since the previous evening certainty had been growing within him that Weizmann would not willingly subject himself to further treatment.

He went back to the last file, taking his coffee with him. On the cover of this one Mimi had printed Inderasagan Reddy, 16 April 1973. Like Barney Tsatse, Reddy had survived to make a statement to the police. His was first in the file. "I was travelling down Smit street in my car at a speed of about fifty kilometres an hour. I had one passenger, my friend, Govan Singh. A car pulled out of a stop street right in front of us and we hit into its side. Some European men got out of the other car and one of them, Mister Weizmann, punched me through the open window. He shouted, 'Why the hell don't you look where you're going?' I tried to get out and the other Europeans started hitting me with their fists. I do not remember anything after that."

Govan Singh's statement followed. ". . . Four white men got out of the car. Mister Weizmann tried to hit my friend through the car's window. I got out and the others came for me. . . . I ran

79

towards Simmonds Street bridge . . . slipped and fell . . . they kicked me . . . lost consciousness. . ."

A third Indian had been involved in the affair and Mimi, like the good government servant she was, had grouped the statements ethnically. Yudel read what Jayendra Naidoo had told the police. "I stopped my car when I saw people fighting at the side of the road. I tried to intervene, but one of the Europeans (I later heard that he was Sergeant Jeffreys) shouted, 'Here's another one.' Sergeant Jeffreys punched me and Mister Weizmann hit me over the head with a revolver. Then Mister Weizmann shot me in the leg. . ."

The statements by Weizmann, Jeffreys and Jansen, who was identified as Weizmann's son-in-law, all told an almost identical story, of how after a minor motor car accident they had to defend themselves against three aggressive Indians. The revolver was drawn in self-defence and accidentally discharged into Naidoo's leg as he charged at Weizmann.

Yudel turned reluctantly to the judgement, but this time he was surprised. The magistrate had found that Weizmann and his friends ". . . are trying to cover their own assaults and no credence can be attached to their evidence." He found all of them guilty and sentenced each of the others to fines of five hundred rands on charges of common assault. Weizmann was sentenced to a fine of one thousand rands, half of which was suspended conditional upon his undergoing psychiatric treatment. Yudel had been growing progressively more sleepy as he worked his way through the files. The last part of the judgement drove all the sleepiness away. ". . . Declared unfit to possess a firearm, the suspension to remain in force for a period of five years . . ."

Yudel looked at the date on the file a second time—16 April 1973. That meant that the suspension had expired two months before. Barely seven weeks after the suspension expired Cissy Abrahamse had died. Yudel went quickly through the dates on the files. The only death during the five-year suspension period was that of Isaiah Zulu, who had apparently had the misfortune to step out in front of Weizmann's car. No firearm had been involved. This was the first time Yudel had learnt about the five-year suspension, but something about it was not right. The Weizmann he knew could no more have restrained himself because of a court order than he could have cured himself. And yet he appeared to have done just that. To Yudel's delicate intuition the pieces were not balancing. He felt, without any strong conscious reason for it, that there was something here that he would have to understand if he was to understand Johnny Weizmann fully. And Yudel was determined that he would understand.

SEVEN

THE PRISSY LITTLE mouth had relaxed somewhat during the interview and Mrs Roberts was starting to admit to the sort of things that Yudel had known must exist. "All right, Mister Gordon," she said. "Graham's relationship with his father is awful. They just can't find each other. I don't know what's wrong."

"Whatever's wrong must have started a long time ago," Yudel said.

"It's always been like that. William is a fine man and husband in every way, but he has never had any patience with Graham at all. He's a fine father to the girls, but he seems to have disliked Graham since he was a baby. It's as if, for some reason, he could just not face being the father of a boy."

"You'd better tell me about it," Yudel said.

"I think I had," she said, "but first I must apologise for my attitude on Wednesday evening."

Yudel shrugged.

"Graham has been much better since Wednesday. You seem to know what you're up to, even if you are a bit . . ." Mrs Roberts's manners had become a problem to her again. There did not seem to be a word to describe this Mister Gordon that would not come out ill-mannered.

"Eccentric," Yudel came to her aid.

"Quite," she said.

"Now tell me about your husband and son."

The story Mrs Roberts had to tell was a long one, about a man who hated the thought of having fathered a boy, and of a son who tried again and again to please a father who could not be pleased by him. "He does everything to find favour with his father, but nothing is good enough."

The tight prim little face was a façade behind which Yudel

82

could sense the real Mrs Roberts trembling. "I need to see your husband," he told her eventually.

"He won't come. He doesn't want me to come and he will certainly not come himself."

"I'll phone him and speak to him," Yudel said. "If he will not come, the boy will have to live with someone else—perhaps go to a boarding school."

"But he's never been away . . ."

"He's lived in the same house as your husband far too long. The root of the problem lies with the man, not with the boy. If the man will not be treated the boy will have to live away from him. Do you understand?"

Mrs Roberts lifted her chin in a quick angry gesture, reminding Yudel somehow of a farmyard hen, looking to the defence of her young. "Yes, I do understand. Inside I knew this all along. But it's not an easy thing to admit . . ." She stopped, not seeming to know how to complete the sentence. "But I'll do as you say."

There was something in her manner and the way she spoke that gave Yudel confidence in her. He felt sure that young Graham Roberts was going to be in better hands from here on. "I know that you will," he said, "but first we'll try to get his father to co-operate."

She nodded in quick agreement before continuing. "There is something else I find very confusing. On some days Graham does everything in threes. Not every day, but on certain days."

"Threes?"

"Yes. He does things three times. He comes in the front door when he gets home from school, goes out again, comes in again, goes out . . . until he has done it three times before he actually comes into the house. It breaks my heart to see him sit down at his homework and write the same line three times before he goes on to the next line, and then write that three times as well. It's a terrible thing, Mister Gordon. I've asked him why he does it, but he doesn't seem to know. He slipped out of his bedroom window one night to go and do something with a few friends. Of course he shouldn't have gone, but he didn't know that I was watching from upstairs. His friends were waiting for him on the pavement. It did terrible things to me, Mister Gordon, to see my boy get out of his bedroom window three times and back in each time before finally running off. His friends didn't know what to make of it . . ."

After Mrs Roberts had left Yudel lifted the handset of the telephone to dial Weizmann. He had to be sure whether the other man was avoiding him. There were voices coming over the line and one of them was Rosa's. "It's so stupid," she was saying, "when you think what Yudel's qualifications are and what they pay him. If you ask me the government are nothing more than a lot of stupid old reactionaries. Do you know what Yudel gets paid?"

"At least it's regular," the other voice complained. Yudel recognised it as that of Irena, Rosa's mournful and obese sister.

"What's so wonderful about that? I'll bet Hymie makes as much in a month as Yudel makes in a year."

"Not quite. As much as Yudel earns in six months maybe, or eight months, and it fluctuates awfully," Irena said sadly, apparently bemoaning her husband's low earnings.

"I hate them," Rosa said. "If the government could only know how I simply despise them."

Yudel listened to the voices in a sort of surprised wonder. He had expected to hear the dialling tone, not his wife and her sister. Then he remembered the telephone Rosa had fitted in the hall. He was noting again that Rosa's obsession with what she regarded as his low earnings was a pocket of immaturity (although he had better not tell her so) when he realised that the two women had stopped speaking. "Hullo," he said.

"Yudel, have you been listening in?" Rosa demanded.

"Good morning, Yudel. How are you?" Irena moaned.

"I'm well, Irena. I hope you are too." He was careful to avoid enquiring directly about Irena's state of health. "No, Rosa, I was not listening in. I wanted to make a call."

"It sounded like you were listening in. Well, we won't be long."

Yudel waited until he heard the one short chirp from the telephone that indicated that the women had hung up, then he dialled the number of Weizmann's shop. The ringing tone had scarcely reached his ears when Mrs Weizmann answered in exactly the same way as she had before. "Hullo, Ja. Twin

84

Sisters." Yudel had dialled the number on the offchance that Weizmann himself might answer. He did not believe that the woman ever intended to be of any use to him. He hung up thoughtfully. It was going to be a problem explaining to Rosa that he would have to go to Johannesburg again today. "Do you know what petrol costs these days?" she would certainly ask him.

There were five or six whites sitting at the tables. In the front of the shop there was a constant stream of blacks, coming and going, being served by Weizmann himself, his wife and daughter. None of the blacks made any attempt to sit down at the tables. They knew the rules without being told. Weizmann saw Yudel as soon as he entered the shop. "I don't have to come any more," he shouted. He stared straight at Yudel, but there seemed to be more of fright than anger in his face. "I've had treatment now. I don't have to come any more."

"Mister Weizmann . . ." Yudel started to say. He had forced his way through the crowd until he was standing up against the counter.

"I've had treatment now." His customers had all stopped talking and were looking from him to Yudel. As for Yudel he was glad that he was in the shop filled with people and not alone with Weizmann in his store at night. "I've had treatment now. I've been twice. I think that's enough. They didn't say how many times I had to go."

"It's not right for you to come in here and follow my husband around." The wife had joined the attack and her anger was cold and hard, bitter and controlled, where her husband's was wild and without control. "It's not right for you to come in here like this. We are hardworking people. We work for a living. We're not loafers. My husband would never be in trouble if people would leave us alone."

"Mister Weizmann, can I talk to you alone?" Yudel said quickly.

"I don't want to talk to you. I want you out of my shop." Yudel could see the heavy film of water all round the edges of Weizmann's eyes. He could see how startled they were and how rigidly they were fixed on him. "I want you out of my shop. There's nothing wrong with me now. I've had treatment. I could

85

have killed a coon last night, but I let him go. There's nothing wrong with me."

Suddenly there was a clattering from the stairs leading to the flat above, followed by the excited shouts of small children. "You are not the only one," Mrs Weizmann was saying. "We know about others who do the same work. We can go to them. We don't have to come to you." Her face seemed even paler than before, accentuating the bright ginger colour of her hair. She had risen quickly to her husband's defence. Yudel had no doubt that it was a role she often filled.

The two little girls came charging from the store into the shop. The front one tripped and fell and the second tumbled over her, both of them squealing with pleasure. A moment later their mother, whom Yudel had seen the night before, followed. She came in fast and fell to her hands and knees, trying to avoid the children who were directly in her path. Immediately she scrambled to her feet, wiping off her hands on the hips of her jeans, her eyes searching for those of her father. Yudel saw the moment of panic in them, the quick assessment of what his reaction would be. Then she swept the two children to their feet and passed behind the counter and out of the shop.

Their passing had diverted attention from Yudel for a moment. He used the moment to speak. "If you won't talk to me I'll have to leave," he said, "but you are making a mistake, Mister Weizmann."

"That's all I want. I want you out of my shop. I want you to go."

Yudel had looked up the name, Malherbe, in the telephone book and checked the address against that in the file. A man had answered and had given him what he wanted to know. There was a new address and a new surname.

The place was a semi-detached house, one of a long row of houses, all without garages, the cars parked on the broad grass-covered pavement. It was old and narrow, but in a good state of repair, the front walls whitewashed and the corrugated iron roof newly painted.

Out front a man in his middle thirties, wearing a blue overall, was tuning the engine of a car, racing it circumspectly as he listened to the exhaust note. He allowed the engine revolutions to drop away to idling speed as Yudel approached him. "I'm Yudel Gordon," Yudel told him. "I phoned . . ."

The man straightened up and looked at him. It was a good honest look, right into Yudel's eyes. The new husband, Yudel thought. After a moment in which the man seemed to satisfy himself about Yudel and nod, more to himself than to convey his feelings, he said, "She's inside."

By the time Yudel had gone down the path to the house Mrs van Wyk was opening the door for him. She was clearly nervous and had obviously been waiting for his arrival. Despite the warmth of the afternoon she was wearing a cardigan and had her hands wrapped round her upper arms as if she was still cold. She looked ten years younger than her husband, but she had already lost the prettiness of youth. She made no attempt to smile at Yudel.

When they were seated opposite each other in the small living-room she looked down at her fingertips and started speaking carefully as if what she was going to say had been carefully prepared. "I don't really want to talk about Kosie," she said. "I've talked about him a lot and nothing has changed. I've been in court three times—the inquest, the civil case and then the appeal and we lost them all. Now I only want to put it behind me. As you can see I'm married again. We've got a baby. I don't want to remember Kosie now. I want to forget everything."

"All I want to know," Yudel told her, "is—might he have tried to break into Mister Weizmann's shop?"

"No." Her voice was firm and decisive and there was not the slightest pretence in it. She was looking at Yudel in very much the direct honest way her husband had. "He would never have done that. You would have had to know Kosie. He wouldn't have stolen a flower from the City Council's gardens."

"That's all I wanted to know," Yudel said.

"Mister Sammel has been dead for some twelve years now," the broad old lady said. "They tried to make me go into an old-age home in Sydenham, but I told them I'm going to go right on living alone." The furnishings in her flat were expensive, most of them old, and had not been selected with an eye to augmenting each other. They were a haphazard accumulation of costly junk, the result of a long and probably prosperous marriage.

87

She was older than her brother, her face deeply lined and her hair drawn into a bun at the back of her head. Her eyes were small and worldly wise, with a hint of slyness, probably the result of helping in her husband's business for many years, Yudel thought. "You want to speak to me about my brother?" The question was put in a very businesslike way and Yudel had the feeling the interview was going to be conducted on that level.

"It's about the trouble your brother's been in during the last ten years."

"If people break into shops they must expect trouble." Her voice sounded very firm and sure and her head nodded in a way that suggested the obvious rightness of what she was saying.

"There's a problem about your brother I hoped you could help me with." He waited a moment to ensure that he had her attention before going on. "Some years ago a court ordered him to undergo psychiatric treatment, but he never went. This week the police sent him to me for treatment. He came twice and then he stopped. If he refuses to have further treatment now, I fear that he's going to get into serious trouble."

"You want me to persuade him?" She laid the accent on the word "me", leaving the idea sounding ridiculous.

"Would he listen to you?"

"No, he won't." It was said quickly with a little shake of the head. "I don't see him often, Mister Gordon. He has even cast our religion aside, you know."

"I know."

"But he won't listen to me. I know Johnny and he won't listen to me, especially not about this."

"You agree with the court that he needs treatment?"

The old lady raised her eyebrows, indicating that this was by no means certain. "A lot of people do," she said.

"But your brother, does he?"

"Perhaps. I don't know. He grew up in a strange way, Mister Gordon."

"Will you tell me about it?" Yudel asked. "I need to understand everything I can about your brother, if I am to help him."

She moved slightly in her chair, looking round the room, her old eyes still quick and intent, passing the many ornaments and

88

pictures that filled the room. She seemed to pause at a far corner of the room and Yudel looked in that direction. He saw a family photograph. It was of an unsmiling couple, neatly dressed in their best go-to-synagogue clothing and with them there was a young woman of perhaps twenty and a small boy. The small boy was standing next to the young woman and he was holding himself very proud and erect. "What do you want to know?" she asked at length.

"I want to know all about the circumstances under which your brother grew up."

"I don't know what you want, Mister Gordon." She fixed her sharp little eyes on him and appeared to be considering his request. For a moment Yudel thought that she was going to refuse, but the loneliness of an old woman who had too much time to remember decided the matter. It was not often these days that anyone was interested in what Mrs Sammel had to say. "All right. I'll tell you," she said.

"We were not like other Jewish families. We were very different. If I tell you what it was like you will understand Johnny better. He's a hard man because he grew up in a hard way. There are so many little things that are different to what it is today. . .

"At dinner times we never sat down at the table with our parents like other families or like families today. Never once did we sit down to dinner with them. My father and mother ate in the dining-room and we sat in the kitchen with the servants. And we didn't eat the same food either. We ate what the servants ate. I remember when I was very small it was the servant that looked after me and saw that I had food to eat, not my mother. The old people were strange, Mister Gordon. It was not as it is today.

"My father would take us all to synagogue regularly and to see him smiling and shaking hands with other people you would have thought that he was the most benevolent old man, but he never brought his friendliness and love home. If I heard him say it once I heard him say it a million times—children must be brought up hard—it's the only way they learn. And he was as good as his word. We grew up hard. We learnt about discipline, Mister Gordon. We learnt nothing about love. I learnt about love afterwards. Johnny never did. That wife of his has been no good to him. He should have married a woman of our faith. But don't judge him too harshly. He is what my mother and father made of him, nothing else.

"When Johnny was born I was already fourteen years old. We had another brother and sister between Johnny and me, but by the time Johnny was ten I was out of the house and married and the other two were dead. Daniel came after Johnny, when he was about three. But from that time on my father concentrated his attention on Johnny, to bring him up in the right way. I think that's why my brother turned out the way he is. My father was never interested in Daniel. Daniel was slow to understand and he was not strong. He never did well in school or sports. So my father ignored him and that was his salvation.

"We had a farm about fifteen miles out of Pretoria near Derdepoort. In those days there were still a lot of farms out there. We were the only Jewish farming family I'd ever heard of. We were different in every way, Mister Gordon. My father would never tire of telling us about what children owe to their parents. It was all right for them to demand anything of us, because children owe their parents everything, life itself, he used to tell us—so they cannot refuse anything. The most important commandment of all is that you honour your father and mother. Once he asked Johnny to go into Pretoria to buy something. I don't remember what it was. Johnny was about eight at the time and he had to walk all the way there and all the way back— thirty miles. And it was one of those hot summer days. He had strict instructions to accept no lifts.

"He got back at ten o'clock that night and he looked terrible. His face was red and he was running a temperature. I put him to bed, not my mother. She had instructions from my father to leave him alone and she never disobeyed him in anything. And all the time he had been away my father had been telling everyone close enough to hear how it was good for children to grow up hard. It built their character, he said. And never once did I hear my mother disagree with him.

"Johnny had dreams. He told me how he used to dream about some sort of monster and it was threatening him. He was terrified of it. He felt that it was going to destroy him. I know nothing about the meaning of dreams, Mister Gordon. I don't know if they mean anything. The old people believed they did.

90

I remember asking Johnny what he thought the dream meant. He cried when he told me. He was a big boy then already, about fourteen, I think. I was married and I was just there on a visit. He said he thought the monster was something inside of himself. I told him that was nonsense, but he said, no, he was sure. The monster was something inside of him and it was going to destroy him.

"If you were brought up in a normal sort of home, Mister Gordon, you wouldn't begin to understand what it is like to grow up in a place like we grew up in. No husband ever had a wife that waited on him hand and foot like my husband did. I treated him like the Messiah. How else could I treat him? He delivered me out of bondage. You don't know what it is like to grow up in a house where, if a little boy does something wrong, he is held down by the servants while his father whips him with a sjambok. I can see you think I'm exaggerating, but that's the way it was. Johnny had a way of dealing with beatings. Before my father even started hitting he would start screaming. Sometimes it seemed to work and my father would not hit him as much as other times. Sometimes it only seemed to anger the old man.

"For his part Johnny did everything my father asked of him. He refused him nothing. He hardly ever even hesitated before doing his bidding. All he ever wanted was to please my father. And that was impossible, Mister Gordon. Nobody could ever have pleased that old man. He just kept on and on pushing Johnny, seeing how far he could go, seeing what he could make him endure. I think he was trying to see how far he could go before Johnny rejected him. And all his life he never reached that point. Johnny was always coming back for more. But what he did reject was everything my father held dear. My father was as orthodox as a Jew can be, and as a child Johnny was unnaturally religious. He made such a point of his Jewishness that he was rejected and scorned by the other children. He must have got into dozens of fights over it. He often came home bruised and bleeding and my father would nod approvingly. That was the way a boy should grow up.

"Now Johnny says he is not Jewish any more. My father lived in the country. Johnny lives in the city. My father used to say all politicians are dishonest. He would have nothing to do with politics. Johnny talks about nothing else if you give him the chance. And his views—you should hear his views. . . My father treated his children callously. Johnny treats those girls as if they are made of gold, not flesh. He is different in every way to his father. But he'll never say anything bad about him, Mister Gordon. Ask him how he grew up and he'll tell you he grew up hard and he'll go right on and tell you that it's the only way to grow up. It did him good, he'll say. The trouble with today's young men is that they didn't grow up hard the way he did. Ask him. He'll tell you.

"They would leave him and Dan alone and go away, sometimes for a weekend, sometimes for even longer. This was after the others were dead and I was out of the house. I heard about it quite by chance. A neighbour of theirs phoned me to tell me that my father and mother had gone away to Bechuanaland, as it was then, for a week and Johnny and Dan were alone. We were living in Vereeniging at that stage. It was nearly a hundred mile drive for me, but I came right away. I can remember it as clearly as if it happened yesterday. My husband had to work that evening and he couldn't come with me. I remember getting there after dark, not the dark of the city, Mister Gordon, with all the lights, the streetlights and the lights from the houses— the dark of the farm where there is no light at all. It was a cloudy night and there was not even any moon or stars. I knew that farm like the back of my hand. I could have found my way around it blindfolded, so when I switched off the car lights unthinkingly I just left them off. I went up to the house in total darkness. I remember that there was just the smallest crack of light coming through between the living-room curtains. I knocked on the door, but nobody answered. Then I knocked again and still nobody. After I'd knocked a few times, louder each time, I went to the window and I could just see through a little opening between the curtains. Johnny was sitting on the couch. I think he was just about ten or eleven and he had my father's hunting rifle across his knees. Dan was only about seven and he was asleep on the floor in front of Johnny. I've never seen so much fear on a face as I saw then on Johnny's. I learnt that night that real fear is an ugly thing, very ugly. It was a bad thing to see, Mister Gordon. I called to him through the window and told him it was me. I had to call again and again. It seemed

92

to take a long time before he heard me at all. Then suddenly he just pushed the rifle to the floor and ran to the door to let me in. He held onto me. I remember so clearly how he held onto me. I don't want to remember it, but some things you can't forget, Mister Gordon.

"Don't judge him. We all let him down, me too. Don't judge him too much.

"Even after he got married nothing changed. One day my father came to his house. Johnny had been married for six months at that stage. And he told Johnny to come with him. Johnny left without telling that wife of his anything. My father took him to a cattle auction in the Western Transvaal where he wanted his help and they didn't come back for three weeks. I think he was wearing a khaki shirt and shorts when they left. During that time he slept in the back of my father's truck and my father slept in the hotel. It sounds like a story I'm making up, Mister Gordon. You don't know anything about the kind of life I'm telling you about. He was never able to refuse my father anything—nothing at all. You have to imagine a home where an eight-year-old boy is fainting with exhaustion, classifying tobacco at four o'clock in the morning, and if he falls over he gets woken up again. You've also got to imagine a home where when a father comes up unexpectedly behind his son the son wets himself at the sound of his voice. My father took that as a good sign. A child should fear the parent the way a man must fear God.

"Only once in all those years did my father show that he wanted Johnny. Only once, and that was when he was dying. He kept calling for Johnny. Johnny was away in the Cape, doing something for him. By the time they managed to contact him my father had already died. He came straight back and, do you know, when he saw the body he cried. Can you imagine that, Mister Gordon? After all that he still only wanted to be able to please that old devil.

"Whatever else Johnny is, he's an improvement on his father. I failed him too, Mister Gordon. When he rejected our religion I rejected him. It was a bad thing that happened, but I had found a lot of comfort in the Jewish community. My husband and I were very involved in community work and I thought it was a terrible thing Johnny was doing. I thought it was ungrateful and cowardly and I told him so. I'm older now and I've learnt a bit more and now I'm sorry, but that was more than thirty years ago and we never managed to heal the damage. And there was his wife, of course. She was never an easy person to like. And in recent years there's been this terrible thing with his hands and his feet.

"During the last year I've been thinking and remembering a lot about those times. They seem clearer to me now than the more recent years. It's all much clearer to me now and much closer. It seems like all of it happened just recently. I think I understand better than I have before. I know it's late now. . .

"I remember something Johnny told me just before I left home to get married. He was a tiny boy, five or six years old. He told me that he had been looking in the mirror at himself and suddenly he could see himself from above, but he wasn't looking at a little boy. Standing before the mirror was an old man. He was seeing himself as an old man. I don't know what it was he saw in the face of that old man, but it made him very unhappy. Thinking back, I fancy he saw the future, Mister Gordon."

The old lady had told Yudel the whole story without displaying any sign of emotion. She had travelled back through the years thoughtfully and without bitterness. It was all too long ago and she was too old for that.

There was a question that Yudel wanted to ask her, but he knew that he would leave it unasked. He wanted to know, why in all of these last ten years since the killings started, knowing your brother, couldn't you have done something? You must have been able to see what he had become. Why did you do nothing?

The question could never be asked because Yudel could see in her face that it was never far from the surface in her mind either. And nothing would be gained by raising it.

The old lady's quick sharp eyes met his and for a moment words were not needed to communicate between them. "What could I do?" she asked. "He's my brother."

The early winter evening had arrived while Yudel was with Mrs Sammel. Outside a gloomy twilight had settled on the city. Yudel looked at his watch. It was only six o'clock. If he drove straight home he would be there shortly after seven and Rosa's displeasure would be of a relatively minor order. He started the car's engine and drove slowly down the empty suburban street with the firm intention of going straight home. It did not work out that way. The shop in the darkness of the little tree-lined street down at the bottom of Hillbrow held an attraction for him that he could not deny to himself. He knew that there was nothing he could do there. Weizmann would not see him. He would almost certainly learn nothing. But Yudel was looking for answers. And the most urgent question of all was how he was going to stop Weizmann killing again. Before he had parked the car two blocks away from the shop in another quiet side street Yudel had made up his mind. He was not going to be able to treat the man, so it would be impossible for him to affect the other man's behaviour in any way. He knew a good deal about the problems of certifying someone insane and he doubted his chances of success there. If it was possible it would be slow and expensive, with Weizmann and his family resisting, hiring their own psychologist. You could always find a psychologist to testify to almost anything in court. There was only one way left to him. He would have to prove Weizmann's guilt in one of the cases so that he could be convicted. And it would have to be the Cissy Abrahamse case. Reopening any of the others would take too long. He would have to do it fast. The inquest was now only six days away. Yudel hated the thought of what he would have to do. Freek had sent the old shop-keeper to him to be cured, not convicted. Yudel believed that punishment was a necessary part of any society retaining its integrity and he had assisted in the conviction of many criminals, but primarily he was a healer. That was how he saw himself and he hoped that was how others saw him. He would have preferred any other way to this, but this afternoon he had run out of alternatives.

From a block away, deep in the shadow of the trees, he could see the door of Weizmann's storeroom. This time it seemed to be closed. The shop was already in darkness, the street quiet. Weizmann's was a daytime trade: lunches for those who could afford nothing better, packets of cigarettes, cold drinks for the passer-by, a gathering place for railwaymen between shifts, bus conductors and pensioners, tradesmen coming off duty, and possibly political friends, others who, like Weizmann himself, were determined to make the streets safe for decent people. By nightfall the businesses were closed, the people of the apartment houses were safe inside and only the sounds of the traffic on the main arteries, not far away in any direction, and the movement of trains down in the station showed that Johannesburg had not gone to sleep.

Across the road from Weizmann's place a double-storeyed block of flats rose a little above the trees. It was the sort of building that would have a flat roof and a fire escape leading up to it.

Yudel found the fire escape at the back of the building in a narrow yard crammed with refuse bins. As he expected it went straight up to the roof. There was no one on the fire escape or the roof. From the floors he had passed he heard only the ordinary domestic sounds, the clinking of cutlery as dinner was being prepared or consumed and the sentimental sound of a woman's voice on a children's television programme. On the roof the cell-like rooms for the building's servants were all in darkness, their doors closed, some of them locked from the outside with padlocks. He crossed to the street side and sat down on the low wall that ran along its edge. Through an opening in the trees he could see into Weizmann's living-room. The curtains were open and Weizmann's two grandchildren were sitting cross-legged on the floor in front of the television set. They were watching a show involving puppets, and behind them, partly obscured by the back of the chair on which she was sitting, a woman was doing some sort of needlework on her lap. Judging by the little he could see of her, she seemed to be the daughter he had seen in the shop. A young man entered the room through a door on the far side. He leant over her and Yudel saw his mouth open and close as he said something. He could see the man's face clearly. He had thick wavy golden-brown hair that receded sharply on either side of his head. It was an unlined, rather immature face, the jaw soft and irresolute, and the eyes wide and almost innocent. Yudel wondered if he was the Jansen who had been fined with Weizmann in the Reddy case and who helped in checking the passes of blacks. He remained next to his wife for only a few seconds, then moved away to a part of the room that Yudel could not see.

96

Moving slowly along the roof until he reached another partial opening between the branches Yudel could see into the next room. It was the kitchen, and there were only light lace curtains in the windows. Weizmann was seated at the table in front of him. He seemed to have his fingers spread wide and to be looking at them. His chin was slightly lifted and he had a disapproving expression on his face.

Yudel was the width of the narrow street from the other man and a floor above him. He could see the disapproval, the shadowed wrinkles of his frown and the glint of light from the little leather caps on his fingers clearly. During the afternoon he had learnt many new things about the shopkeeper. He wondered who Johnny Weizmann really was. Was he the tired and mistreated child, struggling to please his father? Was he the terrified youngster alone with his brother at night on the farm, the rifle lying across his knees, useless because of his fear? Or was he the teenage boy who had striven so hard for a dignity that would never be allowed him? Or was he a dangerous schizophrenic, driven by racialist fears that were not untypical of the country in which he lived and by the fearful decaying of his body? It was possible that the killings had only started after the gangrene had commenced its insidious work on his hands and feet.

Then Yudel understood who Weizmann was and that the shopkeeper must also know. Johnny Weizmann was the child who had dreamed of the monster that was himself, and who had seen the old man that he was to become. He was also the weak-willed young man, unable to shake off his father's hold on his life. And he was the tormented and dangerous man Yudel could now see across the narrow gap between the buildings. There was a frightful continuity here. All the little pieces Yudel had gathered, the fragmentary views of another man's life: they were all part of the same man. To Weizmann who had lived through it all there was no problem. He remembered the childhood incidents as he remembered yesterday's. He had seen them through the same eyes and they were part of the same recollection.

Something moved on the pavement below. Yudel squinted down through branches still heavy with the brown leaves of autumn, but the movement had stopped almost immediately and in the darkness below he could see nothing. He walked slowly along the roof until he reached a point where he could see part of the storeroom door, but the door was closed and as far as he could see there was no one near to it. The movement came again, this time further up the pavement, near the front of the shop. Yudel followed in that direction, steadying himself against the low wall along the edge of the roof and looking down at the pavement, trying to make out any form in the darkness below. He reached the end of the building, bringing himself opposite the front of the shop. There were no trees in Myburgh Street and by the light of the street lamps Yudel could see the pavement in front of the shop clearly. The movement came a third time, a quick shadow-movement under the trees, then it was out in the light and he recognised the alsatian he had seen on the previous evening. It trotted down the pavement and disappeared into an alley on the far side of the shop.

Further up the road on the other side of Myburgh Street there was a new movement, this time in the partly lit entrance to a block of flats. It was so short that Yudel was not sure that he had not imagined it. His imagination had been getting plenty to work on lately. He studied the spot for a few minutes, but there was nothing, only the quiet street and the shadowed entrance to a building where now there was nothing.

He moved back down the roof in the direction from which he had come. In the living-room the scene was just as it had been, the girls watching the television programme, the mother doing her needlework. He wondered about the world in which Weizmann's daughters had grown to maturity. Mrs Sammel had said that Weizmann "treated those girls like gold", but he remembered the woman's quick look at her father's face when she had stumbled over her daughters. The hurried searching of her father's features to discern his mood told its own story. Yudel knew that both observations were probably correct. He probably treated them like gold and gave them reason to fear him too. Without other evidence that would be what Yudel would have expected.

Below the kitchen a small uncurtained window gave him a view of a corner of the staircase, but there was little light and he could see only a few stairs in what seemed to be a very steep flight. In the kitchen Weizmann was still at the table, but his wife was with him now. He was saying something to her and making the small inhibited gestures Yudel had come to know, the movements governed by his need to express himself on the one hand and the need to hide what was happening to his fingers on the other. His wife was nodding and smiling, encouraging him, the mass of frizzy ginger hair bobbing up and down as she moved her head. It was obvious that she was interested in what he was saying. Of all the people in his life Johnny Weizmann had found someone to whom he was truly important. All the good sane and balanced people he had known all his life, Yudel included, had somehow failed him. She had not. To her there was no one in the world of greater importance.

And they were partners. She did not mind that he was a killer. Perhaps to some extent she was a partner in that too. Weizmann's sister had been wrong about her brother not finding love. No one seeing his wife smiling at him, her pale ugly face full of good humour, a human being secure in the place where she belongs, could doubt that Weizmann had found someone who loved him and whose love he was able to return. It was a narrow affection though, directed inward upon a very small group and, as with all love, it had a reverse side, a contrary and balancing emotion. And the reverse side of Weizmann's love was an uncontrollable hostility directed at those he imagined to threaten himself and the small circle of people he held dear.

Mrs Weizmann had placed a basin on the table in front of her husband and she was undoing the leather thongs fastening the sheaths that covered his fingers. Then she was removing them, one by one, her movements very slow and gentle, watching his face for any sign of pain.

And what have you come from, Yudel wondered of the woman, that you should need this man of all men, as much as you do?

What remained of Weizmann's fingers was uncovered and his wife was dipping wads of cotton wool into a solution in the basin and carefully wiping them down. The skin of the fingers was pale and bloodless, but discoloured in patches, blue and grey. The careful movements of the woman's hands and the expression of obvious concern on her face were all one as she cleaned away all that was rotten and decaying, talking to him as she did it, reassuring him, possibly trying to hide from him that for his hands time had all but run out. As an example of domestic care and affection it was almost ideal. Only Yudel's knowledge of the true nature of their relationship made it less than that.

Yudel could see that for Johnny Weizmann there was a division of the night into two parts. It was a time of fellowship and love, of gathering around you those who belonged with you, a time to have his children and grandchildren near, to close out the hostile world beyond. But the night was also a time of fear, violence and sometimes death: far too often it was a time of death.

EIGHT

YUDEL DID NOT recognise the car parked in the drive, but he did recognise Captain Dippenaar and Warrant Officer Marais as soon as he saw them. They were seated in arm chairs in his living-room and they had Rosa sitting opposite them. By the expression on her face she seemed to feel that she was on trial.

Yudel's immediate reaction was to ask what the hell was going on, but he restrained the question. He feared though that they had seen it in his face. "Good evening, gentlemen," he said, deliberately keeping his tone of voice as neutral as he was able.

Rosa started to rise as Yudel came in. "Sit down, Mrs Gordon," Dippenaar said smoothly.

"I'd like a cup of coffee, Rosa," Yudel said. "Would you get it for me?"

Rosa slid out of the chair and disappeared quickly into the kitchen. Yudel knew that for all her pushing ways and vehement manner Rosa was not a brave person. "Your wife told us that Mister Weizmann has been coming to you for treatment, Mister Gordon."

Yudel looked at the Special Branch captain and tried not to remember the fright he had seen in Rosa's face. "Oh really?" he asked.

"Yes. I'm afraid it was essential for us to find out." Dippenaar's face held the same smile Yudel had seen there before. It was a front, a mirthless grimace that did not deceive Yudel in any respect.

"So I wasn't in and you found out what you wanted from my wife?" Yudel was speaking softly, trying to sound at least as polite as the security policeman. "My wife doesn't know my patients. It really isn't her business and it certainly isn't your business."

"We need a little help, Mister Gordon." Dippenaar took it no

101

further. Superficially Yudel was not being threatened, but he could sense something, not a threat perhaps, but the possibility of one. The essence of the threat was in the room with them in case it was needed.

"If it concerns Weizmann I can't help you."

"I think you'd better listen to me. . ." The policeman seemed to be in no hurry to finish what he was saying. He was enjoying himself, savouring his power, letting it reach out to Yudel. This was the last year of the Vorster Government and the security forces, with the Prime Minister's close friend General Hendrik van der Bergh at their head, were at the peak of their power and influence. No doors were closed to them and no secrets hidden. Both Yudel and Rosa knew this as did all other South Africans. The knowledge was often barely conscious, but no one escaped it entirely.

"I have listened to you already." Rosa was still in the kitchen and showing no sign of returning. Yudel had remained standing on entering the room. He could see that Marais, the younger of the two, was beginning to feel uncomfortable sitting down.

"You better realise something. We come first." For the first time the smile was gone. "Whatever we want we can get. Your oaths and ethics come afterwards." Yudel raised his eyebrows in mock surprise. "Don't think we haven't noticed the banned books on your bookshelves." Yudel glanced towards his books. He remembered a reference to them on their previous visit. "There's a penalty for having banned books in your possession." Dippenaar was far nearer to threatening Yudel now, but they had weakened their position considerably by playing on something as innocuous as a few banned books. They knew it and he knew it too.

"I'll answer the charge in court," Yudel said.

"We don't want to make trouble for you. We need a little help. That's all." But the power and the threat were no longer tangible.

Yudel waited a moment, mentally steadying himself. He had not expected them and since he had come in he had been slightly off-balance. This time he wanted to be careful to say exactly the right thing. "Captain Dippenaar, I do not discuss my patients with anyone—no one at all. It's not that I don't want to help you. In this matter it's impossible." Despite his carefulness Yudel

102

felt that he was making a mistake. This time his best intentions were not enough. His anger was overriding his judgement, but there was no way that he could correct it.

"You don't want to get the reputation of being suspect, Mister Gordon. There are some things that are more important than ethics. We need this man and you can help us . . ." What Dippenaar was saying was weak and meaningless, carrying no conviction.

Dippenaar and Marais, and everything they represented in Yudel's thinking, were hateful to him. And they had frightened his wife. "I can't help you. There's nothing else to say. Good evening, gentlemen."

"I hope for your sake that you aren't making a mistake."

Yudel could hear in Dippenaar's voice and he could see in the strained look on his face how insulted he felt. He did not turn to watch them go, leaving them to find their own way out. Rosa came out of the kitchen and looked at him from the far side of the room. "Are you all right?" he asked her.

She almost rushed at Yudel. Holding her loosely in his arms, he was surprised at how she was trembling. She was saying, "Oh Yudel, oh Yudel, oh Yudel . . ." Yudel's own feelings surprised him. Rosa had not been very forthcoming lately and it was not unpleasant holding her in his arms. Her trembling and the breathless sound of her voice made her seem quite feminine. He let his arms slide down to her waist and drew her tight against him. ". . . Oh Yudel, oh Yudel . . ." It was wonderful. Maybe the Special Branch had their uses after all. Yudel was sometimes inclined to forget that Rosa was a person too. So often she seemed to be little more than a sort of animated conscience-cum-cash register. In fact she was not an entirely unattractive woman. ". . . Oh Yudel . . ." The effect it was having on him was astonishing. Yudel loved it. "Don't leave me alone again. You mustn't leave me alone again." He kissed the top of her head experimentally. She turned her face towards his. She was not crying and he kissed her closed eyelids. The sensation was altogether agreeable.

Suddenly Yudel was aware of the open curtains and the window behind him. Unaccountably he felt embarrassed about being seen from the street, kissing his wife. He left Rosa in the centre of the room and went to draw the curtains. When he turned round she was still in the same place, looking at him with anxious eyes, asking for comfort. What the hell, Yudel thought. It was a conjugal right.

"What did they want to know?" Yudel asked her.

"They were here a very short time. They hardly asked me anything."

"Try to remember exactly what it was they wanted."

"They asked about poor old Weizmann and I told them. Oh Yudel, I'm sorry, but I was so scared."

"That's all right, Rosa. What else?"

"They wanted to know about some African. They spoke about him last time they were here. I don't remember his name. They wanted to know if you'd ever mentioned him."

"Muntu Majola?" Yudel asked.

"That's right. Who is he?"

"I'm not sure. Get dressed, Rosa. I think we'll be going out."

From the telephone in the hall he dialled Freek's number. When he had Freek on the line he asked, "How'd our horse do? I was out this afternoon."

Freek answered without hesitation. "She won by a length the way I told you. You want to come round and get your winnings?"

"I'll be right over," Yudel said.

Freek met them in the drive of his home. It was a large stone and thatch house in Pretoria's elite suburb of Waterkloof. Freek was not a man to live contentedly on a police salary and the quality of his house and style of living had more to do with the horses he and Yudel had discussed over the telephone than what the police department paid him. "Magda's inside, watching television," he told Rosa. "Go right in."

They watched Rosa go into the house. Then Yudel told him, "They came again. They wanted to know about Majola again."

"What else?"

"Majola and Weizmann. They asked Rosa about Weizmann, wanting to know if I was treating him. And they wanted to know about Majola. They asked Rosa if I'd ever mentioned the name."

"Where were you?"

104

"I was in Johannesburg, seeing Weizmann's sister and trying to see him. I got back while they were talking to Rosa."

"What did they say when you got back?"

"They wanted my help and I refused it. Dippenaar also said, 'We need this man.' But I never let him get so far as to tell me who it was they needed. I supposed Majola."

"What did they want you to do?"

"I don't know that either. I interrupted him on that too."

"Jesus, Yudel. . ."

"Yes, I know. But they frightened Rosa and they caught me off guard . . ."

"It's done now." Freek moved closer to Yudel, his broad square face troubled by what he had been hearing. "Did you say that you were trying to see Weizmann?"

"He won't see me any more. I got too close to his problem on Thursday evening. He refuses to see me now. He's running away from it."

Freek looked down at the ground. Yudel, who knew him well, could see how he was weighing up the situation, considering what would be the best course of action. "I think it's time we found out all we can about Muntu Majola," he said at last.

"I was hoping you'd say that," Yudel told him.

The apartment block was very big, but the apartments themselves were tiny, row upon row wedged in next to each other, designed to crowd as many human beings into as few cubic metres as possible. They took the lift to the thirteenth floor, then Freek led the way down a long passage, stopping at one of the last doors. He knocked on it as if warning the door not to offer any resistance. After a wait of only a few seconds a slender young man, wearing only a vest and running shorts, opened the door and blinked out curiously. Freek took hold of him by the front of the vest and pulled him into the passage. There was a moment of surprise and resistance as he was pulled through the door, immediately followed by a half-hearted attempt at a salute. "Good evening, Colonel," he said in Afrikaans.

"Wynand, I need some information tonight. I want your help." Despite the choice of words it came across as an order and Wynand seemed to almost come to attention. Yudel thought he could hear him clicking his naked heels together.

105

"I'll get dressed, Colonel."

"Wynand," Freek said, giving the young man the full force of his attention, while Wynand's whole bearing was saying, "Yes Colonel." "Wynand, you know how to get into Security's stuff, don't you?"

"I'm not supposed to know, Colonel."

"I want something out of one of Security's files."

"Will the Colonel come in while I get dressed?" Wynand asked.

"We'll wait here. Do it fast."

Freek was known to the security guards on both the ground floor and the floor that housed the data centre and scarcely needed to identify himself to get the three of them inside. Wynand, who was wearing his uniform now, led this time, taking them down an unlit passage and into a small room that housed only a computer terminal. The terminal was covered by plastic sheeting like a typewriter cover. Wynand lifted it off the machine, folded it and put it down in a corner of the room. Then he reached below the keyboard and switched on the power.

"Wynand, how is it you know how to get into Security's files?"

"The Colonel must excuse me, but there's nothing about the computer that I don't know."

"I suppose you find Security's files very interesting."

Wynand grinned and glanced quickly at Freek. "Very interesting, Colonel. They've even got how everyone likes it, all the members of parliament, everyone."

"Tell us a few."

"The Colonel must be joking. That's classified information."

Freek chuckled. "And don't you think what we're doing now is irregular?"

"Very irregular, Colonel."

"Then why are you helping me?"

Wynand turned away from the keyboard to face Freek. The earlier mischievousness was gone. His face was so young and his eyes so honest that no judge alive could have found him guilty of anything. "I believe that if the Colonel asks me to do it the Colonel must have a very good reason for asking."

"And would you do it for any colonel?"

"Very few, Colonel."

Freek grinned at him. "You'll go far in the service, Wynand."

"I don't think so, Colonel. I'm resigning at the end of the month. I think I'll do better in IBM. What does the Colonel want to know?"

"We want to know who Muntu Majola is."

Wynand's fingers moved rapidly over the keyboard, sorting his way through the protocols of the system in order to interrogate the security police files on Majola. At the first attempt the printer on the machine reacted chaotically, printing three lines of gibberish and then switching off. Wynand tried again. The result was the same. The printer fascinated Yudel. It printed while moving both left to right and from right to left across the page. "What's wrong?" Freek asked him.

"If the Colonel will just be patient a minute while I get it right. . . This is not something I do every day."

"Should it type that way?" Yudel asked him.

"It can print that way because it has a memory," Wynand said. "It stores the information coming from the computer so it can print it both coming and going. In this case we're not getting into the computer so we're just reading a lot of errors." Wynand tried again, his fingers moving over the keys as quickly as before. For a moment the terminal was still, as if the computer was thinking it over before letting out the information, then the golf ball on the printer was shuttling back and forth across the page at a furious rate, hurriedly printing all that the security police had on file about Muntu Majola. Yudel and Freek leant forward to read it as it came out of the machine.

Muntu William Majola.

Born 1935–04–01. Hammanskraal, Transvaal.

Education: Hammanskraal and Fort Hare.

Family. Father, Kaya George Majola, Anglican minister, accused in Treason Trial, 1956. Brother, Kwame Majola, guilty in Terrorism Trial, 1977, serving life sentence on Robben Island. Brother, Albert Majola, deceased while in custody, 1977–06–13.

Career: Employed De Beers as clerk, 1958. Resigned to work full time for Black Social Endeavours, 1972, until banning

of organisation in 1977. Office bearer in African National Congress. 1952–1960. Suspect underground ANC activist 1960 to present.
    Listed communists among associates: Muhammed Thaver, Saths Cooper, Johnston Nene, Steve Biko, Adam Mashabane, David Mdlalose, William Hendricks. . .

Yudel stopped reading. The name, William Hendricks, halted the information-gathering process instantly. Yudel had only seen him intermittently since they had been close friends at university nearly twenty years before. The last time he had seen Hendricks he had been running a small heavily subsidised literary journal that printed only the work of black writers. In the evenings he had been running a night school for domestic servants. Yudel had his own ideas about the personal motives for such an altruistic life. They had everything to do with Hendricks' personality and nothing to do with his politics.

Even at university Hendricks had been almost totally bald. When Yudel had last seen him his head had looked like a large pink egg, the face seeming to be set unnaturally low down in it. "How I admire all your hair, Yudel," he had said.

Yudel remembered involuntarily pressing his own tangled mass of hair down with both hands. "You wouldn't if you had it," he said. "Your style is much simpler."

Yudel drew himself away from his memories and went back to reading the print-out. The list of names of Majola's associates was a long one and not one of the others meant anything to him. Further down the page a passage drew his attention.

    . . . Currently sought for the killing of Lieutenant Walter Bradfield, 1977–08–21, and Warrant Officer Willem Lessing, 1977–09–04, in their homes. Officers Bradfield and Lessing were members of the team interrogating Albert Majola at the time of his death. Also sought in connection with bomb blast, Germiston Post Office, 1978–01–21, in which Mrs May Turnbull, 74, was killed and bomb blast in Roodepoort office of West Rand Administration Board, 1978–03–09, injuring two white female clerks and causing damage to building. . .

The rest of the file had nothing of interest to Yudel. There

108

was not a word that could possibly have tied Majola to Johnny Weizmann whose political involvement would have been at quite the opposite extreme of what was a very wide political spectrum. At the end of it Freek turned to Wynand. "They didn't say how he likes it?"

"They must have slipped, Colonel."

To Yudel Freek said, "I don't see a connection. But they obviously want him badly. That's why they leant on you that way."

"I know Hendricks," Yudel told him.

Yudel got up carefully so as not to wake Rosa. He had stayed in bed until he could see that she was sleeping deeply. The sleeping pills he had given her had taken effect quickly and even the jerky little movements of her body were subsiding now. He put on his dressing gown and went into the study. Something was bothering him. He was not sure whether it was as he remembered it or not. He found the Cissy Abrahamse file in his brief-case and took out of it the statement for which he was looking. The first time Yudel had gone through it he had read it very quickly, skimming over the contents, and there had not seemed to be anything of importance in it. Now he read it again, stopping to read very carefully at the section that was bothering him. "My daughter was staying with me and I went onto the balcony to fetch some baby napkins that had been drying there. I noticed a Bantu man on the pavement on the other side of the road. Then I heard three shots being fired. I saw the Bantu man run away up the pavement and I went straight inside to tell my daughter. . ."

Three points stood out so clearly that Yudel was disgusted that he had missed them the first time. There had been a man on the pavement outside the store. And there had been three shots. Cissy had had two wounds and the shots had been fired at almost point-blank range. Yudel remembered Freek's words ". . . He hardly ever uses more than one bullet. . ." Could he have missed at such close range? The third point was less certain. The person who had made the statement had witnessed the scene from the building where Yudel had looked down on Weizmann's flat earlier that day. Yudel knew that there was little you could see of the pavement outside Weizmann's shop

109

from there. The trees limited your view to small fragments, especially at night. And Cissy Abrahamse had died at night. And yet the person who had made the statement had been able to say with apparent certainty that the person on the pavement had been a "Bantu man". On that same pavement Weizmann's alsatian had been no more than a shadow to Yudel.

The name at the top of the statement was Mrs J. Sinclair. Yudel knew that he was going to have to talk to Mrs Sinclair.

NINE

THE MASSEUSE WAS a pretty teenage girl. The way Yudel was lying down on his stomach he could not see her face, but he remembered it well, associating it in his mind with the strong gentle little fingers that were kneading at the muscles of his neck and shoulders, helping them to relax, slowly smoothing away his tensions.

"Turn over, Mister Gordon." Her voice was a little bell, tinkling prettily in the silence of the room. He complied and she darted lightly to the foot of the bed. There she massaged his feet, doing something to the toes and soles until they were warm, glowing and relaxed. He felt the hands working their way up his calves, past his knees, to his thighs. Now she was close by, an arm's length away from him. To his surprise the little white suit, like a tennis outfit, had been discarded. Her hair and breasts were swaying in unison as she worked her way up his thighs.

"Do all clients get this treatment?" Yudel asked. He had difficulty speaking.

"Oh no, Mister Gordon, you are something special." She was sliding onto the bed next to him, gently wrapping her arms round his neck.

"Is this the way it's supposed to be?" he asked.

"Only for you. For no one else."

"Are you sure?"

"Oh yes, Mister Gordon. You are my special client. This is only for you."

She completed her work in the same perfect way that she had carried out the preliminaries. Yudel felt her slide off the bed and heard her slip back into her uniform. He closed his eyes, savouring the warm relaxation of his whole body.

He heard her coming back towards him, her bare feet padding

111

softly across the floor. He opened his eyes and saw that she was carrying a huge rubber stamp in one hand. "What are you . . ." Yudel started to say. Before he could complete his sentence or move to stop her she had stamped him once on the stomach and once on the left thigh. Both places now had "Serviced by Lucy's" printed across them in large indelible letters. "What did you do that for?" Yudel yelled at her.

"It's an advertisement for the firm, Mister Gordon. We do it to all our customers."

"But my wife . . ."

"She'll understand, Mister Gordon. It's quite in order."

Yudel was in a bath and scrubbing desperately, but the letters on his stomach and thigh were completely unaffected. "Yudel-dear, Yudel-dear." It was Rosa's voice and it was drawing nearer. "Yudel-dear." She was just outside the door and he could not possibly scrub in both places at the same time. "Yudel-dear." The door was opening. "Yudel-dear. . ."

"Yudel-dear." Rosa was bending over him. He tried frantically to cover the places where the stamp had fallen. "No need to look so startled. I brought your coffee."

It was Sunday morning and the sun was shining directly in at the window, falling all around Yudel where he lay in bed. He watched Rosa put down the coffee on the table next to the bed. "Thanks," he said.

"You looked so startled. It must have been a bad dream."

"I don't remember."

"What have you on the programme today?" she asked, sitting down on the edge of the bed. She was wearing a furry pink dressing gown and some of the previous evening's femininity had remained. Her face had a peaceful friendly expression and early morning coffee on Sunday was not normally Rosa's style.

"I'd like you to spend the day with Irena, if it's all right with you," Yudel told her. "I have to go back to Johannesburg again."

"But you were there all day yesterday."

"There was someone I missed that I should have visited and there was someone I didn't know about."

"The petrol's costing a lot." Even this was said in a peaceable way, as if it was a subject she would rather not mention

112

and, in any event, it was not something to fight about.

"I know, but I simply must go. I have to clear this business up."

Rosa nodded slowly. That, at least, was something they agreed on completely.

Yudel knocked on the door of Mrs Sinclair's flat. It was on the first floor of the building from the roof of which Yudel had been able to see into Weizmann's place. In the centre of the door a peephole lens offered Mrs Sinclair a view of whoever was knocking. Yudel heard the sound of someone moving inside. The sound stopped and he could imagine Mrs Sinclair examining him through the peephole. Then the door opened a handsbreadth, the safety chain rattling, and Mrs Sinclair's examination moved to its second phase. She was a small middle-aged woman with a lot of loose skin on her face, who looked as if she did not eat enough. "Yes?" she asked.

"I'm Yudel Gordon," he told her. "I phoned about. . ."

"Oh yes." She examined him for a moment longer before closing the door again to unhook the chain. Then she opened it wide. She was still wearing a faded blue towelling dressing gown and had curlers in her hair. "I was just getting up," she excused herself. The way it was said indicated that it was a shameful thing to be still in her dressing gown at that time of day. "The place is a mess." She closed the door behind Yudel and replaced the chain. "I haven't cleaned up yet." Her voice was thin and uneven in tone. She retreated before Yudel into the small sitting-room, walking backwards so as not to lose sight of him. "The place is a terrible mess, I'm afraid. I feel so embarrassed." There were clothing patterns, bits of crocheting, balls of wool and unfinished pieces of needlework everywhere. In some respects the room reminded him of his study. "I was busy yesterday," Mrs Sinclair explained. "Won't you sit down?" She picked up a book of patterns from a chair to make room for him.

He accepted the invitation and she sat down on a small sofa, sweeping a few balls of wool aside as she did so. "I hope we won't wake Mister Sinclair," he said.

"There isn't a Mister Sinclair. There hasn't been one for eight years, four months and seven days. He walked out on me." It was said quickly with averted eyes as if this too might be

113

shameful. "I wouldn't have him back if he asked though," she added hurriedly.

"You live alone then?"

"Quite alone."

"But last Wednesday night your daughter was here?"

"Yes. She was holidaying with me. She's gone back to Cape Town now."

That pretty well cancelled out the daughter, Yudel reckoned. He would have to get what he needed from Mrs Sinclair. "Two things about your statement to the police interest me, Mrs Sinclair. Firstly, you said you heard three shots. Are you sure about that?"

"Oh definite. There were three shots all right."

"But there were two wounds on the girl. One bullet seems to be missing."

"Mmmm. No." Mrs Sinclair frowned thoughtfully. It was clear that she enjoyed having him ask her these questions. Like Mrs Sammel, it was not often that she was the centre of any sort of attention. It was likely that she enjoyed living across the road from Weizmann. His presence gave much-needed stimulation to her life. "No. Definitely not. There were three shots. I remember it as if it was last night."

"All right," Yudel said. "What about the man on the pavement? You said there was a man on the pavement."

"There was a native on the pavement. I saw him run away after I heard the shots."

"How did you know they were shots?"

Mrs Sinclair smiled. It was a knowledgeable superior expression. "If you live almost next door to Mister Weizmann you learn to know what gunshots sound like. I've lived here for nearly twenty years and I know very well what gunshots sound like. As soon as I heard them I told Leslie, my daughter, there's Mister Weizmann at it again."

"You have a chain on the door," Yudel said. "Have you had trouble?"

"Well, Mister Weizmann has lots of trouble."

"Of course. Do you know him well?"

"Very well. As I said I've lived here for twenty years. Very nice people, strict, but very nice."

"He had no trouble for the first ten years that you lived here."

114

"Oh, this neighbourhood is going to the dogs." She opened her eyes wide as she spoke, to emphasise what she was saying. "It's much worse now than it used to be. Since they took away this petty apartheid business everything has been going to the dogs. The parks, everywhere, are full. . . All the decent people from the old days are moving away. There's only myself and the Weizmanns and a few others from the old days. The rest have all moved away."

"Did you ever have any trouble yourself?"

"Not personally, but I know. . ."

"Yes," Yudel said, "I also know about Mister Weizmann's problems. Could I see your balcony?"

Mrs Sinclair rose quickly, smoothing the front of her gown with both hands. "I'll show you the exact place where I was standing." She crossed the room and opened the door that led onto the balcony. Yudel followed. There was barely room on it for the two deck chairs that were presently occupying it. Yudel had to fold one of them to stand next to her. "I was standing right here. The chairs were not here. I had a small clothes-horse with my granddaughter's nappies hanging on it in this corner."

Yudel looked across at Weizmann's shop. It was almost invisible from the balcony, enough of the brown autumn leaves remaining to form a nearly impenetrable screen along either side of the road. He could see only tiny fragments of the shop's plate glass windows and nothing at all of the storeroom door. In places the pavement was visible below the branches. While he was looking a man in a blue overall passed along the pavement. All Yudel could see of him were his legs from the knees down. "Would you be good enough," Yudel asked, "to tell me again exactly what you saw last Wednesday night?"

"Well," Mrs Sinclair paused, apparently getting her facts straight, still obviously flattered by Yudel's interest. "As I said in my statement I was fetching some nappies when I noticed a native down on the pavement outside Mister Weizmann's store. Then I heard the shots. . ."

"All three in quick succession?"

"No, I don't think so." Mrs Sinclair was trying to remember. "First two and then one, or first one and then two. There was a little wait somewhere though, if you know what I mean."

"Yes, and then?"

"Then the native ran up the pavement and round the corner and past the front of the shop."

"Who do you think he was?"

"He was helping the one Mister Weizmann caught, of course. There were two of them and he was lucky to get away."

"I see. And how do you know the man on the pavement was black?"

Mrs Sinclair stretched her eyes wide and shrugged. "I saw him, Mister Gordon." Yudel was looking down in the direction of the pavement and the little wrinkled woman turned to look in the same direction. Another man was coming up the pavement from the station side, walking quickly. His shoes were black leather and well shone and the crease in his navy blue trousers was perfect. For a few seconds that was all Yudel could be sure of. By the time he had reached the corner at the front of Weizmann's shop Yudel had been able to make out by means of fragmentary glimpses between the leaves that he was white and wearing a pale blue open-neck shirt. "You see. You can tell," Mrs Sinclair said.

"Barely," Yudel said, "but that was at night, eleven o'clock, wasn't it?"

"That's right. The street lights."

"The street lights don't even reach the pavements, Mrs Sinclair."

"Well, I don't know, but I'm sure. . ." Mrs Sinclair tossed her head with a jerky irritated movement, causing the hair curlers to bob quickly once.

Yudel took her by the arm. He tried to look as kindly as possible. "Mrs Sinclair, I am sure that the man on the pavement was black and I am sure you would not have told the police a story that you did not believe, but at eleven o'clock at night you could not possibly have known, watching from the balcony. You could not even have been sure that it was a man and not a woman. Now tell me, why did you tell the police he was black?"

"My servant, Julie, was coming back from the Greek shop. He's still open that time of night." She was speaking very rapidly, anxious to say it and get it behind her. "She saw him run down the pavement in front of the shop. She said he was a

116

native, but I knew it couldn't be a white person. It's only the natives that break into shops."

"This Julie—does she know the name of the man?"

"The native?"

"Does she know his name?"

"I shouldn't think so. He was just some hooligan . . ."

"Where is Julie now?"

"In her room on the roof, but she saw nothing else. I saw everything clearly."

"Have the police questioned her?"

"Yes, they have." Her expression was that of a disapproving schoolmistress. "Two completely different lots of police came to interview her. I don't know what she could have to say that's so important, I'm sure."

"The second set of police were a middle-aged man and a younger thick-set one and they wore civilian clothes?"

"Yes. Do you know them?"

"We're old friends. They only questioned her, not you?"

"Don't tell me you want to question her too?"

"I'm afraid so," Yudel said.

Julie was a broad woman and when Yudel first saw her a sleepy-looking one. She was sitting in the sun against the wall of her room at a junction between that and another wall running at right angles to it. As a result she was shielded from any wind there might be. Her legs were stretched out in front of her, crossed at the ankles, and a warm winter sun, reflected from the walls and windows of the buildings round about, was close to putting her to sleep. "Is your name Julie?" Yudel asked.

"Yes, sir," Julie said. It was a pleasant shy-sounding voice and she wrinkled her forehead a little as she spoke.

"Who was the man who ran away from Mister Weizmann's shop the night he killed the girl?"

Immediately Julie was fully awake. She started getting awkwardly to her feet. "You police, master?" she asked.

"No," Yudel said. He regretted confusing Julie's understanding of the matter, but he knew that few of his black compatriots trusted the police very far.

Julie looked uncertainly at him, clearly unsure as to what to make of this strange little white man with the wild hair and the

117

intent eyes who asked questions like a policeman, but said that he was not one. "Oh master," Julie said. "Too many police and now the master."

"Too many police?"

"Too many. They ask questions and questions and questions."

"And you answered the questions?"

"Yes, master." Standing up Julie was taller than Yudel and much broader, huge fleshy arms and legs protruding from her 'housemaid' uniform, but she was timid, not eager to answer Yudel's question, but anxious to avoid giving offence.

"What did they ask?"

"They ask . . ." Her voice sounded uncertain and she was looking at him doubtfully.

Yudel had seen Julie's difficulty growing and he tried to meet it. "I am a lawyer. The church is paying me to find out what happened. They think Mister Weizmann is not telling the truth." Telling Julie the truth would have been too complicated and far less believable. When necessary Yudel lied with such sincerity and conviction that far more sophisticated victims than Julie believed him without hesitation.

"O-oh," Julie said, the sound long-drawn like a sigh, looking appreciatively at him. Obviously it was a wonderful idea to her.

There was a moment in which Yudel feared that she might ask which denomination, thinking that whichever one it was it was certainly deserving of her support. Yudel continued before the conversation could be diverted onto those lines. "We don't want to let him get away, do we?"

"No-o," Julie said, looking at Yudel out of the corners of her eyes. It was a reluctant admission, the answer slow in coming. It was clear to Yudel that the dominant factor in all her thinking was the desire to stay out of trouble.

"Now you tell me everything they asked you."

Julie wrinkled her forehead in earnest thought. "They ask do I see the old master shoot the gel."

"And what did you say?"

"I say, no."

"What else did they ask?"

"They ask what I see?

"I tell them I am coming down the road by the shop. I hear

the old master shoot. Then I see a man run straight for—coming straight at me."

"Have you ever seen this man before?"

"Oh yes." Julie smiled at what was clearly a pleasant memory. "I know him."

"What is his name?"

"His name Muntu Majola, master."

Yudel looked at the large timid woman, her arms hanging at her sides, her fingers toying with the material of her skirt. He wondered if she realised how important that piece of information was. She smiled her little shy smile and Yudel was sure that she had no idea of it at all. "How is it you know him, Julie?"

"From Alexandra, master. When I was a gel I knew Muntu there. He was Msomi."

"Msomi?" Yudel asked. "What's that?"

"Msomi. That's . . ." It took Julie a few seconds to find the word. ". . .That's gang."

"He was in a gang?"

"He was in a gang," she repeated. "They kidnap me one time." Julie giggled, lowering her head and swinging her body from side to side with embarrassment. It had obviously not been an unpleasant experience.

"How old was he then?"

"He was. . ." She rolled her eyes upward while she thought it over. "He was maybe fifteen, maybe sixteen." She stopped speaking, still smiling to herself, possibly remembering, picturing what he had been like and recalling to her mind what she had felt. Then her expression became serious. "Muntu a big man now, very big man now."

Yudel knew that her calling him a big man had nothing to do with physical size. "How long did he stay in the Msomis?" he asked.

"When he was maybe eighteen, maybe nineteen."

"And then?"

"Then he work." She shrugged. "Grow up, get married . . ."

"How long ago was all this, Julie?"

"Oh, master." The deep brown of her face seemed to go a shade deeper in colour.

Yudel grinned at her. "Two years, three years."

"Oh master. Twenty-five years."

"Twenty-five years. That's a long time. Are you sure it was Muntu you saw?"

"Yes." Julie looked serious now. "It Muntu. I know it Muntu."

"But it was very dark. How can you be sure?"

"He grab me."

"He grabbed you?"

"He grab me. I coming, walking down Myburgh Street. Come past front of old master Weizmann's shop. I hear old master Weizmann's gun—bang, bang. I see somebody is running. I very frightened. I stand still. I hear bang again and I see light from gun. Muntu run straight for me. He grab me and pull me round corner. He say, run gel or don't you want to live any more? I run. Muntu pull me. Then he pull me in the little road, small road . . ." She held the flattened palms of her hands close together to indicate how small the alley had been. "He stop in dark place. Stand very still. I too much scared. Muntu hold me, arms around me, hold hand over my mouth." She cupped a hand over her mouth to show Yudel how he had done it. "Muntu say, quiet gel. You want to live, be quiet." Yudel could see that Julie was recalling the whole thing just as it had happened. "Muntu very big man now."

"Did he recognise you?"

"Master?"

"Did he see who you were? Did he know you?"

Julie shook her head sadly. "He not know. It dark. He not look at me. He look to see if old master Weizmann come. We wait, stand still for a long time. Afterwards Muntu say, you go now, gel. He walk quickly away. I see him stop one time, look back." Yudel looked thoughtfully at Julie. This new bit of knowledge, rather this confirmation of what Yudel already suspected, took a little digesting. "If Muntu not grab me the old master shoot me too," Julie added.

"Quite possibly," Yudel said. "Thanks, Julie. You've been a help."

"All right, master," she said as he was turning to leave. "You catch him now?"

"Will I catch whom?"

"Old master Weizmann—you catch him?"

"I hope so."

"Maybe the church will pray, then you will catch him. Maybe God will listen."

"Maybe," Yudel said.

As he went down the fire escape Julie was again settling herself on her cushion in the sun. She was a simple person who was not truly aware of all that life had done to Majola in recent years. She had only the vague knowledge that he was a 'big man' now. Yudel did not believe that she would have answered questions about him as readily as she did if she understood that the police were looking for him. She certainly had no idea that the more recent pair of policemen to visit her were far more interested in finding Majola than in the death of the girl.

It was Sunday and they had questioned her earlier in the week. It disturbed him to think that Dippenaar and Marais were that far ahead of him. He wondered how much further he would have been if he had let them tell him why they needed him.

One fact was inescapable. There had been a witness to the little mulatto girl's death. Muntu Majola knew exactly what had happened that night.

Yudel sat in the car for a few minutes, watching the front of Weizmann's shop. A few customers entered the front door and came away with their little packets of food. The streets still held little traffic as Johannesburg struggled with the effects of Saturday night. Through the open door he could see Mrs Weizmann alone in the shop, serving her customers with the same brisk movements, the barely suppressed anger that seemed to be a part of her.

He started the car's engine and found his way to one of the main roads, running north. The ugly paint-chipped dirty-concrete littered face of Braamfontein fell behind him and was replaced by the lovely wooded gardens of the northern side of town, the reds, browns and yellows of winter shining among the deep green of the conifers, large solid-looking houses all but enveloped in the foliage of their gardens.

The street in which Bill Hendricks lived was a short cul-de-sac. The house was small and overgrown by a tangled creeper, its leaves bright red and brown. Hendricks was digging in a vegetable garden at the side of the house, his bald head covered by a cloth sun hat that hung down low over his ears. He looked up, resting on his spade, as Yudel came in at the gate and followed the path down the side of the house towards him. His almost elfin face was wrinkled with curiosity and suspicion as he watched Yudel approaching.

Yudel stopped before him and held out a hand. "Bill," he said.

Hendricks hesitated before taking Yudel's hand. Then he shook it briefly. "I just wonder why you're here, Yudel."

"I need your help."

"Everyone seems to need my help these days." He went back to his digging. "I never thought that you had any political morality to speak of, but I must say that I'm saddened that you allow those people to use you."

"No one is using me, Bill."

"That's rather a lot to swallow. They come round and get nothing out of me, so they send you, knowing that we were once friends. It seems logical enough." He paused in his digging to glance at Yudel. "Or is there something I haven't understood?"

"When were they here?" Yudel asked him.

"Don't you know?"

"Tell me."

Hendricks stopped digging altogether, thrusting the spade deep into the upturned soil, and stood erect, looking straight into Yudel's face. "They were here last night." Yudel calculated that they had probably spoken to Julie on Tuesday or Wednesday. By Thursday they were visiting him, looking for help. By Saturday evening they had given that up and were trying a more direct approach, looking up Majola's old friends. "If you aren't after Muntu what are you after?" Hendricks wanted to know.

"I am after him, but for a different reason. You know about Johnny Weizmann? You might have read about the latest shooting in the newspapers."

"Of course, but that old sod will get off scot free again, I'm quite sure."

"Muntu Majola witnessed the most recent killing."

"I don't believe it."

"It's true. It appears to have happened by chance."

"That's incredible."

"Unlikely I grant you, but there it is."

Hendricks dusted off his hands, using the back of his trousers.

He was a small man, no bigger than Yudel, but the way he held his chin up high and looked at Yudel down the length of his nose made him seem much taller—to Yudel, at any rate. "I don't know whether I believe this, Yudel, but come inside. I'm sure Marion will be pleased to see you again."

Yudel followed Hendricks round the back and into the house via the kitchen. Marion was a pale woman who looked paler for not using cosmetics. She was sitting on a sofa in the living-room, marking her students' essays. She was wearing a formless black and red dress and wearing sandals that looked as if they might have been intended for her husband. But that was Marion as Yudel had known her. She dropped the paper she was marking as soon as she saw him, scrambled out of her seat and rushed across the room. "Bill, it's Yudel. It is Yudel, isn't it?" She kissed him quickly and stepped back to look at him. "You're on an adventure, Yudel, aren't you?"

"Hello, Marion."

"Yes, you are. I can always tell when Yudel's on an adventure. His hair becomes even a little wilder because he stops combing it at those times and his eyes become bright, as if there are little hot coals behind them." A long time before Yudel had thought that Marion was his girl-friend. Unexpectedly, at least unexpectedly to Yudel, she had married Bill Hendricks. When he had asked her why, she had said, "He's committed. You aren't."

"Committed to what?" Yudel had asked.

"You aren't committed to anything, Yudel." So Yudel had become committed, but Marion had married Bill and he had married Rosa.

After Marion had gotten over her surprise at seeing him they all sat down in a room that was exactly like the security police description of a communist's home—books everywhere, in bookcases, on tables, scattered around the room . . . It was what Yudel's home would have looked like without Rosa. "And what have we to thank for this rare privilege?" Marion asked.

"I need to know all I can about Muntu Majola. In fact I want to find him."

Marion glanced briefly at her husband and some part of her moved a bit further away from Yudel. "We don't know much about him," she said carefully. She was a poor liar.

Yudel told her why he was looking for Majola and she looked

123

towards her husband again before speaking. "They didn't send you, did they, Yudel?" The expression of her face was saying, please, I don't want them to have sent you. It was also saying, but I can't take any chances with you, not after all this time and not considering who pays you.

"No, they didn't send me. I told Bill why I'm here. I need Majola's testimony. It's the only way I'll convince a court that Johnny Weizmann is guilty of his most recent killing."

"If we believe you," Bill Hendricks said, "of what good will it be? They want Majola. They'd have him before he got anywhere near a court."

"Perhaps he could defend himself in court," Yudel said. "There are organisations that will provide money for his defence. Perhaps he isn't guilty."

"He doesn't need to be guilty," Hendricks said. Suddenly he looked tired. "Yudel, how is it you've lived so long in this country and learned nothing about it? Haven't you heard that they can take him in without taking him to court? Haven't you heard of deaths in detention?"

"Yes, I . . ." Yudel tried to defend himself.

"Muntu is one of those who will not come out of detention alive."

"How can you be sure?"

"Take my word for it. I've been around this sort of thing for a long time. I am . . ."

"Committed," Yudel suggested.

"That isn't what I was going to say, but take my word for it, there's a better than even chance that Majola will not come out of John Vorster Square alive. He knows it and I know it and he won't be able to testify."

"Perhaps he could give me a sworn affidavit."

The way Hendricks snorted indicated that he did not think very highly of Yudel's affidavit. "A sworn affidavit by a so-called terrorist who is being sought by the security police? Don't make me laugh, Yudel. Muntu was as deeply involved in Black Social Endeavours as anyone at the time they banned it. He was a worker, an organiser, not a thinker . . ."

"The security police seem to think he was a political radical."

Hendricks shook his head, seemingly trying to shake himself free of Yudel's ignorance. "Of course he was a political radical.

If a man is that committed to the uplifting of his people, he is also going to be concerned for their rights. He was not a leader of the movement in the true sense. He was more a trusted lieutenant, a slogger . . . And when they banned the organisation, closed its doors and stole its funds he was possibly more embittered than anyone else. You want to know about those bombings and killings? He might have done them. He was that bitter. You know about his brothers?"

"Yes."

"And there was Biko's death and Mohapi's and all the others. They were all friends."

"Where is he now, Bill?"

"Where are any of them? The Black Social Endeavours staff are scattered, running, hiding, trying not to be noticed, trying to stay out of jail, trying to stay alive. He's somewhere on his own and, if the whole security police network with their phone-tappings and buggings and beatings can't find him, I shouldn't think even you have got a chance." He stopped speaking and looked at his wife. She was looking intently at him and Yudel's eyes were darting from one face to the other, studying each of them. He had no doubt at all that they could tell him more than they had.

"What did you tell the security police?" he asked.

"Nothing. Nothing at all. What else can I do for you?"

Yudel looked round the room. It looked very comfortable and homely in its disorder. He looked at Marion. She was looking at him through wide round eyes, her pale face innocent and guileless. Even Bill, despite his anger, looked innocent : a man concerned for others, whatever his unconscious motives were. "Could I spend the afternoon with you?" Yudel asked. "It's either that or spending it with my in-laws."

Bill Hendricks looked surprised, the anger fast disappearing from his face. He turned to his wife and shrugged. Marion was looking pleased with the idea. "You don't need to ask that," Hendricks said.

"Perhaps you can tell me what Majola was like," Yudel said.

The winter cold came early that afternoon so they sat in the living-room, telling stories about the old days and filling each other in about the happenings of more recent times. Yudel told

125

them of a case he had had in Middelspruit the year before where a schizophrenic black labourer had been wrongly accused of a murder and Bill and Marion accepted his invitation to tell him all about Majola. The stories they told and the way they described Majola's position in Black Social Endeavours left Yudel with the impression of a man who had great energy and sense of purpose, given more to doing than rationalising. The photographs Marion brought out interested Yudel almost as much as what they told him. Most of them were pictures of groups of people, sometimes just grinning at the camera, perhaps in front of a building that was soon to be an office or in an empty hall after a meeting was over. In some of the photographs the white faces of Bill and Marion Hendricks could be seen among the darker faces of their friends. And in all of them the broad confident, almost arrogant face of Muntu Majola was in evidence, staring challengingly at the camera in what was certainly the way he looked at the world in which he lived. It was the first time that Yudel had seen the face of the man for whom he was searching. Often there was a girl standing close to him and it was always the same girl. She was pretty, smooth-skinned and looked very much younger than he was. In contrast to the severity of his face she was often smiling and even in the photographs where her expression was more serious there seemed to be a withheld amusement, a possible inhibiting of her natural impulse. This was a woman who found life enjoyable. On this thin evidence Yudel guessed that perhaps she was drawn more to Muntu Majola the man, than to the political activist.

"Is he married?" Yudel asked.

"He was—years ago. His wife died."

There were photographs of the Black Social Endeavours staff and their friends, painting the walls of buildings, erecting partitions, hammering nails into roofs, raising beer glasses and hanging onto each other at parties. This had been no formal, soundly capitalised operation. Every man and woman had helped to renovate old buildings, paint them and get them operative. This had been the high time of all their lives. None of them had ever dreamt that they would live to see such a day and probably all of them had been able to delude themselves that it could go on forever.

Yudel had not knowingly heard of Black Social Endeavours

126

until that time. Like so many of his countrymen he lived in a closed society, bounded by the limitations and preoccupations of the group to which he belonged. Only occasionally through his work did he see beyond that small vista. He knew that his black countrymen occupied a very different world to the one in which he lived and he understood something of what they suffered, but because he did not share it his comprehension of it would always be limited.

When he had learnt all that he reasonably could from the photographs and stories that Bill and Marion had freely offered he began slowly, employing the skill of long experience, to manoeuvre the conversation to crime, then homicide and finally to Johnny Weizmann. He told them about each case in the files Mimi had assembled for him, inventing the less important details that his memory had discarded. Eventually he explained to them that Weizmann would certainly kill again unless he found some way to stop him. And he explained that Muntu Majola seemed to be the only way. When he had finished the three of them sat silent for a few minutes. The Hendrickses knew by that time what Yudel was doing to them. But they also knew why it was so important to him.

"There is a woman in Soweto," Bill told him at last.

"Majola's woman?"

"Yes."

"The one in the photos?"

"That's right. If anyone knows where he is, she will be the one."

"I can't safely go into Soweto at night without a permit, especially not on a weekend. I'll get picked up."

"You can go in at night," Bill said, "but not by the road. There is a way."

127

TEN

"ROSA LOOKS A bit worried," Hymie was saying. "She said something about the Special Branch." Hymie paused to look carefully at Yudel. "You haven't been getting involved in politics, have you, Yudel?"

"No, Hymie," Yudel said. "Have you?"

"Me?" The conversation's change of course threw Hymie off balance. "Why do you ask?"

"Why did you?"

"Well, it's nothing—just what Rosa said about the Special Branch."

"What was it she said?"

Hymie shrugged, stretching out his hands expansively on either side, the palms facing upward, and turning down the corners of a large thick-lipped mouth. "I don't know. Something about them visiting you." When Yudel did not respond he went on. "We're Prog supporters ourselves, you know. I believe we should show our opposition—but within parliamentary limits. I make that clear to the kids too. I tell them you can join university political movements, but I don't want anything radical. The odd protest is all right, but there have to be limits." Hymie was being very wise and he was listening to what he was saying far more carefully than Yudel was. "Opposition, yes. Radicalism, no."

Yudel looked at the one-acre garden with its shrubs, creepers, statuettes and ornamental stone walls. He looked at the hundred-thousand-rand house and the swimming pool that had exactly half the surface area of an olympic pool and he looked at the synthetic-surfaced tennis court. "I like your place," he said.

Hymie was still involved with his political wisdom and what Rosa had said about the security police. "Thanks," he said absently. "Then there's nothing to worry about? About the Special Branch, I mean?"

128

"Nothing at all."

"Just visited you in the course of duty, I suppose?"

"Their duty or mine?" Yudel asked innocently.

"Well, I . . ."

"Sure," Yudel said. "They just visited me in the course of duty."

"I told Irena there was nothing to worry about. Let's go into the house. It's getting cold out here."

Irena, Rosa and two other women, by their dress and bored superior manners clearly more in Hymie and Irena's social grouping than in Yudel and Rosa's, were having tea and looking out onto the empty tennis court. "It's an original Petzer," Irena was saying. "We paid a fortune for it, but it's worth it. There are just no South African artists these days. I don't mind spending money on a real work of art." For a moment Yudel wondered at a tennis court being called a work of art, but the women in the room all turned appreciatively to face a painting of a large orange bull with prominent pink genital organs.

"It's lovely," Rosa said. "He seems to be influenced by Battiss."

Yudel wondered who Battiss was. He hoped Rosa had it right. It certainly sounded good enough.

"I'm sure he was," one of the other women said. "That use of colour . . ."

At that moment Irena noticed Yudel for the first time. "Yudel's here," she said in a way that seemed to indicate that all other events of the day had now been eclipsed. She heaved herself to her feet, the flesh on her mighty upper arms shaking like jelly, and advanced broadly on him. Yudel tried to duck in behind Hymie, but Irena surged round her husband, gently heaving him aside without slowing. Yudel had to turn his head quickly to take the kiss on his cheek. At least it was dryer than usual, he thought. "I hope you're going to stay for dinner," Irena said sadly. To Yudel her voice sounded sad no matter what she was saying.

"I'm afraid we have to leave early," Yudel said. "I have an appointment at home this evening."

"Then let Rosa stay with me. She can go home later in the week."

"That's a good idea," Hymie said. "Let the sisters get together. Give you a break." It was said archly, signifying all the tantalising things Yudel could be doing while his wife was away.

Yudel could see in Rosa's face how she wanted to stay. He knew that it had to do with her being afraid to be at home alone now. The bastards, Yudel thought. If there was some way I could make them pay . . . "Rosa has to be present this evening, I'm afraid. She can drive out tomorrow." He saw Rosa's expression change to one of surprise. It was the first time she had heard about the evening's appointment.

"Let's at least have a drink before you go," Hymie said.

Yudel accepted a brandy. Outside darkness was approaching quickly. Through the high broad windows he could see an almost full moon high above the horizon. He was glad of that. It should make things much easier.

The talk moved to the increasing price of petrol (Hymie was even thinking of selling one of the three family Mercedes), whether helicopter landing ports should be allowed on private property in Bryanston (No. Only the Zietsmans and the Trafford-Smythes wanted them and did the Zietsmans think a killing on the stock market and a chain of discount stores made them royalty?), if in the event of more riots it would be easier to get your money out of the country by means of paintings or diamonds (diamonds—you could never be sure about the value of paintings) and which property values would be least affected by the next round of riots (very cheap ones and therefore of no interest to any of those present, excepting possibly Yudel and Rosa). Rosa tried not to look embarrassed or intimidated by it all, pretending an interest. If Yudel had been paying attention to her he would have known that to Rosa the fact that she had no interest in such a conversation caused an almost physical pain in her. It was, after all, her unattractive sister who discussed these matters with such familiarity.

But Yudel barely heard any of it. In his mind he was going over the way into Soweto and to the home of Thandi Kunene and the difficulties he might have reaching it.

"Where are we going?" Rosa asked.

"You're going to drop me at a place and then pick me up two hours later."

"Where?"

"I'm taking you there."

"Yudel, what's going on?" He could hear the beginnings of panic in Rosa's voice.

"Now listen, Rosa," he said to her. "There's nothing to worry about. I'm going to see someone and I can't go by car. You will drop me and go to a restaurant or something for the next two hours. All right?"

"This is crazy, Yudel."

"I know. Humour me though. I'm getting somewhere at last."

He took the main highway south, turning away into a narrow road that curved to the right into a dense plantation of blue-gums. The trees were set well back from the road on either side. Yudel watched the trees on the left. Their crests were clearly visible in the moonlight, but underneath the hard High-veld ground was in deep shadow. They passed a broad break in the trees, the sand of a track that ran down its centre almost bright with the reflected moonlight. The road itself was quiet. One other car came from the front, passed quickly and then there was nothing, only the road winding gradually to the right and the trees, silent in the windless night. Yudel counted a second firebreak on his left and allowed the car to slow slightly. In his rear-view mirror a car was coming up quickly from behind. He slowed enough to let it pass, then he had reached the third firebreak and he brought the car to a halt on the gravel shoulder of the road. "There's no danger, Rosa," Yudel said. "This is the third firebreak since we left the main road. Be back here in two hours. It's six-thirty now. That will make it eight-thirty. If I'm not here, waiting for you, go away again and come back another hour later . . ."

Rosa was looking at the dark shadows of the trees on the side of the road where they were parked. "And if you still aren't here?"

"I will be."

"But Yudel this is a forest . . ."

"I noticed. Will you do as I told you?"

She was leaning past Yudel to look at the trees on the other side of the road. They looked equally dark and unwelcoming. "You're sure it's not dangerous?"

"I'm certain." Yudel got out of the car and watched Rosa

slide into the driver's seat. "Don't go back to Irena's."

"Give me credit for a little brains." She sounded angry. In Rosa that was a good sign.

Yudel stepped into the shadow of the trees. "Two hours," he said.

"You'd better be here," Rosa said.

He waited till the car was out of sight round the long curve of the road, then he moved off along a track that ran down the edge of the firebreak. The moon was high and straight in front. Ahead he could see the end of the bluegum plantation and just beyond that, directly across his path, a low barbed-wire fence and a single spreading tree with a thin lacy network of leaves. The bluegums were only a few hundred metres deep. Where they stopped the track turned to the right and then left again after going through a hole in the barbed-wire fence. Yudel walked quickly, breathing the cold night air deep into his lungs and aware of the little puffs of steam coming from his mouth each time he exhaled. He was crossing an uneven meadow. Ahead, against the sky, he could see the long flat roof of a hangar. Far away to his right the meadow ended against more trees, bigger than the gums and very dark. They might have been pines.

The luminous hands of his watch told him that it was a quarter to seven. That meant that he had already spent fifteen minutes of his two hours, and heaven only knew how far ahead Soweto was. Yudel lengthened his stride until he was moving at a steady jog. He was no athlete and never had been one, but his body was light, his shoulders and hips narrow and carrying no excess weight. His health had always been good and his stamina was considerable for someone who was not in any sort of training.

In the clear moonlight he could see every bump and pothole in the path. He was able to move as quickly without discomfort as he would have by daylight. The position of the moon meant that he would be able to see anyone on the path ahead of him in sharp outline against a surprisingly bright sky. Conversely anyone following him would be able to do it with little difficulty and almost no chance of his being seen. Dropping to his haunches, he looked back along the way he had come. Everything was grey in the moonlight, the meadow and the gums

132

running into each other so that it was impossible to see where one ended and the other commenced. Yudel reflected that he had no allies on this one. If the authorities discovered him, they would suspect him of being about the business of inciting the citizens of Soweto to revolution. As for the blacks, the '76 riots in which hundreds of them had died had only been two years before. But he also knew that the uncontrollable mob fury that had made a white face a sure passport to eternity on some of those days now no longer existed. He wondered briefly whether he would rather fall into the hands of the citizens of Soweto or those of the security police. It was a short debate. Yudel gave it to Soweto by a long way.

The path skirted the corrugated iron hangar. He could see the long row of ground lights that marked the airstrip, fading into the distance in either direction. Far away to his left the lights of a control tower stood out high above the runway. He could see no sign of any traffic. He took in the airfield at a glance, but out in front of him, dominating his senses, stretching up a hillside beyond another barrier of trees and then over a further hillside and a further one and another and another until they melted into the distance, Yudel could see the bright orange floodlights of Soweto.

Without stopping he moved diagonally across the airstrip, picking up a row of pines Bill Hendricks had told him about at the place where the smoothly cut grass of the airstrip gave way to the rough grass of the veld. There were a double row of big trees, running down a long gentle slope, with a fair footpath between them. The path was slower and trickier for being in the shadow of the trees, but much better than crossing the veld without one, and the trees provided shelter. He allowed the slope to carry him forward, his eyes searching the path for obstacles. Close to the bottom a wall of very cold air seemed to be moving up the slope, enveloping him instantly, chilling the newly-formed sweat on his back and forehead.

He stopped in the gully at the foot of the slope on the sandy bed of a dry water-course. Looking carefully and giving his eyes enough time to work on it, he could see a number of paler spots up the next slope in the direction of the township. It took him a while to realise that they were the lights made by oil lamps shining through curtained windows and a little longer to make out the first row of small brick houses ahead and to his right.

He circled away to his left into a dense plantation of immature gums, staying far from the houses. Hendricks had told him that he would reach the township near a corner. Following a new firebreak he worked his way around the corner, going slowly, his eyes searching the shadows between the gums for any sign of movement. The Soweto noise was reaching him now: the barking of dogs, a wild insistent tribal song, consisting of a curious rhythm beat out on a drum and a hoarse uninhibited chorus of voices, a radio playing rock-and-roll music, the occasional sound of a car. . . After a few minutes he cut back towards the houses. The young trees were growing in dense clusters and Yudel moved from one to another of the clusters, trying to stay in shadow and under cover. Through the trees he was getting brief views of the bright orange floodlights that bathed most of Soweto in an orange twilight that lasted all night every night. The lights were perched on masts tall enough to take them out of the reach of vandals' rocks, the nearest of them just visible above the crest of the first ridge, its light barely effective from so far away.

A bright light flashed in Yudel's face and he dropped quickly to his haunches. The light whirled away through the trees and he heard the sound of the car's engine from close by. A moment later he could see the tail lights, flickering through the trees not far ahead. The sound of a radio, plaintive and distorted, reached him and was gone. He could smell the dust, raised by the car, as it settled round him and he waited a while without moving. He could see the roof line of one of the little matchbox houses on the far side of the road along which the car had passed, but no more than that. Yudel moved forward again over ground devoid of the litter of dead branches that normally cover the ground under bluegums. Fuel was always a problem in Soweto and bluegum branches burnt with a strong flame and made good coals that stayed hot long after the fire had died. When he stopped this time he had a view of the whole length of the road. The little houses were dark silhouettes against the orange glow the floodlights made in the sky. Now the figure of a man was approaching from lower down the road, moving very quickly and evenly. Yudel saw the upper half of his body pass

134

a gap between two houses. In a few seconds the man drew close enough for Yudel to see the pumping of his legs and the outline of the bicycle.

A car came down the road from the opposite direction, travelling slowly. This time Yudel could see the bumping and dipping of the headlights on the bad surface of the road. He crouched still lower, taking the weight of the upper half of his body on his hands. But he needed the lights. Bill Hendricks had told him to watch for a house the front of which was painted black. The car drew abreast of him slowly, weaving back and forth to avoid potholes, its headlights intermittently lighting the leaves above Yudel. The lights were not shining far ahead of the car, but as it passed him it went over a larger bump, the beams of light flashing high into the air. Yudel's view of the house was momentary, but the black walls stood out sharply from the unpainted brick of the others. He waited until the car had turned a corner, then he stepped out into the open. As far as he could see there was still no one on the road or in front of any of the houses. In the windows cheap cotton curtains were drawn to shut out the night. The dull glow of oil lamps or candles, penetrating the threadbare material, formed the pale patches in the darkness that he had seen earlier.

Yudel walked quickly in the direction the car had taken, keeping to the side of the road and near the cover of the trees. As he had been told the black-painted house was on a corner, the side street running at right angles to the one he was travelling. He stopped at the corner, looking down the long side street, dark except for the faint yellow light from the nearest of the floodlights and the moonlight that seemed far less effective here than in the veld. According to Hendricks the house where Thandi Kunene lived was the first one in the third block on the left-hand side. Yudel could not see the end of the first block, but if it was anything like the blocks in other township streets it could quite possibly be a few hundred metres long. He would pass a lot of doors in that time. A lot of probably hostile people would be between himself and the relative safety of the blue-gums. And a lot could happen in the darkness of a street like this one. Even to Soweto's own people these streets were not safe at night. The frustrations of a million insults found expres-

135

sion in daily killings where the victims were any who were not able to strike back.

Looking round one last time, Yudel started down the road at a quick trot, his eyes searching the houses on either side for any sign of life. He would have admitted it to no one but himself, but something within Yudel was quickened by being part of the apartheid society. He loved the stimulation of it, the threat of the police, the excitement of visits like this one, the troubled presence of Soweto, Thembisa, Atteridgeville, Mdatsane, Guguletu, Kwa Mashu. . . There was much that would not exist in any more sophisticated society that contributed to giving Yudel's experience of life a sharpness that in a truly free country it would have lacked. He hated the system under which he lived with its attendant exclusiveness and injustices, but he would have lived nowhere else. Within the framework of this singular society there was much at which he was unusually accomplished. In a certain sense he was a big league player. And this was his home turf.

Somewhere up ahead the brighter glow from an open door showed on his right. Behind him a dog was barking, joined after a while by a second. The houses on either side were low and narrow, separated from each other by wire fences. The nearest floodlight was a distraction, making it difficult for him to see in the darker street. The end of the block was still not in sight, but he had almost reached the open door and now he could hear the sounds of men's voices from within. Yudel considered stopping, but the consideration was brief. Nothing would be gained by it. He would have to pass the door at some time and no one was going to close it for him.

He increased his pace, putting his feet down as softly as he could. He had an oblique view into the open door and the grey-coated back of a man, then a face on the other side, but not looking in his direction, a second coated back . . . Yudel turned his head away as he passed the door to hide his white face. He was past and there was no shout of alarm or any audible stirring from the people in the room.

He could see the end of the block now, only twenty or thirty houses further on. Suddenly, not far in front of him, a door swung open and a small barefooted boy wearing shorts and a heavy polo-neck jersey came running out, carrying in both

136

hands a bundle of refuse wrapped in a newspaper. He and Yudel looked straight into each other's eyes from a distance of a few paces. Yudel grinned at him, not knowing if the child would be able to see the expression of his face. The child stopped exactly on the spot where he had first seen Yudel. Clutching the bundle against his chest, he turned his head slowly, watching the white man come by. Looking back at him after he had passed, Yudel saw that the boy was still in the same position, watching him go. The figures of a man and a woman were approaching out of the shadows of the houses on the other side. Drawing closer, Yudel could see that they were young, the man lean, despite the cold wearing only a white shirt open at the collar and slacks, the woman walking a few steps behind him, wearing what seemed to be a cotton dress with a shawl pulled round her shoulders. Yudel slowed to a walk and the man approached him. It was too dark to see his face clearly, but the uncertainty in the way he moved and the way he craned his neck forward indicated that he felt far more bewilderment at seeing Yudel there than hostility. "Boss?" Yudel heard him say. It was clearly a question. What is the boss doing here tonight? Or, is there anything I can do for the boss? This man was not going to be a problem to him. He waved one hand at the row of houses along the road, and then in the direction of the nearest floodlight, mumbling under his breath the one word, "Lights."

"A-ah," the man said, the sound long-drawn and puzzled.

Now three men, their shoulders hunched as if that would provide some sort of protection against the cold, were coming quickly towards him on his side of the road. They were only a few steps from him when one of them noticed Yudel for the first time. "Hello there," he said, his voice carrying the bravado of one who is normally down near the bottom of humanity's pile and suddenly finds himself in a position of temporary superiority. Yudel said nothing, only making sure that he passed well wide of them, hoping that the coldness of the night would prevent them from stopping to investigate him any further. "Hello there," the voice called again.

Yudel looked back. The three men had stopped and were watching him. "Hello there," he said.

The three men turned and went on their way. And Yudel was no longer afraid. The little identical houses that he was passing, with the colourful tattered curtains in the windows and the old and battered cars in the yards or out front, were places where human beings lived, where they were born and took their first uncertain steps towards adulthood, where dreams were spawned and either flared into something real or more probably died in the reality of Soweto. These were simply the dwellings of a very depressed human community, no more and no less dangerous than any such community anywhere on earth. That they would be hostile towards him was to be expected, but the thought that they would eagerly seek his death if they found him on their streets was based on the collective fears of the group to which he belonged, not on any real knowledge of the people.

A man sitting behind the steering wheel of a car, slouched low so that his head pressed against the backrest, rolled his head in the direction from which Yudel's footsteps were coming. The eyes were vague and unfocussed, probably drunken, seeing nothing.

Yudel found the house he was looking for. It was like all the others, identical except for the number that Bill Hendricks had given him and its position at the start of the third block. He knocked at the door and it was opened immediately by a teenage boy. The boy stepped back quickly at seeing Yudel, his eyes widening in surprise and fear. Yudel stepped into a tiny room full of people. "Good evening," he said. "I'm looking for Miss Thandi Kunene." But he had already found her. She was sitting at the table in the centre of the room, her eyes wider than normal and her mouth hanging open slightly in wonder. As the photographs had shown her to be she was a young woman, the skin of her face smooth and deep brown. Her hair was combed into a crest along the top of her head, adding to the impression of surprise. The room was silent with the sort of silence you would expect when someone has just made an utterly shameful revelation about himself or someone else in the company. The eyes of the others that Yudel's swift glance had taken in all held the same surprised look, but there was also fear in many of the faces. "You are Miss Thandi Kunene," Yudel told her.

The woman nodded slowly. Yudel was looking directly at her, but aware that some of the others in the room were pushing past him to get out of the door. Most of those in the room when Yudel had come in had been young men with a few of Thandi's age completing the gathering. One of the young men answered for Thandi. He was seated at the table next to her and he stammered as he spoke. "Who-who-who is it who wants to know?"

Yudel turned to look at him. The young face was both arrogant and alarmed, afraid and hating the knowledge that he was afraid. "Yudel Gordon," Yudel told him. "I need to speak to Miss Kunene in private if I may." There were a few shouted voices in the street outside and the sound of someone running. Yudel looked straight at the young man. "Is there someone I should ask?" He looked uncertainly round the room as if expecting to find some such person.

The man made no attempt to answer and Yudel's eyes found those of the woman. She was still looking at him and, added to the surprise in her face, he could read the beginnings of curiosity there. She partly raised one hand, a quick furtive gesture to show him that he must say nothing.

The street was suddenly quiet again, the footsteps having seemingly left in every direction. He heard a door slam shut somewhere and then another. Yudel looked round the room. Apart from Thandi and the young man one other woman and two men remained in the room. The men had taken up positions just behind Yudel. A glance at their faces showed him the same mixture of fear and hostility that he had seen in the face of the one who had spoken. Henchmen, Yudel decided, assistants, camp followers even, nothing more.

The footsteps were returning. A young man probably still in his teens came quickly into the room, said something in an African language that Yudel did not understand and took up a position with his back to a wall. Another came in. "There's nobody," he said in English. "It looks like he came alone." Two more came in, and another and the message of each was the same. Returning from their fruitless explorations of the nearby streets they again filled the tiny room. Yudel wondered what they would have done if they had met teams of police reinforcements instead of only the empty streets. Expecting to be searched, he was surprised when no one seemed to think of doing it. The young people in the room were playing a game, a dangerous game not of their own choosing, and as yet they were not playing it very professionally. Yudel knew that it was the sort of game where, if you did not learn fast, you were seldom granted an opportunity to complete your education.

The one at the table looked past Yudel to one of those behind him. "Wha-what do you say?" The first word of the sentence seemed to be bottled up, struggling to break free, but when it was released the others poured out quickly, the obstruction temporarily removed.

"System," the other said.

Yudel knew enough of township lore to know that "System" in this case meant the security police. It was not a mistake he wanted them to make.

The one at the table was now looking at another of his friends. Yudel heard the one word, "System," again describe his probable identity.

It came again. "System." And again, until everyone except the women had been asked their opinions and all the opinions had been the same.

Yudel imagined that what he was seeing was the last distorted vestige of Black Social Endeavours. The organisation that had set out to destroy racism had been reduced to this hunted-looking little band, the grand dreams gone, now trying only to avoid the police. And somewhere, perhaps not far away, Muntu Majola too was hiding, perhaps determined to take his campaign of vengeance still further. "May I join this debate?" Yudel asked politely.

"Ou-our friends wouldn't tell anyone to come here unless they were forced. And nobody here knows you."

"Bill Hendricks told me."

"If-if he told you, he was forced." The young man behind the frightened, but hostile face had made up his mind. Yudel doubted that there would be any room for his arguments. "Who-oo all knows you are here?"

"Bill Hendricks knows."

"Who else?" His confidence was growing and he managed to speak without stuttering.

"His wife."

"Who else?"

"No one else."

140

"You expect us to believe that?"

"I expect you to listen to what I have to say before you make up your mind."

"Talk, white man. Talk quick and talk good if you want to go home tonight."

Yudel talked. First he pointed out that if he was a policeman then surely he was not the only one that knew and they had problems with him dead or alive. And also if he was a policeman there would have been no point to his coming alone. Then he told them what he had told Bill and Marion Hendricks. He expected that most of them would be aware of Weizmann and that that part of the story would be believed, so he filled in the sort of details that only intimate knowledge would reveal. As he spoke he looked from one face to the other of everyone he could see without turning round. They were young, and now they were serious rather than aggressive. They were the innocents, soldiers in ragged shirts and flannels and tennis shoes, who had not been able to accept the end of the organisation that had been of such importance to them all. Now they were probably no more than Muntu Majola's supporters, ready to shield him with their hopeless young lives if necessary. Looking at them, Yudel was certain only that he had their attention. He finished by telling how Majola had saved the life of Mrs Sinclair's servant, Julie.

No one spoke. Yudel sensed that there were those in the room that believed him. He also sensed that the young man at the table whose opinion was clearly of greatest importance did not. He looked past Yudel at someone behind him. "System," he said. "He wants Muntu." Looking into the hostile young face, Yudel regretted the irreligious life he had led.

"He's telling the truth," the woman said. The man turned towards her. "Muntu told me about it. He saw the old man kill the girl. He was there. The door was open and he saw it. And he saved the woman."

The man hesitated, watching Yudel all the time, seemingly reluctant to discover that Yudel was not System. "What are you getting out of this?" he asked.

"It's my job," Yudel said.

"Your job?" The voice was cold and unbelieving.

"Weizmann is my patient."

141

"Your job? This is not your job."

"I want to stop Weizmann killing."

"Why? What's another dead black to you?"

"He's telling the truth, Wilson," the woman said. "How else could he know about Muntu seeing the girl?"

"Somebody saw Muntu. He could still be System."

"And how did I know about Thandi?" Yudel asked.

"How do we know where Bill Hendricks is now? He may have told about Thandi under torture."

"Have someone phone his home," Yudel said. "Find out for yourself."

"We'll see," the man called Wilson said. He nodded to one of those behind Yudel. The door opened and Yudel felt the cold rush of night air against his back that was still wet with perspiration. It closed again almost immediately and he heard the sound of retreating footsteps, quickly fading on the dirt road of the township. He hoped that Bill and Marion had not decided to go out for the evening. "If your story is not true you're finished, white man," Wilson said quietly. There was no doubt in Yudel's mind that the other man would have preferred that as a solution to the problem. His would be at least the partial atonement for many other deaths. It was a solution that would satisfy, at least for the moment, some of Wilson's emotional needs.

"And if you find Muntu?" the woman asked.

"Then I'll want his help to get Weizmann convicted of murder."

The woman's eyebrows lifted high at the thought and a smile both incredulous and amused appeared on her face. It was an attractive face, the quality of humour and warmth that he could see in it reminding him of Bill and Marion's photographs. It was a quality that always seemed to be present to some degree. Inwardly Yudel commended Majola's taste in women. "You want Muntu to appear in court to give evidence?"

Put that way it seemed ridiculous to Yudel too. "He's my only hope. I need to get something definite by this Friday when they hold the inquest. I know he can't appear in court. But he saw what happened. Perhaps he can do something to help me. I'm hoping for an affidavit. There's also a chance that he can tell me something that might lead me to new evidence."

142

"He can run for his life. That's all he can do."

The man who had gone to make the call came back and told Wilson that he had spoken to Bill Hendricks and everything seemed to be all right. "We still can't help you, white man," Wilson said.

"Listen," Thandi said. "I'll tell you the truth." She leant over the table towards Yudel, the amusement still flickering in her eyes. "We don't know where Muntu is. When he leaves me he doesn't even tell me where he is going because he knows that under torture no one can be trusted."

Looking into her honest brown eyes, Yudel was as sure as a man ever can be that a woman is telling him the truth. "Tell him I came and tell him what I wanted."

"I will."

"Thanks," he said. "The existence of this place is safe with me. Am I free to go?"

"Don't come back," Wilson said.

Yudel gave Thandi his telephone number in case she might yet be able to help him. Then he left. He had no intention of ever coming back.

On the slope just below the runway Yudel stopped to look back at the bright orange floodlights, seeming to hang in the sky over the township. He wondered about Wilson and Thandi and Majola, about himself and Johnny Weizmann and the singular convergence of events that had linked all their lives together. In Soweto, as in the little shop on Myburgh Street, there was a division of the night. Here too love and kinship struggled against pain and alienation for dominance. And here too Yudel could see no solution.

ELEVEN

Y UDEL SAW THE lights of the car, slowing, as he came down the firebreak. Rosa had barely brought it to a stop when he was opening the door on her side. "Move over," he said. "I'll drive."

She slid over, leaving the car in gear, allowing it to jerk forward and choke off. "I'm sorry. . ."

Yudel could not remember ever hearing Rosa's voice sound so uncertain. "Everything's all right," he said. "I'm all right." He glanced at her in time to see her nod in acknowledgement, her head shaking in a series of small rapid movements. He felt helpless and uneasy in the face of her obvious distress. He had seen it growing in her since their first visit from the Special Branch on the Thursday before. "Are you all right?" he asked.

She nodded again and turned towards him. "Yudel, how long is this going to continue?"

"Not long." They were coming out of the trees and passing small industrial buildings. "It can't be too long now."

"Please, Yudel. You must do something. Solve it or do whatever you must do, but do it quickly. I can't go on this way."

He reached out and patted her hands where she was holding them tightly together in her lap. "It can't be too long now. I'm making progress." He was trying to reassure her, but knowing that what he was saying was not true. He seemed to have reached the final possibility and that had turned out to be no possibility after all. There seemed to be nowhere left to go. But Yudel knew that he would not be able to ignore Weizmann, not until he was sure that the killings would stop. Punishing the sad old man with the fearful past and the gangrenous hands and feet was a last possibility. He knew only that the killings must stop. "I think you should stay with Irena until it's all over," he said.

"What about you?"

"There's nothing to be afraid of, Rosa."

"I don't understand what's happening."

"I'll tell you everything when it's over. In the mean time you go and stay with Irena."

"Will you be safe?"

Yudel knew that Rosa was only going through the motions of showing concern for him. What she really wanted was to get out of it herself. She was asking about his safety, but what she meant was—Yes, I'll go to Irena. Try not to get yourself killed, but as for me, I'll go to Irena.

As he started the engine Yudel saw Hymie go back into the house, pausing a moment in the doorway for what was intended to be a reassuring wave of his hand. Rosa was already installed in one of Irena's many guest rooms. The explanations to Hymie and Irena had been brief, Irena who was possibly Yudel's greatest admirer nodding as if she understood everything, and Hymie looking puzzled and perhaps a little irritated, finally coming out to the car with Yudel and saying, "Anything I can do—you only have to ask." Yudel viewed the offer on much the same level as Rosa's concern for his safety.

His watch told him that it was a quarter to ten. He had time to go to the Hendrickses and tell them what he had learnt or, rather, what he had not learnt. Perhaps they might be able to suggest some other way that he could find Majola.

The drive from the very wealthy suburb where Hymie and Irena had their home to the happily comfortable one where Bill and Marion Hendricks lived was short, the traffic sparse. It took him through lovely tree-lined streets. Yudel was there in less than ten minutes.

He had not recognised the car the first time he had seen it, when it had been parked in the driveway of his home. This time he recognised it immediately. He braked hard, threw his car into reverse and backed round the corner at the end of the block. He stopped close behind another car parked against the pavement, so that his car would not be immediately visible from the corner. Then he ran back to where he could see the house.

The car was still there, blocking the Hendricks's drive. From where he was watching he could see only the roof of the house, the rest being obscured by a neighbour's fence. Yudel hurried down the street, keeping close to the garden walls on the opposite side. The house directly opposite the Hendricks's place seemed to have a large garden with a lot of dense shrubbery. Yudel made for it, glancing continually in the direction of the security police car and the house. The house he was aiming for was in darkness. He vaulted a low stone wall and stepped in behind a dense shrub that had mercifully kept its leaves through the start of winter. The cover in the garden was not as good as it had looked from down the road, but it would do as long as the owner stayed inside and as long as no one switched on an outside light.

Yudel was only just in time. Warrant Officer Marais was coming down the path from the house with Bill Hendricks following him. Bill was leaning forward, like a man pacing back and forth, deep in thought. A policeman Yudel had not previously seen was following close behind. Marais opened the back door of the car and got in. Yudel saw that Bill seemed to hesitate for a moment and glance back at the house, a quick parting look at what he might be losing. The wrinkles on his forehead went only a little way up the high pink dome of his head. He straightened up suddenly, obviously having been pushed from behind, his head jerking back and his feet quickly taking the last few steps to the car. The second policeman got in after Bill so that he was wedged between them. Now Dippenaar was coming down the path, walking straight upright with a businesslike self-assured manner, clearly a man who saw himself as being occupied by work of some importance. Yudel looked past him to the house, but the curtains in all the windows were drawn and he could not see into any of the rooms. He waited until the car had travelled slowly down the length of the street, Bill Hendricks seeming shrunken between the two big men on either side of him, had turned the corner and was gone.

There was no sign of movement from the house, but if they had seen him arrive their leaving might be a trap. He went deeper into the property in which he was hiding, following a narrow brick-paved path down the side of the house, climbed a reinforced concrete fence at the back and found himself in the back yard of another house. This time the garden was wider and he was able to keep well away from the house on a smooth wide lawn. There was no wall in front and he reached the next street as a dog started barking near the house. He trotted up to the corner, stopping there to look for Dippenaar and Marais's car. His own car was parked half the length of the block towards the street he had just left. Apart from a few other parked cars the street was empty. The only other danger was that they might still have a man at the house. Yudel reckoned that he should be able to judge that by phoning. But he was very tired now and finding a telephone without making all sorts of explanations provided its own problems. What the hell, he thought. If they had a man there he would brazen it out somehow.

He walked the distance back to the house, still on the lookout for the car in which Bill had been taken away. But everything seemed normal. The quiet suburban scene was just as always, the doors and windows closed against the cold of the night and the possibility of intruders, lights in a few windows, the bright square of a television tube shining through a neighbour's curtains. There was no sign that a man had just been taken from his home by force, a man that Yudel knew had committed only one crime: he had cared too deeply for those who were unable to care for themselves.

Yudel had to knock twice before Marion answered. He heard her voice through the solid wooden door. "Yes . . . who is it?" It sounded weak and shocked.

"It's me—Yudel."

He heard the almost frantic scratching sound of Marion unlocking the door, then she was in his arms, holding onto his shoulders for support. Yudel reflected that this was the second time in a few days that the security police had driven a woman into his arms. This time the sensation was less than entirely pleasant and he did no more than hold her against him. Her shoulders and chest were heaving deeply as if struggling for air. Yudel patted her back gently until she detached herself.

As soon as they were back in the house with the door closed and locked behind them he asked, "Are you all right?"

She nodded, reminding him of the way Rosa had done it a few hours earlier. From the mantelpiece she picked up a drink that she had poured earlier and swallowed some of it down. "I'm all right," she gasped. The gasping had nothing to do with the potency of the drink. She was drawing air into her lungs through her open mouth like a person in danger of drowning who had just unexpectedly reached the surface.

Yudel was not the most useful man in dealing with distressed ladies. He wanted to step forward to take her in his arms again, but doubted his ability to do it confidently and gracefully, and he doubted her willingness to have him do it. He also wanted to say something comforting, but nothing sensible came to mind. In the end he took the brandy bottle from the mantelpiece and poured himself a drink. "I'll join you," he said. It sounded weak and like something you might have said at a party, leaving Yudel sorry that he had said anything. Marion was still struggling for air, her eyes closed and the brandy glass held tightly in both hands, when Yudel at last said something sensible. "What are you going to do tonight? Do you want me to sleep here?"

"No." She shook her head decisively. "You're not involved. Stay out of it. I have friends that are committed coming to fetch me." That word "committed" was intruding again, still excluding Yudel in Marion's mind. "I phoned them. Do you know what happened?"

"They took Bill away. I was watching from across the road." Marion closed her eyes, not trusting them to remain dry, and not saying anything, also not trusting her voice to remain steady. "I think you'd better sit down," he told her. He took her by the arm and led her to an armchair. She sat upright on the edge of the seat, her hands clenched tightly round the brandy glass, supporting each other. He sat down on a hardback chair near to her. "Will your friends be here soon?"

Carefully, between breaths, she tried to speak. "They'll be here . . ." Something cracked in her voice and the last word was lost. She tried again. ". . . soon," she said. "They'll be here soon." She turned suddenly on Yudel, the pretence forgotten, not caring that he should see that she was crying. "What are they going to do to him?"

"They'll interrogate him."

"What else?"

"Nothing else. They're afraid of bad publicity." Yudel had

148

heard about the security police methods and, given the circles in which Marion moved, he had no doubt that she knew more about those methods than he did. He imagined that how far they would go would depend on how desperate they were. And if they really believed that Majola had killed two of their officers they might be pretty desperate. He knew—and he was sure that Marion knew—that their surest weapon against bad publicity was that no one, having been through their hands, would want the details repeated. There are some things that a man or woman who has suffered them shrinks from ever reliving. No normal human being readily seeks out his or her own humiliation.

She was shaking her head and had brought her hands up to her face, the action knocking the brandy glass to the floor. "That's not all. You know that's not all." The words were choked and breathless.

"Try not to think about it," Yudel said. It was clearly an impossible suggestion. He was still not doing too well.

Marion did not even attempt to answer. She had not moved from her position, seated stiffly on the edge of the chair. She had changed surprisingly little in the years since he had known her at university. Her face was a little more fleshy, but still unwrinkled. Her figure was as slight as it had been then and her skin as pale. She still cared as little for her appearance as she had in those days. Her dresses looked as shapeless on her and she was wearing the same heavy masculine-looking sandals she had been wearing that afternoon. But much had changed since the days when Yudel had been in something close to awe of her furious uncompromising opinions and actions on what she considered to be social and political injustices. So far as he knew she had never campaigned against bullfighting. It was probably the very quality of certainty in her that had frightened Yudel and made him more than usually hesitant in his dealings with her, and that very hesitance that had persuaded her that Bill Hendricks was the right man. The result of Marion's strength of personality and the force of her convictions had been that in everything that was important to him Bill Hendricks was dominated by his wife, whereas Yudel was dominated by his wife in everything that was unimportant to him. In the things that were important to him Rosa had never questioned the

149

rightness of Yudel's actions and had only tried to influence them when money had been involved.

"Did they say anything to you?" Yudel asked at last. She looked at him uncertainly, almost as if she had not understood the question. "Did they say anything to you? What did they say?"

"They say . . ." Her hands were against her face and speaking was difficult. Her breathing was easing, but the membranes that make the sounds of speech were drawn taut by the tension within her. "They say . . ." It was no more than a painful croak. "They say they'll keep him until I tell them where to find Muntu Majola. They say that if I go to a newspaper or if I don't tell them in twenty-four hours I won't get the same man back . . ."

"This Majola," Yudel started to say. "He's a dangerous . . ."

"If he's dangerous they made him that way." For a moment her voice was angry, but only for a moment, then again it was broken and despairing. "Yudel, what will they do to him? He's not a strong man. What are they going to do to Bill? Do you know? I don't think he would ever have been involved in all this if it hadn't been for me." She looked into his face, searching for an answer and finding none. "What am I going to do? If I tell them what we told you this afternoon they'll take Thandi in. God only knows what they'll do to her. It'll be much worse than what they'll do to Bill. If I don't tell . . . Tell me, Yudel, what will they do to him? Tell me . . ."

Sleep was an uncertain matter, a drifting close to the surface, a running before furious winds, a fleeing from unidentifiable fears, a struggling in shadows and dark places, a grasping after secrets and a numbness, a cold paralysis in the grip of great danger. . . Yudel woke up, tearing off the sheets and running for the door, only to stop half-way across the room, not knowing where he was going or the reason for his fear. He came slowly back to bed. Switching on his bedside light, he saw that it was just after four o'clock. Still shivering slightly with the effects of the dream and not anxious to return to it, he put on his slippers and dressing gown and went to the kitchen where he switched on the kettle to make coffee. Yudel drank coffee at all times: in emergencies and at times of ease, to calm himself

150

or to give himself energy, to put himself to sleep or to wake himself up. In Rosa's view he was an addict. Now he drank it in a probably ineffectual effort to drive away the dream he could not remember and to clear his mind. In all the confusion of the last few days he had to find the significant pieces. He had to frame a course of action.

Even the coffee did not help. Clarity was a problem when he knew about the decision that faced Marion and when his imagination would not ignore where Bill might be and what might be happening to him. The week just past had brought him his first experience of the security police, but in prison he had heard stories. On one occasion he had had to deal with a political prisoner who had been driven close to the outer limit of reality by what he had suffered. Yudel had failed in his efforts. It was normal and desirable for a psychologist to free a patient from imaginary fears, but how could Yudel free a man from the fear of a danger they both knew was still alive? He would have had to induce insanity in the man to have released him from his terror.

He did not want to think about the security police, nor about Marion and Bill. They had known there were risks. It was not his business. He would not think about them. He thought about Thandi Kunene and the young man called Wilson. No. He did not want that either. They would all be distractions now. And there was nothing he could do. Or was there? Yudel hated it. He hated his powerlessness to do anything to help them. He hated the fear he had seen in Rosa and in Wilson. And he hated his own fear.

But he had to think about Weizmann. The other was not his business. He could not afford to be diverted.

When he had finished the first cup of coffee he made himself a second. Then he fetched the Weizmann files from his study. If it was impossible to prove Weizmann guilty in the Cissy Abrahamse case, perhaps one of the others could be reopened. It would take time, but if there was no other way. . . He went through the files again, wondering about his chances of success in each one. The Malherbe case was unlikely. It had gone through an inquest and a long civil hearing and Weizmann had won all the way. The Isaiah Zulu case had not even yielded a witness other than Weizmann. Yudel knew that he could go

151

looking for a witness who might or might not exist, but Weizmann had run Zulu down at night in an industrial area. The place was not likely to be swarming with witnesses. According to the file Weizmann had been the only witness in the Nkabinde case. In the Qumbisa case the victim had had a friend with him, but the Attorney-General had decided not to prosecute. Whatever the friend had said had obviously not affected that decision in any way. The only witness to Oscar Mbhele's death had been Weizmann. Henderson Mhlope had a friend with him. The friend had gone to jail and Weizmann had remained free. Barney Tsatse had survived to make a statement to the police, but no charges had been laid. Only the Reddy case had gone against him, but no one had died and he had paid the fine the magistrate had imposed. None of them looked promising. In each there was likely to be a lot of work, a lot of time spent and no result. And in the mean time Weizmann might kill again.

It was all too much for him to deal with. He found his thoughts moving away from Weizmann and the others, retreating before them, looking for an area in which to operate where a solution was possible. He found himself thinking about young Graham Roberts and his strange behaviour where actions had to be repeated three times before they satisfied him, lines of homework rewritten three times, doors being opened and closed three times before he felt able to pass through. . .

Yudel was aware that the number three had a special significance in the unconscious mind. Over thousands of years men had invented mythologies and godheads that were dependent on that number and the result had been to impress its importance indelibly on the human psyche. Or perhaps he was seeing things in the wrong order. Perhaps some deep-rooted unconscious knowledge within man had made him see the eternal in the form of a trinity. Whichever way it was three seemed to be the number of completeness, perfection, wholeness, the number of eternity. Ancient Babylon, struggling out of a harsh tribal past to a glory such as the world had not previously seen, had its triad of Ana, Bel and Ea. Egypt had called them Isis, Osiris and Horus. Christianity sought to relieve its self-imposed guilt and suffering by way of a Father, Son and Holy Spirit. Three kings with three presents had visited the new-born Jesus. He remembered learning about the Slavic tradition that God was the sun, the sky and fire; and a rabbi once telling him that the soul had three parts. In religions and social systems everywhere three parties, the mother, the father and God, were seen to be necessary to life.

Yudel's memories of childhood were filled with fairy tales where the hero had to do three brave deeds before he could marry the king's only daughter, or was allowed three wishes before a clash with a giant, a dragon or some other evil force. In the tabernacle there were three divisions of the sanctuary. Even Freud, exploring the deep caverns and tunnels of the human subconscious, had decreed that the human psyche had three parts, the Id, the Ego and the Super-ego. The ancient mystics had taught that the three parts of a candle flame, the blue flame, the white flame and the heat, were representative of the three parts of the soul. The scriptures that long before had been forced into Yudel's reluctant brain were full of three feasts for three years, third-born sacrifices, a universe that was heaven, earth and abyss . . .

To young Graham Roberts the word, God, had three letters, so did the word, man, and the word, boy . . . He was a boy. The father that he so desperately tried to please was a man. God was perfect and man was in his image. Graham Roberts was obsessively trying for perfection. Somewhere far below normal rational thinking was the knowledge that three meant perfection and, if he could be perfect, perhaps then he would be acceptable both to God and to his father. And in his mind the two were probably synonymous anyway.

Suddenly Yudel was shivering violently. He could not believe it, but he had learnt that nothing was too strange to be accommodated in the mind of a fellow human. He started scratching feverishly through the files, writing down the dates of each killing, ignoring those where the intended victim had survived. Weizmann had also had an obsession to please his father. He remembered Mrs Sammel saying, "All he ever wanted to do was please my father." He remembered Weizmann himself trying to defend his father. "If a man grows up hard he learns to live the right way." And he remembered Weizmann's reaction under hypnosis when he had been told that his father was approaching him, reaching out his hand to touch him—the

153

sudden unexpected attempt at flight and his urinating with fear.

He had the dates of the killings written out and immediately Yudel could see the pattern. 18 September '67, 28 January '68, 5 May '68 . . . the first three killings were within eight months of each other. Then there was a break of more than four years. 21 October '72, 16 December '72, 9 February '73. . .three killings in less than four months this time. Yudel scratched out the Reddy case where no one had died. On the 16th of April 1973 Weizmann had been forbidden to carry a firearm for five years. That meant that the ban had expired two months before, but he had knocked down and killed Isaiah Zulu on the 15th of February just before the expiry date. He had seemed to be almost preparing the ground for the return of his gun when he would be able to complete a new trio of killings. Cissy Abrahamse had been the second. The third was still outstanding.

When he killed again, as Yudel knew he would kill again, there would have been three lots of three killings each. Yudel asked himself if the cycle would then be complete. Would Weizmann be able to relax in the knowledge that he had achieved perfection? There was no way Yudel could know. But of something he was certain. The present series would have to be completed.

TWELVE

THE CHIRPING OF the telephone slowly penetrated the protective layers of an uneasy sleep. Yudel was very tired and he was sitting on the edge of the bed, looking absently round the room for his dressing gown, before he realised what it was that had woken him. He went into his study to answer it. "Gordon here," he said into the mouthpiece.

"Mister Gordon?" The voice on the other end of the line was soft, female and definitely African. He thought he knew to whom it belonged. He waited for her to speak again, wide awake now. "Mister Gordon?" The voice was hesitant, questioning. The I in mister was pronounced sharply, almost meester. Yudel was sure that he was listening to the voice of Thandi Kunene on the other end of the line. He hesitated for a moment, not wanting to lose the contact between them. Then he hung up. Freek's warning that when dealing with certain people it was wisest not to use the telephone was suddenly fresh in his mind, so was Bill Hendricks' reference to the security police network with their phone tappings. None of this had been in his mind when he gave Thandi his number. Now no matter what she wanted to tell him Yudel would not be able to listen to her. It would be impossible for them to even arrange to meet somewhere. To deliver her into the hands of those who might be listening was unthinkable.

The telephone was chirping at him again. Yudel sat at his desk and waited for it to stop. The sound seemed to continue for a long time, but when it stopped this time it stayed silent.

The dull-grey light of early morning was coming in at the window. He opened a curtain to look out over the rooftops of the partly awake city. He wondered how many of the people in all of those houses—brick-and-tile, carpeted, coal-fire-in-the-living-room, servants-quarters-out-the-back, neatly kept gardens

155

lush with shrubs and flowers—how many of them had any idea
at all of the things that were done in their defence?

He went back to the bedroom and started to get dressed.

Getting away from Doctor Williamson was a problem. Eventually Yudel invented a complicated lie about the mental state of
a paroled prisoner living in Johannesburg and convinced the
old psychologist of its urgency. "Come back as soon as you're
finished," Doctor Williamson had said.

"Of course," Yudel had assured him as he fled from the
office, his thoughts already occupied by where he was going.
Coming back was a matter of less importance and would be for
later consideration.

He took the road he had travelled the night before, this time
not following the turning that led into the plantation. Instead
he drove straight into Soweto by the main road. He reasoned
that in daylight a car with government number plates would
draw no attention and no embarrassing questions about permits
would be asked.

The voice on the telephone had said only two words, "Mister
Gordon," but they were in Yudel's mind so clearly that he
could still hear the sound of them. The question of why she
would have telephoned him so soon after he had been with her
was uppermost in his thoughts. What did she have to say that
was so important? Perhaps she had already spoken to Majola
and wanted to arrange a meeting. His recollection of Thandi
Kunene had to do with her face in the photographs, always close
to Majola, the sound of her voice on the telephone and the
quick sure way she had come to his defence on the previous
night. More than any of those things it had to do with the
knowledge that she was Majola's woman and now she wanted
to speak to him.

The road carried only one lane of traffic in either direction
and was very busy, delivery vans, government vehicles, old
much-used cars and the occasional newer models all hurrying
either into or out of the huge network of identical little houses
that to live in must have been something between a city and a
concentration camp. Yudel turned off the main road as soon
as he reached the first houses. He took a road that skirted the

156

edge of the township, driving slowly and watching for the place where he had entered the night before. The houses all had white asbestos roofs and red-black brick walls. Many had their fences built up to more than head-height, the upper strands always of barbed wire, to protect the little peach tree next to the house, the few rows of vegetables round the back and of course a man, a woman and their young.

The streets were quiet: a few old people who were no longer considered to be employable, a number of children of less than schoolgoing age, a group of boys who should have been in school and were kicking a plastic ball, a work gang consisting mainly of women that was cleaning up the litter along the road and a few young women in front of the houses, some of them with babies in their arms: all went about their business barely turning to see the government car coming past. By daylight his fears of the night seemed ridiculous. The quiet streets, the few bored-looking people and the relative immunity from prosecution provided by the government car had restored everything to a superficial normality.

Away to his right at the top of a steep rise he could already see the long flat stretch of veld that was the airport's runway and a section of the hangar's iron roof. He turned right to stay on the edge of the township, following a road named after a government-supporting Johannesburg city councillor, past a house with a sign in one of the windows saying "Tents for Hire". Ahead and to his right he could see the row of pines he had followed. Then he was passing the straggling bluegum plantation he had used for cover. A moment later he was alongside the black-fronted house and had turned the corner, now following the same route he had taken the night before. Like the other streets this one was quiet, only a few small children playing in a drift of loose sand that had been washed across the road in one of the summer storms and had never been removed.

The door of the house where Thandi Kunene lived was closed and the curtains in the windows were drawn. A young man in a red sweater, blue denim trousers and tennis shoes was leaning against the wall of the house. He grinned as Yudel came through the gate, his upper lip curling right over to reveal pink gums and yellow teeth. "Is Miss Kunene in?" Yudel asked. The

157

grin remained unchanged and the man pushed himself away from the wall with a shrug of his shoulders. He lifted his hands in front of him, knocking the knuckles of his clenched fists together so that Yudel heard the sound they made. "Is Miss Kunene in?" Yudel asked again. "I want to see Thandi Kunene."

The young man in the sweater nodded vigorously, still knocking his knuckles together and grinning. "Thandi Kunene," he said to Yudel.

"I want to see her. Is she inside?"

"Inside," the young man said.

"May I go in?"

"Inside," he said again.

A woman had come out of a house on the other side of the road and was coming towards them. She was lean and tired-looking, a shapeless black and brown dress hanging limply on her body. "Can I help you, master?" she asked. "He can't hear."

"He does hear," Yudel said, glancing quickly at the young man to see his reaction. "He answered me."

There was no discernible reaction from the other man. He looked as friendly as before, his upper lip still curled over in a friendly grimace. "Inside," he said again. Obviously it was a word that sat easily in his mouth.

"He can't hear, master," the woman repeated, tapping the points of her fingers against the top of her head.

Yudel looked again at the young man, this time understanding the sort of hearing to which she was referring. "I want to see Thandi Kunene," he told the woman.

"She's not here."

"Are you sure? I spoke to her last night. May I go in to see?"

"You can go inside, but she's not here. The police came." It was said evenly, without any special emphasis, as if it was such an ordinary matter that comment was hardly necessary.

"Police in uniform or without uniforms?"

"Police with uniforms and police with no uniforms."

"When did they come?"

"Maybe six o'clock."

The thought registered in Yudel's mind that that must have

158

been just about the time she had tried to phone him. "Did they take her away?"

"They take Thandi away and they take Wilson away."

"Inside," said the man who could not hear.

Yudel looked from the woman to him. At least there was something he had got right.

It had taken them just a few hours after arresting Bill to get what they wanted. Yudel wondered if it had been Bill who had been unable to endure their attentions, or if it had been Marion who, tortured by her imagination and guilt, had been unable to leave her husband in their hands? He wondered what Bill and Marion would say to each other when next they met. Would they talk about Thandi?

The public prosecutor showed no interest in what Freek was saying. Clearly he felt that Yudel and Freek were trespassing on Department of Justice territory and the sooner they got back onto their own ground the better. His department did not need Prisons and Police to tell them how to do their job. "I don't think we prepare to take action in this case," he said. He spoke English badly and with a pronounced Afrikaans accent. The way he held his head, tilted slightly back, the way he tried so hard to look both thoughtful and superior, and the way he was careful never to concede a point: all reminded Yudel of Doctor Williamson. The prosecutor was young, but he had learnt quickly. Yudel reckoned that his future in the civil service was secure.

"I'll speak to your senior," Freek said.

The superior unamused face looked surprised at the idea of a policeman suggesting such a thing. "What I am giving is a departmental decision, not what I view the matter personally."

"I'll speak to him."

"The senior public prosecutor is busy at the moment . . ."

Yudel thought he saw the beginnings of a sneer on the face of the Department of Justice official.

"I'll wait," Freek said.

"Perhaps you'd like to wait in the passage."

"I'll wait here."

"I got work to do. You not allowed . . ."

"We won't bother you," Freek assured him.

159

The public prosecutor rocked back in his chair, the movement defensive, as if he was trying to put as much distance between himself and them as possible. Now there was nothing superior in his manner. He seemed to be considering the possibilities, at least one of which seemed remote. The two on the other side of his desk, the big grim-looking one and the little sharp-looking one were not going to go away quietly. He got up and left the office without saying anything further.

"What do you think?" Yudel asked.

"We'll see his boss now," Freek told him.

They had waited less than a minute when a young woman came into the office. "Mister van Jaarsveld will see you now," she said. Her manner was businesslike and her expression reproachful. Without doubt she felt that she was dealing with a severe breach of protocol.

In keeping with civil service status requirements the senior public prosecutor's office, desk and carpet were all bigger than those of his junior, who was nowhere in sight. He was a large grey-haired man who extended a hand to shake hands with each of them in turn. "I believe if I don't see you two you won't go away," he said in Afrikaans. It was said in a way that indicated that they were old friends already.

"Something like that," Freek said in the same language, chuckling briefly as he shook hands.

"Pleased to meet you," Yudel said.

"Now yes," the senior prosecutor said. "Sit down, Misters. It's this Weizmann business, is it?"

"That's right."

"And what do you now actually want?" It was said in the same friendly way in which he had greeted them and by now Yudel doubted that this man was going to be of any use to them. There was a government service type that assured you that he was going to help, gave you plenty of friendly encouragement and no assistance at all. Yudel feared that they were dealing with one of them now.

"There is a court order against him, saying that he has to have psychiatric treatment. I want to enforce it."

"Have you seen the court order?" He was smiling, still friendly and obliging, but with one eyebrow raised enquiringly and by now Yudel was sure that they were wasting their time.

160

Freek had not seen the court order, but down the years he had dealt with many van Jaarsvelds. "Would you like a copy?" he asked.

Van Jaarsveld shook his head. "No, no, that's not necessary." Both his expression and his tone of voice said, please, gentlemen, I am not doubting you. "It is best to see the exact wording of a court order sometimes," he explained.

Freek smiled broadly. He was playing the prosecutor's game. "Quite true," he said. "We should have got you a copy. What it says is that he has to have psychiatric treatment. We want to force him to comply."

"Most probably it won't do him any good any way," van Jaarsveld said. "But why are you two tackling this old man?"

"You know about his case?" Yudel asked.

"He shot some burglars if I'm not mistaken."

"We only have Weizmann's word that they were all burglars."

Van Jaarsveld shrugged. "Why would he have shot them if they weren't burglars?" It was said in a way that suggested that no answer was necessary.

"In the Singh case," Yudel told him, "there was no burglary. It started with a motor car accident and the magistrate ordered him to have psychiatric treatment. He ignored it. We want to enforce it. Do you understand that?"

The brutality of Yudel's way of speaking and his choice of words cut through the other man's bland reassuring front. His face lost some of its friendliness. "Now yes. Are you sure he hasn't had treatment?"

"I'm the psychologist."

"If you're the psychologist then he has had treatment."

"Two visits," Yudel said.

Van Jaarsveld's eyebrows and shoulders came up in unison. "The court order says he must have treatment and he went twice. It's a matter of interpretation. Perhaps twice is treatment."

"That would be for the psychologist to decide."

"Who says that, you or the court order?"

"Obviously a mental patient does not decide when he is cured."

Freek had listened to the exchange between Yudel and the prosecutor, frowning at the lack of progress Yudel was making.

161

"Mister van Jaarsveld," he said, "why don't you want to help us?"

Van Jaarsveld's eyes widened and he raised his hands in protest. "It's not that I don't want to help you. This is not an easy case though. . ."

"Then you're not prepared to do anything?" Yudel asked.

"It's not that I'm not prepared to do anything. I don't think there's anything I can do. There's an inquest coming up soon, I think."

"Friday," Freek said.

"Why don't we just leave things to the inquest?" van Jaarsveld suggested.

Freek and Yudel got up to go. Van Jaarsveld winked at Yudel. "Business is a bit bad at the moment, hey?"

The woman looked to be in her middle forties. Years of practice had her looking superior without any effort. Her lips were pursed into a neat little rosebud, her hair firmly lacquered into position. Her clothing looked tailor-made, the cut smart and conservative. "You need an appointment to see the Deputy Attorney General," she said. "He is very busy."

"I understand that," Freek told her, "but the matter is urgent. I had hoped he could see us today."

She consulted a diary. She was manifestly unimpressed with Freek's urgencies. "Wednesday afternoon. What about Wednesday afternoon? If anything comes up that he cannot see you then I'll give you a ring. Leave me your number. . ."

On their way out Yudel asked, "Why didn't we use the same tactic that we did with the other one?"

"Because I've only got one neck," Freek said. "A prosecutor and the Deputy Attorney General are not the same thing."

"Let's try the Attorney General himself." The look Freek gave him answered Yudel well enough. It did not seem wise to pursue that line.

"What the donner, Freek, wait till Friday," Brigadier van Zyl said. "We can't always do what we want to, you know."

"It's just that we don't have much confidence in what will happen on Friday and in the mean time there is this old court order. Also it seems to be urgent."

"Why is it urgent? I understand that you don't want this Weizmann shooting people. That's good, but what's so urgent?"

Yudel explained about Weizmann's precarious state of mind, how he might kill again at any time, finishing with the significance of the number three in Weizmann's mind. Before he had stopped speaking he realised that the last part had been a mistake. The brigadier's eyes were opening wider and wider in unfeigned scepticism. When Yudel finished the policeman said, "Well, that's very interesting, Mister Gordon, from a psychological point of view, I suppose. . .but I'm an ordinary policeman." He turned suddenly to Freek. "Freek, old brother, do you believe this?"

Freek shrugged helplessly. Yudel thought he looked a little embarrassed doing it.

As they left Yudel said, "Thanks for the help in there. You were great."

"Do you realise how far I've stuck my neck out over this business?" Freek asked. "And this thing about the threes is rather a lot . . ." Yudel looked sharply at him. ". . . For an old policeman like Brigadier van Zyl to accept," he finished.

Yudel had left his office around mid-morning to go in search of Thandi Kunene. Then the afternoon had passed quickly, with his fruitlessly trying to interest someone who occupied a position of sufficient power in enforcing the court order against Weizmann. The evening had arrived early as if it had been blown suddenly over the city by a cold wind that had come up with the disappearance of the sun. By the time it was dark they were still in Freek's office, where Yudel had been telling him about Julie, Bill and Marion Hendricks, and about Thandi Kunene. Freek listened in silence. He would rather not have been confronted by the rebellious men, women and organisations that had been spawned by the social system his people had devised.

"What I don't understand is—the CID man must have picked up from Julie that Majola was there when the child was killed. And he must have contacted the Special Branch. So why didn't he tell you?"

"It could happen. He may have thought that I wouldn't be interested."

"But it should have been in his report."

The thought troubled Freek, but he was unwilling to see it as being significant. His apparent conflict of interests with the security police was enough. He was not anxious to mistrust his staff. "I think I know the reason," he said. "I've also been busy. I found out that Dippenaar and Marais's boss is a colonel by the name of Tollie Nieuwenhuysen. I was Tollie's sergeant years ago when he was a constable."

"He caught up to you."

Freek sighed, looking a little chagrined. "They always get promotions faster in Security. It's the glamour department in the police."

"Have you spoken to him about Weizmann?"

"Not yet. I only found this out today. I found out some other things too." Freek's frown deepened and he spoke reluctantly. He was moving onto a subject that he did not enjoy discussing. "I found out that Tollie is a member of an anti-communist organisation called the South African Freedom Campaign and Weizmann is a member too, and so is Louis Pienaar, my man on the Weizmann case. I don't think there was any deliberate attempt to exclude me. They just seem to think of each other first. This anti-communist business is just more important to Pienaar than his job. He'll probably find himself in the Special Branch one of these days and in a few years he'll be a colonel too. I don't think we must see too much in this." Yudel said nothing, but he was in agreement. An anti-communist movement would by its very nature attract policemen and especially security policemen. It would also attract Weizmann. "I also found out that they're having a meeting tomorrow night in the George Hotel. You want to go?"

"Is it open to the public?"

"You have to be a member, but I'll fix us membership cards."

"Weizmann will be there. He'll see me."

"We'll slip in late—after they've started."

"Freek, if they're all friends—Weizmann, Nieuwenhuysen and the rest and they want to use Weizmann, why do they need me?"

"We'll ask them," Freek said.

"It won't do us any good to talk to those people."

164

"It won't do us any good to just sit around."

"I think it'll be a mistake to contact them, Freek."

"I don't think so. They were all ordinary policemen at some stage. And they can all be moved back to ordinary police duties at any time. They're policemen like me, Yudel."

Yudel thought that Freek was talking as much to convince himself as for any other reason. "They're not ordinary policemen," Yudel told him.

"I'm going to talk to them."

"It'll be a mistake."

"I don't think so." Freek sounded tired. "For a change let's follow *my* hunch."

"Are you going to try to talk to Nieuwenhuysen tomorrow night?"

"If I get the chance. We'll buy him a drink and get him into a friendly mood."

"This Nieuwenhuysen, do you still have any influence with him?"

"At one time what I said was law to him, but that was a long time ago. Now—I don't know. I'd be surprised." Freek got to his feet. His face was still troubled. "Let's go home," he said.

An earlier doubt awakened in Yudel. He got up to follow Freek. "What about Weizmann's brother's death? You know how he claims his brother was beaten to death."

"A lot of bullshit, Yudel. He made such a noise at the time that our people took photographs of the body. I wondered about the same thing and drew them to have a look. There wasn't a mark on the body."

They made their way to the lane behind the building where Freek's car was parked. Yudel had come to Johannesburg that morning in an official car that had been taken back by someone else in the afternoon. He had arranged with Freek to travel home to Pretoria with him. After they had got into the car they sat for a few moments in the darkness, a feeling of helplessness and ineffectiveness, unbeckoned, having descended on them. Both Yudel and Freek were men who enjoyed being faced with problems because they found a special pleasure in the solving of them. Occasionally when either had a problem that presented special difficulties, and most of Yudel's special problems came to him from Freek, he would discuss it with the other. It was a system of co-operation that served both of them well and seldom led to a total frustration of their efforts. Their talents and spheres of influence supplemented each other well, filling the gaps in their abilities that even the best-equipped of men always possess. Neither was consciously aware of the extent of his dependence on the other, but at times like this each automatically turned to the other for support, an extra brain or pair of hands—whatever was needed.

"Let's go past Weizmann's place," Yudel said.

"What's the point?"

"Let's go anyway."

"Is this one of the famous Gordon intuitions?"

"Let's just go there."

Freek parked the car a few blocks up the hill from Weizmann's café. "And now?" he asked. Yudel got out with Freek following reluctantly. "It was warm in the car," he said.

"You see that building across the road from Weizmann's place. From its roof you can see right into the flat. I'll show you."

"I'll take your word for it," Freek said.

"Come on," Yudel said.

The rooms of Weizmann's flat that Yudel had already identified as the kitchen and the living-room were in darkness. A light was burning in one of the other rooms, probably a bedroom. Downstairs the shop was closed, the windows in darkness. The door of the storeroom was closed and the pavement in front of the shop was empty except for an old, probably illiterate black woman, wearing a sweater with the legend "I choked Linda Lovelace" in large letters across the chest. She was walking slowly in the direction of the station.

Yudel led Freek round the back of the building opposite and up the fire escape onto the roof. In one of the little rooms used by the servants a light was burning and Yudel thought he heard Julie's voice as she sang softly to herself. He showed Freek the view of Weizmann's kitchen and the corner of the stairs, both in almost total darkness and, from further along the roof, the view of his lounge where light from the bedroom was coming in through an open door, outlining the television set and a small table in the centre of the room. Freek looked patiently

166

first at one, then at the other, then he looked at Yudel. "Tell me, Yudel," he asked eventually, "what are we doing here? What are we after? Are we looking for something?"

Yudel looked helplessly at him. "I don't know."

Freek had his hands deep in the pockets of his overcoat and his arms pressed in tightly against the cold. "I think we've gone as far as we can go. At the meeting tomorrow night I'll talk to Tollie and we'll see what we pick up there. Perhaps we'll be lucky."

"I've got no faith in that."

"Well then what? If we find nothing there we've still reached the end. We have to face it."

"There must be some way to sort it all out."

"Sort what out? Weizmann? Your friends who are in trouble with the Special Branch? Majola? It's impossible, Yudel. There are some things that you and I can't sort out." Yudel did not answer. He continued to look down at the dark interior of Weizmann's flat without seeing it. There had to be a way. His life was built around the premise that nothing was insoluble. "This is crazy," Freek said. "We're standing up here on this roof, freezing, when we could be warm in bed . . ." He paused reflectively. ". . . with someone else's wife."

"That's a stupid thing to say," Yudel said. "It denotes a pocket of immaturity in your make-up."

"Don't preach, Yudel. I'd rather be in bed with someone else's wife than up here, dying of cold."

"You shouldn't pamper this sort of immaturity in yourself."

"Stop preaching. Do you mean to tell me you've never been unfaithful to your wife?"

"If I have I don't glory in it."

"Ah." Freek was making little silent jumps in an effort to keep warm. "So you have. I always wondered about that. With whom?"

"Hell, Freek. Mind your own business."

"Don't be such a prude, Yudel. I'm your friend. Who'd you do it with?"

Yudel was silent. By the light coming up from the street he could see Freek grinning at him. "It's a funny thing . . ." he said and then stopped, possibly editing the admission he had been about to make.

167

"It's a laugh all right. Tell me about it."

"You know . . ." Yudel looked at him again. He wished Freek would stop grinning. "It's a funny thing, but whenever I've been unfaithful to my wife it's been with Afrikaans girls. I think it's a matter of dominance. By sheer weight of numbers you buggers are dominant in everything else. I think it's revenge, in a manner of speaking."

"Ah, dominance is it? How many girls have there been?"

"I don't see what that has to do with it."

"Come on, Yudel. What's there to hide."

"I don't see the relevance." Yudel was aware that he was sounding pompous, but it was difficult to do anything about it. However he defended himself it was likely to come out sounding pompous. "It's the principle that's important."

"Come on, Yudel. I'm interested from an academic point of view." Freek's teeth gleamed in the light from the street. If his grin grew any wider, Yudel thought, it would go right round to the back of his head. "How many girls have there been?"

"It's not relevant."

"Of course it's relevant. Scientists are always counting things —how often a wife screams at her husband, how many times a lion copulates—things like that. The number of times is very important."

Yudel was not taking seriously any part of Freek's dissertation, but he was growing tired of the conversation. He took a deep breath before answering. "Two," he said.

Freek tried to restrain his laughter by pursing his lips tightly closed. The result was that his cheeks puffed up like bellows, the air escaping like steam being blown off by a coal engine. He went straight over to coughing, trying to smother the sound with his handkerchief. "Two?" He struggled to get the word out between spells of coughing. "Dominance?" The coughing completely overwhelmed him so that he had to support himself on the low brick wall running along the roof's edge.

"You're making a noise," Yudel grumbled.

"Two?" Freek wheezed. "As an attempt at dominance, don't you think it's a pretty small attempt?"

"The principle is one of dominance," Yudel tried to say. With Freek still laughing he sounded pretty foolish to his own ears.

Freek put a hand on Yudel's shoulder and shook him back and forth in what was by Freek's standards an affectionate way. "As revolts go," he said, "I don't think yours poses an immediate threat to Afrikanerdom."

"Freek," Yudel said, but something in his voice had changed. The embarrassment and the pomposity were both gone. "Freek, the door's open."

Freek had to crouch to get a clear view of the storeroom door. "Are you sure?" he asked. "Wasn't it closed when we got here?"

"Yes. I looked at it when we were down on the street."

Yudel's eyes searched the windows of the building on the other side of the street, but the kitchen and the living-room were exactly as they had been earlier. There was a trace of light on the stair that had not been there before. He could see no sign of movement. "Do you suppose someone has broken in while we've been here?"

"Either that or someone has opened the door from the inside."

"Willem Roelofse told me Weizmann does that."

"A very superior source of information," Freek said.

The street and Weizmann's flat were both as quiet as they had been ever since Freek and Yudel arrived, but now the storeroom door was open. It was hard to believe that anything had changed, that someone had moved to open the door, that Weizmann was being robbed or that he had come downstairs to lay a trap and might now be waiting. . . Everything was quiet, only the relatively distant sounds of traffic and railway station intruding. But the door was open, not all the way, just enough for a man to squeeze through without disturbing it.

"Should we go down?" Yudel asked.

"Yes." Freek's voice was hard, the word clipped short. A moment later he was running for the fire escape. Yudel took a few steps, following him, but returned to the wall. It was no more than a second before he saw what Freek had seen. A young black man, wearing an old grey overcoat, had stopped under the tree immediately in front of the open door. Now for the first time Yudel saw a movement from within the flat. It came from the stair and in the faint light it was no more than

169

a dark low shadow, moving quickly upwards. Without doubt it was the form of Weizmann's alsatian.

The man on the pavement came out of the shelter of the tree. Yudel saw him glance up and down the road and then move right into the doorway. He waited for a moment, looking into the store, then he backed off to look up and down the road a second time. He returned to the door and was pushing it slowly open with one hand when Freek dashed into the road. "Hey, what are you doing there?" Yudel heard him shout.

The young man in the coat turned and ran down the road towards the station without looking round to see who had shouted. There was someone on the stair again. This time it was Weizmann, stumbling quickly past the open window, his toeless feet working badly on the steep staircase. For a moment Freek was framed in the doorway with Weizmann only a few steps from the bottom of the stairs. Then he threw himself to the side, flattening his body against the wall. Weizmann rushed out onto the pavement straight into Freek's smoothly thrown right hook. Yudel saw the shopkeeper disappear back into the store, his arms outstretched on either side grasping for a support that did not exist, and he saw the alsatian leap out of the darkness, straight for Freek's throat. Yudel ran for the fire escape. It was a move that was long overdue.

By the time Yudel had run across the street and into the store-room a degree of peace had returned to the evening. Weizmann was sitting in the centre of the floor, shaking his head slowly from side to side. There was no mark to indicate where the punch had landed. His wife was standing close behind him, her eyes wild and alarmed, and she had the alsatian by the collar. The dog was growling, his teeth bared and the hair along the ridge of his back standing up like the quills of a porcupine. Freek was leaning against the shelves to Yudel's left, his normally carefully combed hair hanging loose over his forehead. He had his coat off and was rolling up the bloodied right-hand sleeve of his shirt. He grinned at Yudel. "Thanks for the help in there," he said. "You were great." To Weizmann he said, "It's lucky for you that Mister Gordon and I were passing. We came round the corner just as the burglar hit you. I'm sorry to say that he got away."

Weizmann was still shaking his head to clear it. His wife's eyes were moving back and forth between Yudel and Freek. She was too startled to be able to hide the fright and suspicion in them. It was clear that she did not believe any part of Freek's account of what had happened. It was also clear that she was afraid. Yudel wondered if her fear had to do with her knowing that the storeroom door had been opened. "Thank you very much, Colonel Jordaan," she was saying, the words bearing no relation to her feelings.

Yudel helped Freek to get his sleeve up as far as the elbow. The dog's canines had made two parallel tears each about a centimetre long in the fleshy part of his friend's forearm. He took out his handkerchief and stopped what was no more than a trickle of blood. "It doesn't look too bad," he told Freek.

"Thanks," Freek said. "Next thing you'll be saying it suits me."

Weizmann got slowly to his feet, first turning over onto his knees, his hands pressing down onto the cement floor. The little caps on his fingers reflected the light sharply as if they were newly polished. His wife knelt to help him. Yudel saw him reach up and take her arm, leaning heavily on her as he came erect. That's the way it always is, Yudel thought, leaning on her, relying on her. . . He looked at the woman, seeing both hatred and strength in her face. And he looked at Weizmann, still resting on her shoulder, his eyes as fearful and defeated as ever Yudel had seen them. Do you kill for her too? Yudel wondered. Weizmann was looking puzzled, not altogether sure of what had happened. Yudel was not surprised at that. He had seen Freek's punch land and a state of confusion on Weizmann's part was to be expected. Then Weizmann looked straight at Yudel, for the first time becoming aware of his presence, the confusion on his face growing. He was straightening up, deliberately pulling back his shoulders, lifting up his head, but averting his eyes. Yudel was again looking at the little boy in the presence of his father, determined not to be humiliated, the young man refusing to classify any more tobacco. . .

171

THIRTEEN

THE GEORGE HOTEL was an old double-storeyed building with a sloping corrugated iron roof, ornamental steelwork along the balconies and banisters, and pressed-steel ceilings in the rooms. Inside it gave the appearance of being well maintained, the carpets and paintwork new, the light fittings and wood panelling freshly polished. The conference room where the South African Freedom Campaign was meeting was on the first floor.

As they went up the stairs Freek handed Yudel a small green card, bearing the signature of a P. Nortje and a badge with the letters SAFC. "What's this?" Yudel asked.

"Your membership card," Freek said.

"Who's Nortje?"

"The bloke who lent me the card."

"Looks like me, does he?"

"Relax, Yudel. He's one of my sergeants and he's been a member for years without ever attending a meeting."

"Whose card have you got?"

"I joined for the occasion."

The man at the door was young and frowning, his hair cut short along the sides and at the back, wearing a tweed sports coat, a tie and carefully pressed fawn-coloured trousers. In appearance and dress he looked like any other young man from twenty years before. He glanced at the cards Freek and Yudel produced before stepping aside to let them in.

The hall was just big enough to seat perhaps fifty or sixty people. It was almost entirely full when Freek and Yudel entered. The audience rose and started applauding as they came in the door. Yudel was reasonably sure that the applause was not for him and Freek. Peering between the heads of other members of the audience, he saw that the clapping was for a

172

small unsmiling man who carried his hat in one hand and was mounting the steps to the low platform at the end of the hall. Without acknowledging the applause he sat down at the table on the platform. Of the two other chairs one was filled by a man who looked to be in his early thirties and who wore a rather similar frowning expression to the one who had let them in at the door. The other was occupied by a middle-aged man in a light suit who was leaning back in his chair with one arm hooked over the backrest.

Freek prodded Yudel down the row of seats at the back of the hall so that by the time the rest of the audience was seated they had reached the empty chairs at which he had been aiming. The man with the frown got to his feet. "Gentlemen. . ." Glancing round the hall Yudel was interested to note that there were no ladies present. He wondered if their absence had to do with the movement's constitution or if they had not been able to recruit any ladies. "Gentlemen, we are very fortunate tonight . . ." If his expression was anything to go by their good fortune seemed to bring him no pleasure. "We are fortunate tonight in having two very distinguished guests. First of all we have, all the way from Arkansas in the United States of America, Mister Wilbur Hartman who has a very special message for us. Mister Hartman is the sort of real ambassador for his country who has come all the way to see us at his own expense. And tonight he's going to correct a few popular misconceptions about his great country." While he was speaking he had turned slightly towards Mister Hartman. Now he paused and faced the small unsmiling man whom the audience had applauded. Yudel thought he lowered his head a little before continuing. "And our main speaker tonight—we want to thank him very, very sincerely for giving up his very precious time to be with us here in person tonight." The small man stared out over the audience as if he had heard no part of what the speaker was saying and remained unaware of their gratitude. He had eyes that were permanently half-closed, possibly protected against inquisitive outsiders who might want to read something in them. To Yudel they were the eyes of a man who also hid the true nature of at least some of his actions from himself. In the Departments of Police and Prisons Yudel had known many ambitious men who had subdued and eventually

173

all but eradicated in their minds what they knew to be right. In departments where ruthless actions were sometimes required a man with a conscience that operated only selectively was always at an advantage. The initial impression the main speaker of the evening made on Yudel was that he might be such a man. "We know how important every minute of his time is," the chairman of the meeting was saying. "We know with what momentous decisions of state he wrestles every day. And we know that for him to come here to be with us is a real sacrifice. . ." The unsmiling face was impassive, the guarded eyes unblinking and turned away from the speaker, not acknowledging him or the audience in any way. "So we say a deeply heart-felt and sincere welcome to the Right Honourable, the Minister of Justice. . ." His name was drowned by the applause that filled the hall and suddenly the audience was on its feet again.

Yudel was lifted out of his seat by Freek. "Clap," Freek whispered. He was applauding vigorously and, looking at his face, Yudel would have thought that he was thrilled with the idea of listening to a speech by the Right Honourable, the Minister of Justice. Yudel applauded.

"Before I hand over to Mister Hartman I would like to draw attention to the excellent books and periodicals that will be available at the back of the hall when the meeting is over. Among those that make excellent gifts for friends and relatives overseas to give them a better perspective of the real situation in our country is *The Terrorist Behind the Cross,* an exposé of the World Council of Churches and their auxiliaries in our country. . ."

Yudel was looking at the faces of the members of the audience. There were men of all ages. Young men barely out of their teens and determined to save their country, pensioners who had memories of other more patriotic times and were sitting up near the front where they might be able to hear, businessmen who were willing to put their money where their mouths were to make their country safe for decent people to live in, men with steady hands who could shoot straight, had practised to make the margin for error minimal and were eager to exercise their skills on those they saw as their country's enemies: they all had earnest faces, their expressions grim and worried. The world was after them. There was a communist

174

threat, a big-money threat, a liberal-Jewish threat and a black threat, a permissive society threat, a pornography threat, a newspaper threat, a women's liberation threat. . . It was no wonder that their faces reflected the seriousness of the position. They were the clearsighted ones who understood these dangers, who hankered after a more disciplined age where trouble-makers who went against the government would be dealt with firmly and no nonsense about it, where not every liberal-commie journalist would be allowed to go around shouting the odds about things he knew nothing about. . . They had come from the workshop and the office, the gun club and the bar room, the consulting chambers and the pulpit, and they had all come to make South Africa safe for decent people.

"Another excellent book that we have available tonight, one that meant a great deal to me is *The Net Around South Africa,* dealing with the Capitalist-Communist plot to seize South Africa's mineral wealth. . ."

Yudel's eyes, searching the faces of those he could see, found Weizmann's. The shopkeeper was two or three rows in front of him on the other side of the hall so that Yudel could see him in profile. Unconsciously Yudel slipped a little deeper into his seat, drawing his head back so that if Weizmann turned he could hide behind Freek. He was afraid that if the old man saw him it might disturb what was already a dangerous and deli-cately-balanced condition. After his sudden and unexpected appearance the previous night, if Weizmann saw him again now, he might start to occupy a new and unhappy position in the old man's tormented thinking. A new element of persecution might be added to Weizmann's state of mind.

On either side of Weizmann two younger men were seated and Yudel recognised one of them as the man he had seen in the flat, the one he had taken to be Jansen. On the near side of them a young policeman occupied the next seat. It was clear that they had come to the meeting together. Yudel assumed that two of them were Weizmann's sons-in-law and he remembered that there had been a policeman, a Sergeant Jeffreys, involved in the Reddy case. There was something about the attitude of the younger men and the way they clustered around Weizmann that made Yudel see him as the centre of the little group. And that was logical. He was the one who did what the others only dreamed of. He actually killed in the defence of his people. To the serious-looking young men on either side of him he was a hero and, seated among them, his head proudly raised in the determined imitation of worth and self-esteem that Yudel had got to know, he could see himself that way too. Johnny Weizmann had made his own world of which he was the centre. To his wife and young friends, perhaps to his daughters as well, he was a fearless patriot, not a demented killer.

Mister Wilbur Hartman had taken over and was explaining to the audience that American policy on South Africa did not reflect the attitude of the great American people. American policy, he explained, was ruled by the unpatriotic liberal press, the big money lobby, the black lobby, the treasonous actions of certain movie stars. . .but, in fact, the American people were right behind South Africa. The average down-to-earth middle American did not want to see communism get a foothold in Southern Africa. They knew the white South Africans were indispensable.

The American had a way of leaning backwards as he spoke, accentuating a broad chest and stomach, his jacket hanging open unbuttoned and his thumbs hooked into his belt. His face wore a little confident smile, indicative of the accuracy of what he was saying and how acceptable he knew it would be to his audience. He completed his explanation of the views of the majority of his countrymen and went on to describe the totally false impression of South Africa created in his country by the untrustworthy liberal press and how when he got back he was going to put the record straight. When he got back he was going to see to it that Mister Average America learnt just how much was being done for South Africa's blacks. In fact, when he got home South Africa's troubles would be just about over.

Yudel was growing tired of Mister Wilbur Hartman. The world's Wilbur Hartmans were not an uncommon sight in the republic. Dredged up from the lunatic fringe movements of their countries' politics by organisations like the South African Freedom Campaign, they were paraded around the country for the benefit of the faithful. It was important that the people should see that there were still white men in the world who thought like white men. ". . . and if there are a few bad things that happen here from time to time— why, this is true of every country . . ."

Yudel nudged Freek gently. "Which one is Nieuwenhuysen?" he whispered.

"Second row from the front, third from the right," Freek told him.

All Yudel could see of the security policeman was a full head of wavy grey hair in which the original colour did not remain in even the smallest trace. That he was a tall man, his head higher than most of the others in the hall, was obvious. A previously unconsidered thought slipped into Yudel's mind by the back way. He started searching the hall for Dippenaar and Marais, but as far as he could see they were not present.

Nieuwenhuysen and Weizmann, members of the same élite organisation, fellow travellers in a common school of thought, sufferers from a common insecurity and possessors of a mutual determination: what could one of them want of the other that required Yudel as the intercessor? The bonds that held them together were far closer than any they shared with him. In terms of their preoccupations he was an outsider.

The American patriot finished his speech and sat down in the midst of prolonged applause. When it subsided the chairman got to his feet and said, "Gentlemen, the Minister of Justice." It was said simply, but the note of reverence in his voice was unmistakable.

The small man rose to his third round of applause of the evening. He waited until the hall was completely silent before starting to speak. "It's a privilege to be here. . ." The way it was said made it seem that it was the audience that was enjoying the privilege. There was no doubt in Yudel's mind that the audience felt more privileged than the Minister. ". . . particularly to hear those comments by Mister Hartman." He was speaking English for the sake of the visitor, inclining his head towards him as he continued. "When I hear comments like those from patriotic Americans like Mister Hartman I say to South Africa's enemies—beware!" Mister Wilbur Hartman was watching the face of the Minister of Justice and at his words he lifted his chin a little higher, at the same time turning down the corners of his mouth. Clearly the enemies of South Africa were to beware of Mister Hartman as well as the Minister. "We live in troubled times," he told the audience. Remembering the faces of the men around him Yudel felt sure that piece of information was unnecessary. There was not a face among them that did not look troubled. "We live in times when for the first time in the history of South Africa a government cannot trust the official opposition. We have definite documented proof that the official opposition has dealt with South Africa's enemies behind the back of the government." Around the hall heads were being shaken and a few muttered "bastards" could be heard.

Where, Yudel asked himself, did Bill and Marion Hendricks or Thandi Kunene or Wilson or Majola, himself, fit into all this? In the world of these men Soweto and all the places like Soweto might not exist as places of human habitation. They existed only as threats to themselves. But in Soweto the world of these men existed in all too vivid a reality.

"I spoke to Buthelezi," the Minister told his audience. "I not only spoke to him I listened very carefully to what he had to say." It was clear that this was a major concession to the Zulu leader. "I said to him, Chief, you talk. Let me hear what you have to say. Do you know what he said to me?" He paused to allow the audience to consider what the Chief might have said. Yudel could sense the indignation growing in the members of the audience. "He said to me. . ." Another pause. Whatever Buthelezi had said he was going to be in trouble with this outfit. "He said, I'm not a Zulu. I'm a South African."

"Jesus," a man in the row in front of Yudel said. Yudel was watching Nieuwenhuysen and the security policeman half-turned his head at that moment, revealing a fleshy face, the cheeks loose. He was smiling broadly. From scattered parts of the hall there was muted laughter. Clearly Buthelezi's claim to being a South African was too ridiculous to warrant reasonable consideration. The expression on Weizmann's face was unchanged. To him it was not a matter for laughter.

"So I said to him . . ." He paused again and again his audience responded in the way that was expected of them. There was a general tendency to lean forward, an expectancy in the faces, a possible eagerness. This was where Buthelezi was going to get his come-uppance. "I said to him, you don't want to be a South African. You just want to gang up against me so that you can say, I am the majority. You don't want to be a South African—you want to force me into the position where I am the minority." It was said forcefully and conclusively so

178

that now the ultimate truth was revealed and there would be no point in the Zulu leader trying to hide it. "You don't want to be a South African. You want to be the boss." The audience erupted briefly into clapping, laughter, hear-hears and angry mutterings that were directed against the man who wanted to be the boss.

The speech rolled steadily on through a maze of confused rationalisations and stern warnings, the audience responding as if on cue, having learnt their part in many such meetings. At last the small man with the private eyes drew to the end of what he had to say, sure in the knowledge that the South African Freedom Campaign was again fortified against the threats from without. They would continue to be a pocket of permanence in a changing landscape.

He turned again to Mister Wilbur Hartman. "We know that you will take with you everything that is good in South Africa and ignore the few things that are bad . . ." Yudel was thinking of Bill Hendricks coming down the path of his home, being pushed towards the car by the policeman behind him. He was thinking of the frightened little group that gathered in Thandi Kunene's home and he was thinking about the life Johnny Weizmann had lived and was still free to live. "We know that you will correct the untruths spread abroad about our country and we want you to know . . ." The unaltered expressionless face of the speaker, the bureaucratic evasions of the Justice Department, the tear-rimmed eyes of Johnny Weizmann and the unsmiling determined expressions of the men in the audience were fusing into each other in Yudel's mind and becoming one. He doubted that anything had been gained by attending the meeting. All his doubts had become more clearly established. The man on the podium was the Minister of Justice. In sympathy with him, listening carefully to every word as if they were life-giving, was Johnny Weizmann. A little way away Tollie Nieuwenhuysen, the man who was directing the search for Majola, was seated. The spiritual bond between all of them was close, far too close for an outsider like Yudel to disrupt. "We want you to know that South Africa, all the peoples of South Africa, deeply appreciate what you are prepared to do for us," the Minister was telling Mister Hartman. "Go in peace and our good wishes go with you."

The speech was over, the members of the audience including Mister Hartman were on their feet and applauding yet again. The small man who was the Minister of Justice left, still without smiling, without acknowledging the applause and without looking to either side. He came down the steps and passed out of the side entrance with the audience still on its feet and without once turning his head to look at any of them. A number of men who had been seated in different parts of the hall left with him.

All that remained was for the chairman to encourage members to buy the books and pamphlets to send to overseas acquaintances, again express everyone's appreciation of the now-absent Minister and Mister Wilbur Hartman, and the meeting was over. Freek got slowly to his feet and Yudel slipped in behind him, trying to keep his friend between himself and Weizmann. He saw in glimpses between the moving bodies that Nieuwenhuysen was moving purposefully across the hall. There seemed to be an inclination among the other members to make way for him. It took only a few seconds for Yudel to realise that he was aiming for Weizmann. The shopkeeper, surrounded by his own personal bodyguard, was already nearing the door. Nieuwenhuysen caught him in the doorway. To Yudel's regret they passed through it, Nieuwenhuysen holding onto Weizmann's arm and thus slowing him, talking all the time, his head inclined towards the older man.

Unlike Weizmann most of the members were not keen to leave. They gathered in groups in the aisles, each explaining to his neighbour how best to save South Africa from the evils that threatened it. Yudel made his way along the outside aisle, trying to position himself opposite the door in the hope of getting a clear view of the conversation between Nieuwenhuysen and Weizmann. Disjointed bits of wisdom reached him from the little knots of men in the aisles. "It's easy for Vorster to be *verlig* with Rhodesia and South West. They're not his country. . . One thing we've got to get rid of is the United Nations. That's just a bastardised mixture. . . America is being run by the communists—that's the trouble. . . The sooner the churches start sticking to religion and leave politics alone the better. . . We're too soft. We let terrorists waste the time of the courts. . ."

Yudel got to the centre aisle where he was opposite the door. He could see out into the passage where Nieuwenhuysen still had Weizmann by the arm and was talking. And all the time, while he talked, the shopkeeper was shaking his head. Whatever it was that the security policeman was saying it was having no effect on Weizmann. The level of noise in the room and the distance between them made it impossible for Yudel to hear any part of the conversation. He could see the face of one of Weizmann's sons-in-law, his eyes moving uneasily between his wife's father and the policeman. Yudel had only watched the conversation for a few seconds when Weizmann pulled himself free and, with a final shake of his head, set off down the passage, his entourage in pursuit. Nieuwenhuysen came back into the hall, his annoyance reflected on his large fleshy face. Yudel looked for Freek. He caught up to him as Freek reached Nieuwenhuysen.

"*My wêreld*," Freek was saying in Afrikaans. "Tollie! And how goes it with you, old friend?"

Nieuwenhuysen smiled at Freek and held out a hand to him. The smile was less enthusiastic than Freek's and the extended hand looked limp, the fingers touching each other, not spread as they are when a man intends taking hold of something firmly. "Hullo, Freek. I'm glad to see you here."

"Yes, *jong*. I decided I must stop being so lazy. A man has also got certain duties."

"You chose a good night to come—with our minister speaking." It was said smoothly, knowing that the sentiments expressed were what was expected. It may have been that what he said reflected his views, but it may as well not have been so. It was a guarded careful way of speaking that had as its reason for existence the need to hide what the speaker was thinking.

"But I'm glad to see you again, Tollie. How long have you been a member?" Then without pausing and while Nieuwenhuysen's mind was still occupied by his question Freek half-turned towards Yudel. "This is Piet, one of my boys," he said.

Automatically Nieuwenhuysen held out a hand and Yudel shook it. "Pleased to make your acquaintance," he said. The security policeman's hand was soft and smooth and did not return the pressure of Yudel's. He barely glanced at Yudel. He was not the sort of man to waste time with subordinates while in the presence of a more senior man. His eyes were pale blue and they looked past Freek while speaking to him.

"First class speech tonight," Freek was saying. "The minister made a lot of good points."

"Yes," Nieuwenhuysen said, his voice tone reluctant and unconvinced. "I'd like a bit more force on some of the issues though." Like his handshake his voice was soft and lifeless.

Freek nodded thoughtfully. Yudel wondered what he was thinking. He knew Freek well enough to know that what he was trying to convey had nothing to do with his real feelings. "Why don't we have a beer?" he suggested. "So long since we've last seen each other, Tollie."

Nieuwenhuysen smiled, a tight inhibited expression. "If mine can be a brandy, I'd like that."

"Yours can be a whisky if you like," Freek said.

"Brandy's my drink."

Yudel followed them down the stairs into the hotel lounge. Nieuwenhuysen walked smoothly with a little too much hip movement. His hands were carried at just below hip level and held in loose fists. "When last did we work together?" Freek wondered aloud. "Must have been nearly twenty years ago." The other man turned his head partially towards Freek and smiled his weak smile without saying anything.

In the lounge they sat down at a table far from the door. Yudel noticed that other groups from the meeting were arriving in the lounge and ordering drinks. The waiter came and Freek ordered beers for himself and Yudel and a brandy for Nieuwenhuysen. "Those were good old days, Tollie," he said. "We had some good times. . ." From the start Freek guided the conversation, going from one subject to another, continually resurrecting the old days to remind Nieuwenhuysen of what good friends they were, insisting on paying for every round of drinks, telling his wide range of jokes and slowly, with the assistance of the brandy, breaking down the reserve that was part of most security policemen. It took him an hour to reach the question at which he had been aiming. "And how is your work going, Tollie?"

"Not bad. And the CID?"

"Good. We have our troubles, but it goes well. I'm busy with an inquest at the moment. The old man who's got to appear was at the meeting tonight."

"Old Weizmann?"

"That's the one."

"Straightforward burglary, I thought."

"The trouble is Weizmann has been involved in so many of these cases. I'll have to put in a good word at the inquest to get him off this time."

Nieuwenhuysen's eyes were moving continually now, seeking out Freek's then avoiding them. "Are you willing to put in a good word for him?"

Freek looked doubtful. "The case doesn't look good."

"But it was a clearcut case of burglary. You can't send a man to jail for shooting an in-breaker. Nothing has been proved against the old man. And he's all right. His heart is in the right place. You see him here at our meetings."

"I don't want to act too fiercely, but I'll have to have good reason to talk in his favour."

"Suppose I gave you a good reason."

Freek looked straight at Nieuwenhuysen and now it was his turn to look suspicious. He had taken control of the conversation so completely, bringing the security policeman to the point where he wanted him, that Yudel who knew him so well was again surprised at his skill. Freek said nothing, leaving Nieuwenhuysen to explain himself.

"Suppose I said that I need Weizmann's co-operation on a matter of absolute importance. He's a difficult old bugger and won't help us. Suppose I told him you'll talk for him at the inquest, if he agrees to help us."

Freek raised his eyebrows. He managed an expression that indicated that this sort of thing was irregular and he had his doubts, but that he could possibly be persuaded. "I would have to be sure that this was very, very important." He spoke slowly, pausing on each word in what was a typically Afrikaner way of emphasising something.

"You have my word."

Freek's eyebrows remained raised and he looked directly at the other man. The security policeman was left in no doubt that he would not have a deal unless he expanded substantially.

"Listen," he said, "do you know about this kaffir, Muntu Majola?" His use of as crude a term as kaffir seemed incongruous with his appearance and manner of speaking.

"Naturally," Freek told him.

183

"He was there when Weizmann shot this in-breaker? You know how he revenged himself in the past. Maybe he'll go back. I want a man inside that shop every night for the next six months. If that bastard comes back I want him to walk into my man."

"Won't old Weizmann agree?"

"The old bugger says he can look after himself."

"Why don't you just put somebody on the roof across the road?"

"Because there are three ways you can get into that flat. You could force the front door of the shop so that you won't have to open the storeroom door to reach the stairs. And there's also a fire escape on the other side of the building. I'd need three men to guard the place, and then he might notice one of them and get away. If I can get a man inside it'll be different. Then it won't be easy for him to escape. In any event I can't spare three men. Do you know how many communists there are in Johannesburg that we have to watch?"

"No," Freek said.

"Thousands, let me tell you. I've had a man watching his place from time to time but it's not satisfactory. I've got nobody there at the moment. . ."

Freek still looked doubtful, but now it was a doubtfulness that was close to being persuaded. He was even nodding slightly, the movement of his head barely perceptible.

"I tell you what," Nieuwenhuysen said. "I've got something that might crack tonight. If it doesn't I'll need your help."

"The Majola case?" Some uncertainty as to Freek's willingness to co-operate remained.

Nieuwenhuysen was leaning forward, eager to persuade Freek. "You want to come along? I'm going there now."

Freek paused just long enough to show that he was not overly enthusiastic. "Now yes, good. If I'm going to help I'd better see what I'm going to help with."

FOURTEEN

THE BUILDING TO which Nieuwenhuysen took them was old and on the east side of the city. The ground floor was occupied by an electrical wholesaler, a small café that advertised the cheapest takeaway meals in town and a dry-cleaning depot. The entrance lobby was blue-tiled, the tiles showing signs of the fine hairline cracks of age. The stone floor had been worn into uneven patterns by the traffic of the years. At the sight of Nieuwenhuysen a uniformed guard at the lift stepped aside for them to pass. The lift was as old as the building, a concertina-type steel cage door having to be drawn closed before it started moving.

They got out on the third floor into a poorly lit passage. When the passage ended a cement staircase turned away from it at right angles. Nieuwenhuysen went up the stairs quickly, ducking to avoid a low concrete beam that Yudel and Freek passed beneath with no trouble. He knocked on a steel door at the top of the stairs with the flat of his hand and a small hatch in its centre opened, a pair of eyes satisfied their owner as to Nieuwenhuysen's identity and the door was opened. The uniformed policeman who had opened the door stepped aside to let them in. They were in a short passage that led to three more doors and Nieuwenhuysen took them to the furthest one.

The second door was open as they passed and Yudel had an instantaneous view of Bill Hendricks on the naked mattress of a bed. He had his back to the door and was pushing himself up into a sitting position, the movement slow and weary. Yudel saw by the sudden surprised turning of Freek's head that he had also seen Hendricks.

They followed Nieuwenhuysen through the third door and into a room where the only light came from an angle-poise lamp in its centre. Nieuwenhuysen and Freek stopped just inside the

185

doorway, initially obscuring Yudel's view of the room. He was aware of other men in plain clothes to his left, standing outside the circle of light. Freek moved a step to his right. Between his friend and Nieuwenhuysen Yudel had a momentary view of a long dark-brown leg, a woman's leg, the toes bunched up under tension. He pushed past Freek to see what was happening.

Thandi Kunene was on a chair in the centre of the room. She was naked except for a broad rubber band that looked like the inner tube of a truck tyre. The rubber band was fitted tightly round her abdomen and the back of the chair, pinning her arms to her sides, her large breasts hanging heavily over it. The lamp was positioned close in front of her face, shining straight into her eyes. Yudel could see the perspiration where it had formed along the top of her forehead and down her temples. Her upper lip was twitching in a series of grotesque sneers, first on one side, then on the other. Her legs were held slightly apart, the thighs tied separately to the two front legs of the chair so that they could not be brought together. She seemed to be trying to lean forward and move her buttocks back as if that might somehow shield her naked clitoris, but the attempt at movement was restricted by the insistent presence of the rubber band. She also seemed to be trying to see past the light, perhaps to identify or remember against some future opportunity the faces of her tormentors.

A young man in civilian clothes, kneeling close behind her, was the only other person in the light from the lamp. He had his jacket off and his shirt sleeves rolled up. Like the woman, he was perspiring, the sweat probably caused by a combination of the heat from the light and whatever it was he had been doing. Yudel recognised the deliberately bored look on his face, a manufactured expression the purpose of which was as much to deceive its owner as the other people in the room. His left hand was resting on Thandi's naked shoulder in a way that seemed almost intimate. His right hand was doing something behind her.

Thandi groaned, a long-drawn thin reedy sound. She had closed her eyes, but her upper lip was still twitching as it had been when Yudel came in. The seemingly intimate placing of the policeman's hand on her shoulder and the strangeness of the sound she was making combined to bring a thought, half-

186

formed, into his imagination. In that uncertain instant the sound she was making and the apparent gentleness of the gesture together created the brief illusion that she was having an orgasm.

Then he knew what the sound was. It was a groan caused by great pressure being applied to her body.

Freek moved a step, blocking Yudel's view again. Vaguely in the corner of his field of vision Yudel was aware of Nieuwenhuysen moving to the left so that he would be directly in front of Thandi. He squeezed between the security policeman and Freek. For him to have turned his head to look at the other men in the room would have been impossible.

The young policeman crouching behind Thandi was doing something with the hand held behind her back. Yudel could see the movement of his right shoulder and the slight compression of his lips as he made the effort. Thandi groaned again, longer than before, her eyes tightly closed, still seemingly trying to pull back her buttocks, trying to hide the femininity that should never have been revealed this way, that was kept only for Muntu Majola. The sound continued for longer than Yudel would have thought possible, stopping only for a quick sucking in of her breath before going on. The policeman's shoulder moved again and Yudel saw the rubber band tense. He stopped and seemed to rest his right hand on the ground to steady himself, but the groaning continued, punctuated only by the almost convulsive sucking-in of her breath. The policeman's left hand was still on her shoulder. In the bright light from the lamp Yudel saw it move slightly, but stop before the movement had been completed as if the natural impulse of the white hand was to massage the brown shoulder, but was inhibited by the company. The impression of intimacy in Yudel's mind was strengthened, but it was of a frightful and frightening nature, not the intimacy of lovers. But even that was not true.

He could see that there was something of the lover in the hand on the woman's shoulder. For years Yudel had doubted that the link between sadism and sex was as strong as Freud had made it. He had seen it more as a distortion of the drive for power. What he was seeing now was altering and adding to his understanding of human cruelty. He wondered what would have taken place between the policeman and the captive

187

woman if they had been alone. The movement of his hand on her shoulder, the gently applied pressure of his fingers, were barely perceptible, but Yudel could not avoid them. And yet the drive for power was also present. She was his victim and almost his lover. Her submission might not have been willing, but it was no less real because of that. Every time he tightened the pressure of the rubber band around her body, every time she groaned, the sound she was making so much like that of sexual pleasure, she was submitting further to his will of her. And the hand on the shoulder gripped more firmly, the tips of his fingers massaging the soft flesh of her upper arm more urgently.

Yudel moved to his right, passing behind Freek, a few hesitant steps that took him out of the shadow and into the edge of the light from the angle-poise lamp. From his new position he could see the policeman's right hand. He had passed a wooden baton through the rubber band and was turning it slowly. As it turned the band drew gradually tighter around the woman's body. With Yudel watching he turned his wrist through ninety degrees, then held it still, leaning slightly forward to see the look on her face.

Again she groaned, thin and brittle, this time coming from deeper in her throat. Her head fell back, the lips apart, her eyes closed, an expression almost of ecstasy except for the uncontrollable twitching of her upper lip. The policeman was holding his hand steady, allowing the pressure of the rubber band to do its work, watching her face, the very small tightening and easing of his hand on her shoulder still obvious to Yudel.

Besides Yudel, Freek, Nieuwenhuysen, Thandi and the policeman behind her chair there were four others in the room, all standing well back, deep in the shadow and close to the far wall. Nieuwenhuysen was a step in front of the others. In the indirect light from the lamp Yudel could see his face clearly. His mouth was open as if in anticipation of something and Yudel thought that he saw the tongue moving. The policeman closed his mouth and swallowed quickly a few times, his adam's apple bobbing. The fingers of his large fleshy hands were rubbing restlessly against their palms as if eager to be a part of this. Yudel wondered if what they were doing to Thandi was Nieuwenhuysen's invention. Looking at the almost total fascination on the policeman's face, the unblinking eyes, the little movements of his mouth and the futile swallowing, Yudel could have believed that something like this had been the fruit of his imagination. He was standing directly in front of Thandi, his pupils barely remaining still for a moment as they moved between the woman's face, her beautiful pain-racked submissive almost ecstatic face, and the clitoris that she was still trying hopelessly to shield by thighs that were held too firmly in position.

She was groaning again, the sound coming from deeper within her, seeming to have its origin right in her lungs. The young policeman was turning the baton again, the movement of his hand very slow, edging round in a circle, degree by gradual degree, the heavy rubber band tightening perhaps a millimetre each time. As Thandi groaned she was gasping, trying to draw air into lungs that were not being allowed to function normally. Every time she exhaled the persistent band squeezed more tightly than before, restricting her ability to inhale, making each breath marginally more difficult than the previous one. Her rib cage was shivering with the strain as it struggled against the pressure. Her large drooping breasts, hanging heavily over the band, were shining wet with perspiration and jiggling slightly, and the sound of her groaning was being forced out of her. She could not have stopped making the noise by any effort of will.

The baton was being turned no faster than before, drawing in the band. Yudel could see the corrugations of her ribs through the thick layer of rubber. Below her ribs it had drawn her stomach almost completely flat, level with the protrusions of her pelvis on either side.

Suddenly the smell of excrement was strong in the room as it was crushed out of her, spilling over the edge of the chair and dropping to the floor. Yudel could see the slightest wrinkling of distaste on Nieuwenhuysen's upper lip, but the policeman's eyes were still fixed on the body of his victim like those of a man hypnotised. The deliberately bored expression of the young policeman behind Thandi was not any more as good a disguise as it had been. Yudel saw a sudden half-closing of one of his eyes that came close to wincing. He was sure that he also saw a further tightening of the grip on her shoulder as if the police-man was trying to transmit strength to her, to give her some-

189

thing with which to fight the pain they were inflicting on her. To Yudel the increased pressure of his hand seemed to say, "Be strong a little longer so that we can break and humiliate you more fully. Be strong so that when you submit your final submission will be more complete."

Thandi's face was an agony of convulsing muscles, her eyebrows twitching in sympathy with the frightened sneering movements of her lips, her forehead wrinkling and unwrinkling, the perspiration pouring from it in a steady stream. She had stopped trying to see past the light and had even stopped trying to close herself to the eyes of her tormentors. Now she was conscious only of the pain.

Nieuwenhuysen spoke, his voice soft and indifferent. "Who is he?" He did not try to follow it up or even repeat the question. He let Thandi's pain do the work for him, her pain and the humiliation that was reducing her to something less than a woman.

Yudel looked for Freek, his eyes finding his friend's face, unconsciously searching for someone to stop what was happening. Freek's eyes were hard and staring fixedly, but in a completely different way to those of Nieuwenhuysen. His mouth was a straight line, the hinges of his jaw white and bloodless with pressure.

Behind Nieuwenhuysen one of the security policemen moved, coming forward a step to stand next to his boss and for the first time Yudel noticed Captain Dippenaar. Like the others Dippenaar had been too interested in the spectacle in the centre of the room to pay attention to Yudel's entry. Now Yudel searched the shadows behind Dippenaar and Nieuwenhuysen for the faces of the others. The three of them all seemed to be younger men and were all close to the wall in deeper shadow. Two of them Yudel had never seen before. He had to look at the third for a few seconds before he was sure that the broad body with the feet planted confidently apart, the head held forward, belonged to Warrant Officer Marais. The warrant officer was hunching his shoulders slightly forward and had his hands deep in his trouser pockets, his arms held straight at the elbows. There was much of confidence, much of belligerence and something of both tension and excitement in his stance. As Yudel watched he made a quick adjustment to his trousers that could only have been to accommodate an erection.

The young policeman's hand had been still a while. There was no doubt that he knew his work well. He increased the pressure so slowly that there was not likely to be any early fainting. The victim was brought along gradually, moving slowly, very slowly, from one level of pain to the next, over thresholds of fear that she had never known existed. Sometimes the pressure would even be released slightly, a partial and relative relief, a tiny source of hope that would make the next tightening of the band the more awful for having existed at all. But no small measure of relief was allowed to last more than a few seconds then the pressure would be increased again until it reached the same intensity, and went on beyond. . .

The knuckles of the hand holding the baton were white as the policeman struggled against the tension of the band. He removed his left hand from Thandi's shoulder, allowing the tips of his fingers to trail lightly over her skin and brought it down to support the other hand. Then, holding the baton with both hands, he kept the pressure even and the baton's movement steady. He was turning the baton more slowly than at any time before. Thandi's groaning had risen in pitch and become hoarser. It was surprising to Yudel that there was still any air in her lungs with which to groan.

Nieuwenhuysen spoke again, the question the same as before and the voice as indifferent and lacking in emphasis. "Who is he?" The security policeman's fingers were moving, rubbing against the palms of his hands as if he was trying to wipe away clinging bits of cobweb.

Who is who? Yudel asked himself. If he was talking about Majola he would not be asking, who is he? He would know who Majola is. He would not be asking that question of Hendricks. He knew him too. But Yudel did not know how many others were involved and Nieuwenhuysen could be talking about anyone.

A bubbling sound had started in Thandi's throat. With her face lifted upwards she might have been gargling. Then there were bubbles bursting just inside her parted lips, the blood erupting from her mouth, dribbling out of the corners and over her chin. She tried to breathe in, but the sound she made was like sucking the last drops of a cold drink through a straw. An

191

abortive attempt at coughing without the pressure of air to make it effective sprayed enough blood out of her throat so that she could breathe again, the liquid still gurgling in the air passages.

Yudel looked at the face of the young policeman who was now holding the baton stationary, apparently satisfied for the moment that he had gone far enough. Yudel expected to see him unwinding it, perhaps appalled at what he had done. But the two hands holding the baton were unmoving except for the vibration reaching them from out of the woman's body. Her body was shaking more than before, the loose flesh of her breasts and thighs shivering, the smell of excrement strong and the blood trickling out of the corners of her mouth, running down the sides of her lower jaw and her neck and down the insides of her breasts.

"Who is he?" Nieuwenhuysen asked. It was all that interested him. There was nothing forceful about his voice tone. The force was in the rubber band. Thandi must have known that they were killing her and that if she wanted to live she would have to tell them what they wanted to know. They were killing her and Yudel knew that they were leaving no marks on her body to show what they had done. If the body was examined later there would be an internal haemorrhage, but there would be nothing to show what had caused it. "Who is he? Who is the white man who visited you on Sunday night?"

Yudel could not easily believe what he had just heard. All they had wanted to know was who the white man was who had been with her. Thandi knew his name and nothing else. She had no special reason to trust him, but she was ready to die rather than tell them who he was. "I was with her on Sunday night," he said. He heard a dry grating quality in his own voice. "I visited her." Thandi's eyes opened and she raised her head, half-turning it in the direction of his voice, the blood that had been welling into it spilling out in a flood as her head came upright. "You can release the pressure on her," Yudel said. "I was the one that was with her on Sunday night."

The policeman manipulating the baton had turned to look at Yudel, but there was no movement on his part to release the pressure. "My God, what the hell's he doing here?" Yudel recognised Marais's voice. Nieuwenhuysen's head was cocked

192

to one side as if he had had difficulty grasping what Yudel had said. His eyes had narrowed and the suspicion on his face was total. Yudel had been aware of Freek glancing quickly at him and then turning to face Nieuwenhuysen, his face stern and set. Yudel was very glad to have him in the room.

Nieuwenhuysen took a while adjusting to the new situation. He was looking at Yudel in a way that suggested that he was giving him serious attention for the first time. "I'm the one," Yudel repeated. "You can take off the pressure." He wondered briefly if Thandi had seen and recognised him. She had turned her head long enough to look at him, but her eyes had seemed vague and sightless. A mixture of blood and saliva was trailing in long strands from her mouth onto the outside of her left thigh. The sound of her breathing was still filled with the bubbling of her blood as was the continual groaning, but the shaking had partially subsided. "You can take off the pressure," Yudel said to the policeman with the baton.

At last Nieuwenhuysen seemed to understand what was happening. He gestured towards the door with a quick movement of his head, his eyes travelling between Yudel and Freek. The movement was clearly an order.

Yudel tried one last time. In the corner of his field of vision he could see that Freek was already moving towards the door. "I'm the one who was there," he said. "You can release the pressure." The policeman with the baton looked uncertainly between Yudel and Nieuwenhuysen. While he looked at Yudel he removed his left hand from the baton and replaced it on the woman's shoulder. The action seemed to be almost comforting, saying, Never mind. We'll chase the bad man away. You don't need to worry about him. We won't let him take away what I'm doing to you. It's all right. There's no need to worry.

As it had earlier the policeman's hand massaged the woman's shoulder with tiny barely perceptible movements. Yudel glanced at the other security policemen in the room, Marais, Dippenaar and their two colleagues. The faces he saw were unalterable in their solidarity. They were the ultimate in-group. You could reach no nearer the core of any group than these men were. They were the protectors and defenders of their people. They were entrusted with the very future existence of Afrikanerdom. There could be no yielding by them, no uncertainties and no

193

disunity. All the faces were resolute and mistrustful of Yudel. He looked quickly at each one in turn, then towards the door where Freek and Nieuwenhuysen were waiting for him. He turned finally back to Thandi who had closed her eyes and was again trying to cough through the blood welling into her throat and mouth. At once he felt very tired and defeated. There was going to be no releasing of the rubber band even though they knew who her visitor had been. They would simply go on to other information they wanted from her. And even if they had everything from her that they wanted, perhaps even then they would not release her. The young policeman's hand on her shoulder and the unconscious movements of Nieuwenhuysen's mouth as he watched her torture were an indication that perhaps information was not the only criterion.

Yudel and Freek had been left in an office on the outside of the steel door that isolated the interrogation rooms. With them was a uniformed policeman who was preparing a statement for Yudel to sign. The sound of the steel door opening and closing to readmit Nieuwenhuysen reached them and then the passage was quiet again. The policeman who was writing the statement was a small lean man with hollow cheeks and temples. "Name please?" he asked.

"Yudel Gordon," Yudel said.

He stopped with his pen raised. "Which part is the surname, the Yudel part or the Gordon part?"

"The Gordon part."

"I just wondered." He flashed what was intended to be a reassuring smile at Yudel. "Gordon sounds like a first name. And I've never heard Yudel before. How do you spell it?"

Yudel spelled it.

The security policeman smiled again. "Sometimes they put the surname first—Gordon comma Yudel, you know."

Yudel said nothing. He was listening, imagining that he could hear sounds coming from the other side of the steel door in the passage. He was hearing a high thin groaning, laboured uneven breathing and a sound like the sound of gargling. . . And yet he knew that he was not truly hearing those sounds. What he heard was no more than an echo, perhaps an extension of the reality of the interrogation room, perhaps there was an ear of

194

the mind that could reach beyond the steel door. All that Yudel's ears could hear was the scratching of the policeman's pen on the paper as he wrote and the movement of his chair on the floor as Freek changed position. He glanced quickly at his friend. Freek was looking past the man at the desk, his face set hard, his teeth clamped rigidly together.

"Your address?"

Yudel told him his address, where he worked and his telephone number.

"Now can you tell me what you were doing in Soweto?" The pen was poised expectantly to take down the statement.

Yudel reached out towards him. "I'll write it," he said. The policeman only hesitated a moment, then he handed the paper to Yudel.

Yudel wrote fast, briefly explaining that he had been looking for Muntu Majola and why he was looking for him. He was far past the point where he would be able to hide behind his professional ethics. To refuse them what they wanted to know surrounded by the normality of your home was not the same as refusing them when you were seated in one of their offices and a few steps away a woman was being tortured and might be dying. To refuse them might be to kill Thandi. In many ways Yudel was not a cowardly man, but he knew that he would never be able to do what Thandi Kunene was doing.

He wrote that he had learnt that Majola had been a witness to the killing of Cissy Abrahamse and he was looking for him for that reason. He started writing that he had learnt where to look for Majola by talking to the Hendrickses, but changed his mind before he got to their names and drew a line through that part of the statement. Then he signed it and handed it back to the policeman.

The Hendrickses. Bill Hendricks was in the cell two doors down from where Thandi was being tortured. He had no doubt that was deliberate. They wanted him to hear the sounds of what was happening to her. If there was anything they still wanted from him this could be guaranteed to weaken his resolve. He had often heard it said that white opponents of the regime were more harshly handled than blacks. And that the Afrikaner opposition suffered more than any other. It was not true, not in any respect. Yudel knew how strong the bonds of the group were, making the Afrikaner who resisted the system no more than a freak to be avoided. The Englishman who made his voice heard too loudly was only a bit of nastiness to be kicked aside. But the black man or woman who thought that they should have rights and vigorously pursued those rights ran the risk of visiting interrogation rooms such as the one Yudel had just left. And they ran the risk of dying in them. The racial and language differences, the different and conflicting histories, the diverse societies existing next to and excluding each other, the divergent interests: they all made it safer and easier to be white and in the hands of the security police than it was to be black and in their hands. Bill Hendricks might suffer and come out of it a broken man, a shadow of what he had once been and totally unable to talk about his humiliation. But Thandi Kunene might die and the manner of her dying would be what Yudel had just seen.

The security policeman had left the room, taking Yudel's statement with him. He had said something that Yudel had not heard clearly, only the name, Nieuwenhuysen, registering in his mind. He heard the policeman's footsteps in the passage, rapid and neat as he went up the stairs. He could imagine him passing beneath the concrete beam under which Nieuwenhuysen had to duck. Then he heard him knock sharply on the steel door and he heard it swing open, the hinges squealing softly. The door must have stayed open because Yudel heard the door of the interrogation room being opened. Suddenly, unexpectedly, he was hearing Thandi again. The sound she was making was softer than before, almost choking, but still full of the bubbling of liquid in her throat. Yudel's body tensed at the sound as if the torture was his own. Unconsciously he turned his head towards the door of the office as if expecting to see something there.

There was a new sound, a sharp sudden crack, like a stick being broken. For the first time Thandi screamed, a short wild cry, weakened by the constriction of her lungs. Yudel got to his feet, using the edge of the desk to pull himself upright. He had reached the door when Freek got hold of his arm. His fingers were hard, digging into Yudel's arm, dragging him back into the office. "Where do you think you're going? There's nothing you can do in there."

"What was that sound?" Yudel was surprised to hear himself panting.

"I don't know." Freek's eyes like his face were hard and set. "I think it was a rib going."

"Christ." Yudel made another attempt to break free, but Freek was holding his arm tight and with his free hand pinned him against the wall.

"There's nothing you can do in there, Yudel."

"Jesus Christ, Freek." The breathless frightened sound of his voice was disturbing to Yudel. He wished that he could bring it under control.

"There's nothing you can do." Freek slowly released the hand in Yudel's stomach that was holding him to the wall. He led him back to the chair and made him sit down. Down the length of the passage the sounds Thandi Kunene was making were coming to them. There was a rattling element in her groaning now, almost like something loose flapping around noisily in a wind. The door of the interrogation room closed, shutting out the sound. They heard footsteps in the passage and the steel door closed heavily.

Nieuwenhuysen came into the office first. He sat down at the desk where the other policeman had been sitting, leaving him to stand near the door as if he was guarding the room. "I've read your statement, Mister Gordon, and I accept what you were doing." His eyes were narrowed and his lips pursed. He did not look directly at Yudel while speaking. "I must say that I am surprised that a man in your position has been so reluctant to co-operate with my staff. All we wanted was a man on the inside of Weizmann's shop." To Yudel he looked weak, strangely vulnerable. He looked like a man who would crack very soon under the sort of treatment that his staff were applying to Thandi Kunene. Even now, with everything in his favour, he looked uncertain, possibly even afraid.

Yudel gestured briefly towards the interrogation room with one hand. "Is that necessary?" His voice was little more than a croak.

"You don't know these people the way I do," Nieuwenhuysen said. The expression of his face seemed to indicate that the whole matter was distasteful to him. These were things you did not mention in polite company. It was as if Yudel had been

197

ill-mannered in referring to it. "They aren't just going to admit to things because I want them to. You don't know the types we deal with. You don't think we do this because we enjoy it?"

Yudel did not answer. He was searching for something that would have an effect on the other man. You don't think we enjoy it? he had asked. That was exactly what Yudel had thought. To tell him that would have profited neither Thandi nor himself.

"There's an old saying—every police station needs a sadist," Nieuwenhuysen said. Yudel was searching his face. He could see both bitterness and weakness in it. One of the large lifeless-looking hands was raised briefly to emphasise the point and the gesture was almost effeminate. "I suppose you've heard the saying," he said to Yudel. Then nodding towards Freek he said, "Freek knows that's true. Don't you, Freek?"

Yudel saved Freek the need to reply. "I don't suppose that even you consider it necessary to have a whole staff of sadists."

Yudel had not intended to say that and its effect was a shock to Nieuwenhuysen. For a moment his eyes were startled. Then he was again the same soft-spoken almost effeminate man, his mouth twisted with bitterness, looking past Yudel as he spoke. "What would you know about it?"

"I'm a psychologist. It's my business to know about these things."

The security policeman lifted his head deliberately, withdrawing from this sort of cheap mud-slinging. "I must advise you that as a civil servant what you saw here is subject to the Official Secrets Act. This place is also a prison so it is also subject to the Prisons Act and the Police Act. If you speak to any outsider about what you saw here you will be subject to prosecution under all three acts." Nieuwenhuysen's eyes moved to Freek. They were questioning him, asking, And what sort of company are you keeping these days? Where did you dig up this little Jew? And what are you thinking about, bringing him in here? "You called this man Piet at the hotel," he said.

"I always do," Freek said evenly.

"You said he was one of your boys."

"We work together all the time."

"It seems strange." Nieuwenhuysen was probing for a weak-

190

ness in Freek's position, a hold that would put the other man under his control.

"Come on, Yudel," Freek said. He was standing up and Yudel could see the anger in him. It was a carefully controlled anger that Freek could only let free on rare occasions. Yudel could also see the concern in his face. "Come on, Yudel. We're going."

Yudel got awkwardly to his feet. His limbs seemed sluggish in their movements. "How long are you going to keep that thing on her?" he asked.

Nieuwenhuysen looked towards the door. "We took it off long ago," he said. "We took it off just after you left the interrogation room."

Freek was driving steadily, both hands on the wheel. He seemed to be in complete control. It was an impression that had been of great use to him and that he had carefully fostered since his early days as a policeman. After tonight both of them knew it to be no more than a front. He looked towards Yudel and again Yudel could see the concern in his broad sturdy Afrikaner face. "I'm sorry," he said. "We shouldn't have gone. You were right."

"It's okay."

"No one should have to see that."

"You've seen such things before?"

"Yes."

"Many times?"

"On occasion."

There was a question Yudel did not want to ask. He was sure that he already knew the answer, but not so sure that he could avoid it. If his friendship with Freek was to continue, and he very strongly intended that it should, he would have to ask it. "Have you ever ordered something like that?"

"God almighty, Yudel." The shock on Freek's face was the best answer he could have given.

"All right," Yudel said. "I didn't have to ask that. Now I'm sorry." He looked carefully at Freek's face as he asked, "How are your promotion chances going to be affected by tonight?"

Freek was looking at the road. He had asserted an unconcerned expression on his features. Yudel had no doubt that this

199

too was a front. "What the hell." He had learnt the expression from Yudel. "Colonel is not a bad rank."

"The man in the cell we passed was Hendricks."

"I thought he might be." They drove on in silence for a while, then Freek spoke again. "No one should have to see that."

"It's all right," Yudel told him. "I suppose this was one of the ugly things the Minister of Justice did not want Mister Hartman taking back to America. Perhaps I needed to see it."

In the light from the dashboard Yudel could see the puzzlement on Freek's face. He allowed his eyes to leave the road for long enough to glance quickly in Yudel's direction.

FIFTEEN

YUDEL WAS SITTING in the lounge of his home, the only light coming from the fitting in the passage. Next to him the sliding glass doors were open, letting in the cold night air. He was drinking coffee that he had made himself and he was too deep in thought to be aware of the cold.

He had not contacted Rosa in any way since he had left her with Hymie and Irena forty-eight hours before. He had got through the day by telling Doctor Williamson that he was going to visit a number of newly paroled prisoners. Instead he had parked the car in the shade of a cluster of thorn trees on a quiet dust road some thirty kilometres north of town and tried to restore some sort of order to his thinking.

Too much had happened since the previous Wednesday when Weizmann had come to see him for the first time. His thoughts were alive with fresh memories, jumbles of images and words, pieces of information, all of them valueless. In two days there would be the inquest and Yudel knew that it was going to change nothing. A man had been defending his property against attack from without. The magistrate would be a man who kept a gun against just such a need, so would the prosecutor who would be leading the evidence, and Weizmann's counsel: they were all essentially of the same group and subject to the same fears. A man, a white man, a good dependable citizen, a man of substance, the owner of a shop—surely he was allowed to defend his family and property from attack—a man who was married to a niece of Jan Moolman? He was one of us.

Never mind that his assailant was a fourteen-year-old girl, never mind that she was thin and underfed, wearing a cotton dress that was all but worn through and little protection against the cold of the night; never mind that a five-year-old boy never saw his sister come back again. . .

There was too much. Yudel tried always to fit every new piece of information into place in his thinking, whether he was sorting through a patient's troubled state of mind or following the tracks of a murderer, but this time there had been too much that had affected him too deeply. It was not easy to be objective when you saw Bill Hendricks being taken from his home late at night. Nor was it easy to be objective when you remembered the frightened little gathering in Soweto or the sound Thandi Kunene had made, trying to breathe through her own blood. And the sound of the rib breaking. . . Had it been a rib? Please God, let it not have been a rib.

Where was she now? Could she still be alive? And where was Majola? And when they got him, as they surely would, what would they do to him? And Bill Hendricks? And Marion? And Wilson?

I have shot at them. I'm not saying I haven't shot at them, Weizmann had told him on the first visit. Yudel's thinking, searching for an anchor, fastened onto the image of the old man in his mind. How much of the guilt was his and how much of it had been fostered by the society of which he was a part? What part had been played by magistrates who had been unwilling to recognise the obvious and politicians whose vote-catching racialist speeches had seemed to justify Weizmann's actions in his own mind?

Weizmann, like Majola, was a victim of the circumstances surrounding his life. The shopkeeper had rebelled against the inferiority he had been made to feel all through his childhood. And Majola had rebelled against an inferiority that was entrenched in the constitution of his country. That their lives should meet at this time and, in their meeting, entangle Yudel was simply part of the game played by forces larger than and beyond the understanding of prison psychologists.

He could not keep his mind away from Thandi Kunene and what he had witnessed on the previous evening. Why had she tried to protect him? Had she known that if she once started talking it might be impossible to stop? He had been with her in the room and had seen it done to her. Could he not have done anything? If he had thrown a punch, even though his punches were not very effective, or shouted at them to stop, even though no one would have listened, if he had done any-

202

thing at all, made any sort of gesture, it would have been better than doing nothing at all. And, as Yudel remembered it, he had done nothing.

And what of Majola, ravaged from within by his own fury and despair, utterly resolved to avenge himself wherever he had the opportunity? . . . One brother had died in the hands of the Special Branch and another was a prisoner on Robben Island. Now there was Thandi—what would his reaction be when he learnt what had happened to her? Yudel asked himself how he would describe Majola's state of mind. Was the black consciousness advocate insane? Could you classify a man insane when there was a rational basis for his behaviour? Or would a sane man have ignored the death of his brother?

Yudel got up from his chair, went over to the record player and put on a recording. He was not a practising Jew in the sense that he attended synagogue or saw some special destiny for the Jewish people, but Yudel loved the music of the synagogue. Often when he was tired or depressed he would take out one of his many recordings of cantorial music and allow the beauty and strength of the music to work its wonders on him. The music of his people possessed so much more than the trivial love songs with which the world seemed to be obsessed. Yudel heard the sounds of eternity and mortality, suffering and survival in the music. It seemed to bring him closer to the foundation of his existence.

The recording was one of Jan Peerce singing Rosh Hashanah songs. He sat back in the armchair, trying to blank all thoughts from his mind, allowing the voice of the great American tenor and the glory of the music to dominate his consciousness and drive from it the horror of the past week. If he had been less involved with the music Yudel might have heard through the open door one of the neighbours' dogs barking excitedly and then stopping when the object of its excitement had passed on its way. He might also have heard a car pass slowly on the street, its engine turning over at little more than idling speed. The music went on majestically, rising and falling, filling the night and the limits of his awareness. It may have been because there was little light in the room or possibly because of the music, but it was a long time before Yudel saw the figure of a man, resting patiently against the frame of the sliding door.

The experience of the previous night had left him strained and fearful. He scrambled from the chair and stumbled across the room, looking for the light switch. "Leave the light alone," the man's voice told him. Yudel stopped in the centre of the room. The voice was definitely African.

Immediately Yudel knew with whom he was dealing. "Good evening," he said. He had been searching for Majola, but since the previous evening he had given up all hope of meeting him. Now that his quarry was before him he felt inadequate. How do you talk to a man who survived with adversaries like those of Majola? And how do you approach a man whose woman had the day before suffered what Thandi had suffered? Yudel felt like a child in the presence of a man.

"You were looking for me," Majola told him. His voice was deep and strong and Yudel could hear the anger in it.

"Yes. I'd given up though."

"I heard that you were looking for me, so I came."

"You know why I've been looking for you?"

"Of course." Majola had not moved from his place in the open door. He was still nothing more than a broad dark figure outlined against the tiny patches of light that penetrated the shrubbery from the road. "I know why you were looking for me, but I don't understand."

"You of all people should understand."

"Why should I understand?" Majola asked. He stepped through the sliding door and came into the room.

Yudel turned down the volume of the record player. "Would you like me to close the windows?"

"It's not important. Leave them open."

"I thought they might bother you in case someone came."

"If someone comes there'll be more ways to leave with them open." Majola sat down in a chair close to where Yudel had been sitting. Only later did Yudel reflect that he had chosen the only chair that gave him a clear view of every way into the room.

Yudel sat down in his original chair. Now the light from the passage was falling directly on Majola and for the first time Yudel could see his face. It was a strong face, broad across the temples and cheekbones, the nose wide and prominent, the jaw strong, just as he had seen it in the photographs. It was unlined, but mature, making it impossible to judge his age accurately. He was wearing a dark suit and tie and a white shirt. In dress he looked more like the new breed of rising black executive than a fugitive client of the country's security forces. "Now, what exactly do you want from me?" he asked. He did not look at Yudel as he spoke, but it was not the subtle averting of the eyes of the habitual liar or the used car salesman. Nor was it the security policeman's inability to meet with the soul of another human being. It was an arrogant turning of the head so that he would not have to see Yudel, a deliberate challenging rudeness. But for all the disdainful manner Yudel had the impression that he was being carefully watched, perhaps even judged.

"I want your help. I believe you saw Cissy Abrahamse die."

Majola's head was turned away from Yudel, facing almost at right angles to him. He blew through his nose in something that was almost a snort of disgust and turned his head so that he would be looking past Yudel on the other side. "Certainly I saw her die. What of it?"

"I hoped you might help me get Weizmann convicted."

"You want me. . ." He paused to let the idea gather effect. "You want me to go down to the police station with you and make a statement?"

Put that way the idea was ridiculous. "I thought there might be some way," Yudel said uncertainly. "I thought perhaps we could make a tape recording. . . I could get another witness who would testify to your being here. You could make a sworn affidavit. I have a friend who is a lawyer. . ."

"And this will be acceptable to a court?" Majola blew through his nose again, the sound conveying as much disgust and disbelief as it had the first time.

"I don't have anything else," Yudel said. "An affidavit from you coupled with Weizmann's history might have some effect. . . You are the only one who was there."

"Weizmann was there. And the child was there." The anger was strong in Majola's voice again.

"You were there," Yudel said.

"Yes." The broad arrogant face, its features clearly illuminated by the light from the passage, was still turned away from Yudel, but still leaving him with the impression that he was

205

the object of close scrutiny. "And you? How do you know what happened? Perhaps Weizmann is telling the truth. He's a white man. Why don't you believe him?"

"Because I know him."

"You knew him before?" Added to the anger in his voice there was now the possible intonation of a threat. The other man's eyes had narrowed slightly. If Majola ever believed that he was a friend of Weizmann's they would no longer be of any use to each other. He continued with barely a pause. "You knew him before he killed the girl?"

"No. He came to me for treatment afterwards. The police sent him."

"The police." Again the disgusted blowing through his nose. "You met him a few times and you think you know him?"

"I know him well enough to imagine what happened."

"You don't know him. I know him." Majola was keeping his voice down by an effort of will. "I saw what happened that night. I know Mister Johnny Weizmann."

Does he know? Yudel asked himself. Does he know that they took Thandi in? And does he know what happened to her? Should I tell him? Should I tell how I was there and saw it done to her?

The straining restless anger in Majola was clear for Yudel to see, but it was not the anger of a man who knew that his woman had been tortured and might not still be alive. The anger he could see was always part of the other man. No. Yudel told himself. He doesn't know. Should I tell him? I can't.

Yudel had spoken to Thandi on Sunday evening. On Monday morning a little after she tried to call him she had been picked up by the Special Branch. For Majola to have known about him he must have spent Sunday night with her, left before the raid and had no contact since. It was possible that an hour before Thandi was arrested she and Majola might have been making love.

The girl was in the room with them. Yudel could almost see her image transposed on the face of her lover. He could hear the thin reedy groaning and the gargling. He could see the hand of the policeman on her shoulder. He wondered if Majola's hand had ever caressed that shoulder in quite the same way.

"Tell me," Yudel said, trying to draw himself away from his thoughts. "Tell me what happened."

The other man did not answer immediately. For a moment Yudel thought he was being ignored, that Majola was showing him that the matter was not his business. Why have you come here tonight? Yudel's mind silently asked the other man. What do you stand to get out of it? "It's me who knows him," Majola said. "You want to know Mister Johnny Weizmann—you've first got to see him at work."

"You saw him clearly?"

"I saw clearly and I saw everything. I was a long way down the road, coming up from the station side, when I saw the girl. I saw her come across the road and stop close to the door of that old murderer's place. It was very dark. I could only see her up against the lights of Myburgh Street. Then I saw her go into the shop. I knew about Weizmann of course, but I never knew where his shop was otherwise I would have stopped her."

"You knew what she was up to?"

"Of course I knew what she was up to. I thought she was a black girl. I only saw that she was coloured when I got to the door of the shop." Majola stopped speaking suddenly as if everything had been said and there was nothing left to add that would be of any consequence.

"What did you see?"

"Why is it important to you?" The words burst out of him. "He's white and you are white. Your interests are the same. How do I know what you want out of this?" The high expectation of life that Black Social Endeavours had generated was all gone. Only the resentment remained.

"I've told you what I want."

"How do I know that you are telling the truth? What are you willing to suffer for the truth Mister Yudel Gordon? Have you ever suffered for the truth?"

Again Yudel was a boy, being chided by a man. He had no answer to Majola's questions. He had no way of knowing what he would be willing to suffer for the truth. There were not many facets of life where Yudel was absolutely certain of what the truth consisted. He had a fair idea of what Majola would consider the truth to be. It would be closely bound in the other man's mind with the fight for power in his country, "The

207

Struggle" as he and his people called it. "I don't think I can answer. . ."

The uncertainty in Yudel's voice and the ineffectiveness of his response were soothing to Majola, confirming his dominance. He went on with his story as if he had never interrupted himself. "When I reached the doorway the child was on her knees and Mister Johnny Weizmann was standing in front of her. She was saying, 'Please mister, please mister,' over and over again. He just put two bullets into her. There's nothing else to tell. She was on her knees and he just put the bullets into her."

"A woman across the road heard a third shot," Yudel said. "What about the third shot?"

Majola laughed shortly, and there was a trace of real mirth in the sound. "That was the shot he aimed at me," he said. "He saw me in the doorway and chased me. Out in the street he shot at me."

For no clear reason clusters of thoughts were forcing themselves upon Yudel and he was beginning to understand much that had puzzled him. He was remembering the conversation between Nieuwenhuysen and Weizmann the night before. He was thinking of Majola's strong and vengeful spirit and he was thinking about the number, three. Thoughts and impressions were crowding in upon him and he had to tear himself away from them in order to follow what Majola was saying.

"He hides from the world above his shop, too guilty to show his face, cowering behind his police guard." Again Majola seemed to be straining to keep his voice low.

"He has no police guard," Yudel said. He was surprised that for the first time Majola was looking straight at him, his face alert and intent.

"I'm sorry that I can't help you, Mister Gordon, but the reasons are obvious."

"Aren't you willing even to try?"

Majola blew through his nose again as if trying to clear something out of it. "Why should I try? To what purpose?"

"A child was killed. Doesn't that bother you?"

"A child was killed?" Majola moved forward slightly in his chair and for the first time Yudel thought that he might be in some danger. "A child was killed." The words were spoken harshly as if they were some form of blasphemy and were only

208

used under great stress. "I saw it happen. I've seen it before. Where were you in 1976? Were you in this country in 1976? Where were you?"

"I was here." To his own ears Yudel seemed to be making an admission of guilt.

"You were here." The words were spoken with disgust. "If you were here then you know what happened in 1976. The schoolchildren went to complain about their schooling and they were met with guns. Where were you that you don't know this?" His head was turned even further away from Yudel than before. It seemed that he could not bear to look at Yudel's white face. "Don't talk to me about one coloured child. The lives of black children are cheap in this country. Don't you know that? Where have you been that you know nothing about your country?"

Yudel had no answer. But something was changing in Majola's manner. He was not interested in or expecting an answer from Yudel. What he was saying he had said many times in the past. Now it was little more than a recitation, his attention held by other more important considerations. The disgust and fury were present in his voice and face, but by this time they were habitual, a part of his personality. "Where have you been that you don't know how cheap the lives of black children are?" He was preoccupied, barely listening to himself.

"Hendricks told me," Yudel started. "He told me that you were a friend of Biko's. From what he told me I don't think Biko would have refused me help."

"The bastard," Majola said. "He gave us hope. And where is he now?" He was going through the motions of a man who had been deeply moved, but it was for Yudel's benefit. Majola's mind had moved on to other matters. "He gave us hope—the son of a bitch. He said Black Social Endeavours was going to be an empire. I can't believe he's gone. I never thought anyone would be able to kill him." The sorrow in Majola's voice was not false, but it was not what was occupying his attention. "He let us all down, the bastard, the son of a bitch." At once he was on his feet. He was just above average height, half a head taller than Yudel, broad in the shoulder, his hands also broad and powerful. "I'm sorry. There's nothing I can do."

Majola started towards the sliding doors and Yudel got to

his feet. He searched for something that might persuade the other man to help, but he knew that nothing would be of any consequence. Majola went through the open door without stopping or looking back. His movements were sure, purposeful and determined. In a moment he was only a darker patch against the uneven darkness of the shrubbery, and then that too was gone.

For a few minutes Yudel stood at the open doors, looking into the garden. Eventually he followed the path that Majola had taken onto the drive and then into the street. By the intermittent light of the street lamps he could see no one. A large doberman came out of a garden higher up the road to investigate an especially appealing scent at the base of a lamp post. Apart from the dog all else was quiet under the jacarandas that lined the street on either side. From the next street Yudel heard the sound of a car's engine start.

Why had he come? Yudel asked himself. What possible reason could he have had? He had known why Yudel had wanted him and he had come, knowing that he had no intention of helping. Then why had he come?

Suddenly, without warning, Yudel knew the reason. He turned and ran for the house and the telephone in the hall.

SIXTEEN

YUDEL HAD LOCKED the house and was waiting on the pavement when Freek arrived. The car had barely stopped when he had slipped into the passenger side and Freek was accelerating hard down the street again. The policeman looked tired, his eyes bloodshot as he glanced across at Yudel. His shirt was open at the neck, still screwed into the shape of the tie that had been discarded during the evening. He was wearing an old brown sports coat that had probably been the first that had come to hand as he left home. "I hope there's a good reason for this," he said.

"Muntu Majola visited me tonight. He's on his way to kill Weizmann now."

"What are you talking about?" Freek turned his head to look at Yudel for longer than he should have and had to brake to avoid a car coming from the front.

"Don't slow down," Yudel said.

"You'd better explain what's been going on."

"I'll explain. You just drive fast."

Freek pushed the car hard through the tangle of quiet suburban streets that separated them from the Johannesburg highway, no more than slowing for stop signs and intersections. "What do you mean Majola visited you tonight?"

"I was sitting in the lounge with the doors open and suddenly he was there, standing in the doorway."

"Are you sure it was Majola?"

"It was him, Freek. I recognised him from the Hendricks's photographs."

"And he said he's going to kill Weizmann now?"

"That's not what he said. That's what I say. I'll explain it to you, but I think you should radio ahead first and get them to place a guard outside Weizmann's shop."

211

As he glanced at Yudel again Freek's eyes told him that he was going to need a lot of convincing. But he unhooked the microphone of the VHF radio set and brought it to his mouth. "Control, come in please," he called in Afrikaans. It was the language spoken by almost all white policemen. He was answered by a sudden burst of static interspersed with broken bits of a man's voice. "I won't be able to get him from here," he told Yudel. "The station is up near Voortrekkerhoogte. We're in the shadow of the hill. We'll get him from the other side of the monument."

They were travelling up one of the main arteries that leave Pretoria on the south, cutting through the long ridge that borders the city on that side. On the left the buildings of a university climbed straight out of the ridge, a massive shadow overhanging the road, and on the other side, half-way up a steep hillside, Yudel could see the lights of a train, flickering intermittently through a screen of trees. The steepness of the hill would cut them off from the radio station until they had passed it, but that would only take a few minutes. Freek had hung the microphone on its bracket and was giving his attention to his driving, except for the piece of it that he was reserving for Yudel. "Talk, Yudel. Let's hear what this is all about."

"I think that tonight for the first time I understand fully what this is all about." Yudel was speaking fast, his voice excited, eager to tell Freek what he had learnt. "While Majola was with me I started to understand. A lot of little things that had been bothering me started to come clear. But only after he had left did all the bits really come together."

Freek was trying again to get through to Control. "Calling Control. Come in please, Control." Again there was only the crackle of static with a man's voice somewhere in the background, vainly trying to answer Freek. They had turned off the main highway onto a narrow twisting road that followed the edge of a tree-filled park on one side and the rail tracks on the other. "Yudel, let me get clear of these little roads and get hold of Control and then you can tell me everything. Spare me the introduction about your thought processes though." In the dark interior of the car Freek's face, lit only by the glow from the dials on the dashboard, looked tired and troubled. Yudel knew that the reason was almost certainly their experience of the

212

previous night. The effect it had had on Yudel had been immediate, but it was possible that the effect on Freek would be deeper. The policeman felt very strongly that the government, being an Afrikaner body, should conduct itself in a civilised fashion. Ever since Yudel had first known him Freek had been quick to defend the government against criticism, but there were times when Freek's will to defend the system failed him. When faced with the worst consequences of government actions he seemed to feel personally responsible. Yudel had seen it in the past and reasoned with Freek on occasions to free him of it. The reasoning had never been successful. The lapse of Freek's normally confident and orderly manner was the result of guilt that he was trying to suppress. It was a guilt that Yudel shared.

Freek swung the car right at an intersection and they passed under the railway line in a subway crossing. A moment later they were climbing steeply up the access ramp of the Johannesburg highway. Freek was trying to raise Control again. "Come in, Control. Come in, Control."

"Control here. Reading you."

"Who's that? Is that Flippie?"

"What's your call sign please?"

"Jesus Christ Almighty," Freek told the VHF set. "DS 635 here. Who's that?"

"Reading you, DS 635. Is that Colonel Jordaan? Over."

"Yes, it's me—the Lord knows."

"It's Flippie Lochner here, Colonel. I'm just following orders about the call sign, Colonel. What does the Colonel want? Over."

"Flippie, listen carefully. I want you to call Johannesburg. I want a guard placed on a shop there within ten minutes. You hear me?"

"I hear the Colonel, but I can't help. My main transmitter is out. We're trying to fix it at the moment. I'm using a mobile to talk to you. Over."

"With that aerial you've got up there you should reach Johannesburg even with a small transmitter."

"It's not connected to the main aerial, Colonel. It's just got an ordinary mobile aerial and I'm sticking it out of the window while I talk to the Colonel. The Colonel must realise that I'm doing my best. I think an output transistor has gone. Over."

"Jesus Christ," Freek muttered to himself before speaking into the microphone again. "In heaven's name, Flippie, there must be something you can do."

"Is the Colonel on his way to Johannesburg himself? Over."

"Yes. I'm just coming out of the Fountains now."

"Well, when the Colonel reaches Halfway House, the Colonel should be able to speak to John Vorster Square direct by that time. Over." Flippie sounded very friendly and helpful and unconcerned.

"Don't you understand that it might be too late by that time?" Freek shouted into the microphone. Whatever his uncertainty about the chase Yudel had brought him on, Freek knew by experience that it would be unwise to doubt either Yudel's deductions or his intuitions.

"I'm only trying to be helpful, Colonel. Over." Flippie's voice over the VHF link sounded hurt and humbly reproachful.

"I'll tell you what you do, Flippie. Phone John Vorster Square and tell them I want a man guarding the Twin Sisters café, Myburgh Street, Braamfontein, immediately. Over."

"Just a moment, Colonel, while I get my pen out."

Freek read the address a second time to the man called Flippie and told him that he was going over and out and to report back to him when he had spoken to Johannesburg. Then he turned his attention to Yudel again. "All right, Yudel, I'm sticking my neck out. Let me hear why."

"I hope they get a man there in time," Yudel said.

"They will. Now let's hear it."

Yudel paused a moment, trying to assemble his thoughts in a more or less coherent form. "From the beginning this evening Majola thought the idea of him giving evidence was ridiculous. All the time he was with me I was bothered about why he had come. He knew what I wanted and he knew he wasn't going to help me. So why had he come? Only after he had gone did I realise what it was all about. He went to a lot of trouble to tell me that the death of Cissy Abrahamse was nothing to him. He said that the lives of black children are cheap. . ."

"All right, Yudel," Freek said. "I don't want to hear that. Stay with the point."

214

"The point is that while we were talking he suddenly said something about Weizmann hiding from the world behind his police guard, being too guilty to show his face."

"And you said that he has no police guard?"

"How do you know that?" Yudel asked.

"I know you. You're that innocent." Freek smiled tiredly and shook his head.

"Well, after that he seemed to have lost interest in what we were saying. He seemed preoccupied. It was obvious his mind was busy with other things. He left very shortly afterwards and the way he moved—I was sure there was a special purposefulness in it. It's a hunch, Freek. You're going to have to trust me on this one."

Freek smiled again. The expression was weary, but there was warmth in it. "I've grown used to that," he said.

"Colonel Jordaan, come in please. Over." The voice of Flippie Lochner burst in on them.

"Reading you, Flippie," Freek told him.

"Colonel, the duty officer there says they have no one to send at the moment, but they'll get someone there as soon as they can. They say the Colonel must understand how short-staffed they are at the moment. Over."

Freek's tiredness and his desperation at having been faced by the worst side of the Security Police performance on the previous night had cut his tolerance to a low level. He shouted into the microphone in answer to the operator's message. "You tell them that this is a matter of the greatest importance. Tell them I say so. Tell them it's on my responsibility and I want a man there now, not tomorrow morning."

There was a pause while Flippie Lochner waited to be sure that he was finished. It was not the sort of message he cared to interrupt. "I'll tell him immediately, Colonel. Over and out."

The road had flattened substantially, the highway running straight across a gently rising and dipping countryside. Freek had his foot all the way down on the accelerator and the car was flashing past traffic moving at the national speed limit of ninety kilometres per hour. Yudel went on with his story: "Last night Nieuwenhuysen told us that all he wanted from me was to get him a man on the inside of Weizmann's place. He had asked Weizmann before he tried to get me to help. Last

215

night after the meeting he asked him again. I saw the old man refuse him. That was why they needed me. Who better than a man's psychologist to persuade him?"

Freek was nodding thoughtfully. "And they knew Majola had seen Weizmann kill the girl so they reckoned, considering his past record, that he might be back to get Weizmann."

"They followed very much the same route that I had followed, talking to very much the same people. Some places I was there before them. Some places they got there first.

"That Mrs Sinclair lives right across the road from Weizmann. She heard the shots. Two different sets of detectives visited her and the second set were not interested in what she had to say. They only wanted to talk to her servant, Julie. Julie had known Majola in her youth and she had seen him leaving Weizmann's place in a hurry straight after the shooting and recognised him. When Nieuwenhuysen found out that Majola had been there they had every reason to expect Weizmann's assistance. He is a fellow member of their organisation. Their views on people like Majola are identical. But to their astonishment he refused.

"In Weizmann's most recent cycle of killings there had so far been only two victims. He needed a third and I think this time he had chosen Majola. And he didn't want the Special Branch doing his killing for him.

"One night before I took you there I watched Weizmann's place from the roof of that building opposite and I thought then that I saw someone else watching his place, but I wasn't sure. I think it must have been either Majola himself or one of Nieuwenhuysen's men watching for him."

"You're sure about this thing of the cycles of three killings?"

"Freek, for years at a time Johnny Weizmann had no trouble. I wouldn't be surprised that if we could find someone who knew we would discover that his storeroom door stayed closed at night during those years. But each time there was a killing, and in view of his personality this was always a danger, there would have to be two more to make things perfect."

Freek did not answer this time. He was speaking into the microphone of the VHF set again. "Control. Come in, Control. What the hell's going on there, Flippie?"

After a few seconds Flippie's voice, sounding breathless,

reached them again. "Just a second, Colonel. I've got them on the phone now. I'll be back in a second. Over."

"Standing by, Flippie," Freek told him.

The traffic on the highway was thin and Freek was able to keep the accelerator down, weaving the car easily between the slower-moving vehicles. He seemed to become occupied with his own thoughts, for the time being forgetting Yudel's presence. His face was set, his hair hanging loose over his forehead and his eyes staring unblinkingly at the road. Only the smallest movements of his hands on the steering wheel were necessary to direct the car along the broad highway and between the thinly scattered traffic. When he spoke into the microphone again his voice sounded abrupt, the words cut short. "Come in, damn it, Flippie. What the hell's going on?"

This time Flippie answered immediately. "I've spoken to them, Colonel. And they say they'll send somebody. Over."

"When are they sending them?"

"I told them it's urgent and they say they'll send someone immediately. Over."

Freek inhaled deeply, rocking his head back on his shoulders as he did it. "Good, Flippie, you did well. Over and out."

"Out, Colonel," Flippie said.

Freek had been sitting upright, leaning forward over the steering wheel. Now he rested back, more relaxed, but still tired and determined. Neither he nor Yudel spoke. Both were wondering what they were going to find in Johannesburg when they got there, Yudel afraid that his guess might have been wrong and all of this unnecessary, and both of them afraid that he might have been right. Freek was pushing the car as fast as it would go, its nose vibrating slightly with the movement of the suspension. Yudel knew how determined Freek would be to reach Weizmann's place before Majola got there. Knowing Freek, he knew that he would want to be at the centre of the action to avert, if he could, whatever disaster might be threatening. The policeman was not a man to avoid responsibility of any kind.

Away to the left an avenue of tall bluegums was black against the soft glow in the sky caused by the lights of the East Rand towns. At a break in the trees the few scattered lights of Half-way House disturbed the monotony of the night. Freek allowed them to pass before reaching for the microphone again. "Johannesburg Control. Johannesburg Control, come in please."

"Control here. Over." The voice sounded young and sleepy.

"Freek Jordaan here," Freek told him. Freek often announced himself without giving his rank, thereby causing much confusion among policemen trained to obey orders and desperate not to upset higher-ranking officers. As a young detective sergeant it had at times led to his orders being painstakingly obeyed by officers far senior to himself. "Freek Jordaan here. Has that guard been placed on the Twin Sisters café?"

"I'll check, officer." Across the twenty-five kilometres of flat Highveld the signal was strong, the voice clear. In a few moments he was back. "We haven't yet got the guard at the café, but they'll be there soon, officer. Over."

When he answered Freek's voice had grown harder than Yudel had ever heard it before. "What's your name?"

"Constable Willem Labuschagne, officer. Over." The sleepiness in the voice had gone and it had become defensive.

"Constable, I gave a clear order that a guard has to be placed outside that café. Is there any reason it hasn't been done?"

With Freek not telling him when he could take over the conversation the man at Johannesburg Control had an extra problem. When he did answer he spoke very quickly as if afraid that he might be interrupted. "We sent out a squad car, officer, but before they got there we had to divert them to a break-in at a bazaar in Joubert Park. As soon as another car is free we'll send them across there until we can make arrangements for a permanent guard, officer. Over."

"Who decided your priorities, Constable? Whose idea is it that your break-in is more important?"

"My idea, officer." The policeman sounded as if he was being strangled. "Over, officer."

"Constable, you find an armed guard for that café in the next five minutes, you hear?"

"I hear, officer. I'll try hard."

Freek saw no need to reply. To Yudel he said, "He sounds like a good man. He thinks for himself, even if he did think wrong this time." Ahead and to the left Yudel could see the lights of Johannesburg's outlying suburbs. If Majola was on his way to Weizmann he would probably have travelled slowly, anxious not to draw attention to himself. Even though he had left well before them it was still possible, even likely, that they would get there first. What their course of action would be when they got there was something that Yudel had not even considered. This was Freek's territory and Yudel would not even try to discuss it with him, knowing that his friend's thoughts were probably occupied with just that subject.

Johannesburg's northern suburbs were passing quickly on either side when Freek tried the radio again. "Come in, Labuschagne."

Labuschagne came in quickly. "I'm here, officer. Over."

"Have you got my guard on that shop?"

"Yes, officer. We've sent a car. I'm sure they must be there by now. Over."

"Good shot. I'll be there in a few minutes myself and I'll call you from there." Freek paused as if to consider. "Over and out," he added in a belated gesture in the direction of conformity.

The highway network took them right into the heart of Johannesburg and to within a few hundred metres of Weizmann's place. They picked up Myburgh Street a few blocks from the café, Freek slowing the car for a set of traffic lights that were against them, pausing long enough to glance both ways and then accelerate over the intersection. From more than a hundred metres away Yudel could see the front of Weizmann's place, the trees in Hayes Street peeping out between the buildings. On the pavement in front of the café a figure was moving, but it was only a thick-set white workman in denims, carrying a metal lunch-box in one hand, his free hand deep in a trouser pocket. Freek slowed sharply in front of the café and swung the car into the side street. There had been no police car in Myburgh Street and there was not one here either. Freek braked hard, stopping across the road from Weizmann's storeroom door.

From the moment they turned the corner Freek and Yudel had been trying to see the door of the storeroom. This was the place at which they had been aiming. It was the point upon which the whole investigation, even the whole of Johnny Weizmann's story, had been focussed. And now it was standing open. It was not just a little way open, left ajar as a temptation

219

to the unsuspecting, but wide open as it may have been left by a man in a hurry. The store was in darkness, but upstairs one light was burning, only a faint reflected glow reaching the foot of the staircase.

The car had scarcely stopped when Freek was out, throwing the door open wide so that it rocked against its hinges and slammed shut behind him. Yudel scrambled out on his side to follow.

He had taken the first few steps that would carry him round the front of the car, one hand pressing on the bonnet to steady himself; Freek was entering the door of the storeroom and was turning to leap for the stairs; from somewhere above Weizmann's dog snarled; then all else was obliterated by four gunshots, the first separated from the others by perhaps a second and the other three so close together that they seemed to roll together into one sound.

Yudel was halfway across the street when he saw Freek pass the small window on the stairs. His friend had his head lifted to look at the landing above, the light from the flat highlighting his face. In that moment Yudel could see both the tiredness that had been there earlier and the resolve in his face. Then Freek was gone and Yudel could hear the sound of his passage as he leapt up the remaining stairs.

Yudel was through the door, reaching for the banister to guide himself onto the stairs. He could see the landing on the floor above and the cheap plastic chandelier with a single electric light bulb glowing in it, and he could hear Freek's footsteps, thunderous on the sprung floor of the old building. Before he was halfway up he could hear other footsteps and another gunshot, seeming to come from just above his head, so close that he thought he felt the concussion of the shot. He stopped, one hand holding onto the banister. The footsteps were directly above him and Freek was falling headlong backwards on the landing, one hand raised to shield his face. At almost the same moment Majola was leaping over Freek where he had fallen, then he was coming down the stairs towards Yudel, slipping and stumbling with the urgency of his descent. A heavy shoulder took Yudel in the middle of the chest, thrusting him backwards and against the banister. Catching hold of a vertical wooden railing in one hand, he steadied himself in time to see Majola reach the ground and start for the door. Unthinking, he turned to follow. In his mind he had a picture of Majola's face, its normal expression of restrained anger having become one of panic and fury, his eyes wide open, their whites startlingly prominent in the dark face; and a picture of his broad frame in the doorway a moment later. Both images were frozen into Yudel's awareness, seeming to be fixed there while he moved towards the door, the second or two that he took to get out onto the pavement stretching, the moment growing longer as if he was barely moving at all.

Then he was outside. Majola was running for the corner, his form black in the darkness under the trees, but outlined sharply against the bright lighting of Myburgh Street at the intersection. His arms were working hard, the hands folded into fists and pumping, his shoulders hunched and his head forward.

Freek had arrived on the pavement next to Yudel and he had an automatic pistol in his right hand. Yudel wondered where the gun had come from. He heard Freek shout, "Stop," the word short as if the time spent saying it could not be wasted. Then, "Stop," again and Freek's face was desperate as Yudel had never seen it. The death of Cissy Abrahamse and all the others, the torture of Thandi Kunene, the breaking of Bill Hendricks were all with them on the pavement. Yudel could see it all in the expression of Freek's face. "Stop or I'll have to shoot."

Majola was at the corner, his shoes slipping on the paved surface as he tried to get round it. Freek had turned side-on and raised the pistol to shoulder level, his right arm rigid to absorb the recoil. Yudel saw Majola look back, the broadness of his face still strong in that moment. Freek only fired once, the pistol held steady. Majola was still looking back, but the moment was too brief for the look on his face to change. He went down hard on his right shoulder and suddenly where there had been a man there was only a dark formless heap at the side of the road. There had been no visible buckling of the knees, no upraised hand to cushion the fall. There had been a man and now there was not a man, only the dark object filling the gutter that could not possibly still be a man.

Nothing that remained of the night was clear to Yudel afterwards. The incidents of which it consisted had seemed to merge into each other until he was not sure what their order had been or even if everything he remembered had taken place. He was left with the vague image of Majola's body curled up in almost a foetal position, his hands tucked underneath his chest, his head bent forward and his knees drawn up. There had been a lot of blood in the gutter, dammed up behind the dead man's shoulder, slowly trickling away, soaking into his clothing and congealing.

He had an uncertain picture of a squad car stopping at the pavement outside the shop, two young uniformed policemen arriving to protect the café in accordance with Freek's order and trying to question him about Majola's death, for some reason assuming that he had been responsible. He remembered a woman's voice screaming from the flat above, "They've murdered Pa. The kaffirs have murdered Pa." And blending with and confusing all the other images was the gathering crowd, sleepy and dishevelled, some in pyjamas and dressing gowns, a number of black labourers sullen and silent, looking at the body on the ground and being careful to hide whatever it was they were feeling. Among them Julie had appeared, wearing a plastic raincoat over a long blue dressing gown. She had bent over Majola and had recognised him again, the second time in two weeks. The image of her face, the eyes rigid, both frightened and sorrowing, were part of all the other memories, as uncertain as any of them and yet as true in his recollection of it all.

One of the young policemen had come close and asked, "Do you know who is this dead Bantu?"

"Yes. His name was Muntu Majola."

"The communist?"

"I don't think. . ." Yudel had started to say, but there had seemed to be no point to questioning or debating what Majola had been. "Yes," he had said, "the communist."

The stairs inside Weizmann's place had been steep and badly lit, the dog lying dead on the landing, looking like a pile of ruffled untreated fur, a slight bloodiness at the back of the neck marking the passage of the bullet, and the sound of a woman's voice, not a young woman, coming soothingly from the bedroom. "There he is. There he is. Never mind, Pa. We're

222

going to fix him. We're going to fix him all nicely. Never mind, Pa. There he is." It had sounded like she was talking to a child, using the third person as Afrikaner women often do when talking to their young. Her voice had been encouraging and loving, patient and protecting.

Weizmann himself had been sitting on the edge of a double bed with his back to the bedroom door. He had a bloodsoaked towel wrapped round his left shoulder and under the arm. His wife had been bending over him, wiping blood off his face with a second towel that she had been dipping into a basin of hot water, the liquid already pink and deepening in colour. "Doesn't Pa want to lie down?" the woman had asked, her voice very gentle, the pale ugly face full of love and concern for the man she was tending. "Doesn't Pa want to lie down on the bed?" It had been barely the same face that Yudel had seen behind the shop counter. The hardness and bitterness were gone as though they had never existed. He had been left with the certainty that he had been looking at two unhappy people who had found refuge in each other. And the knowledge had numbed and frightened him.

More strongly and clearly than any other part of it Yudel was left with the memory of Freek, moving resolutely through it all, giving orders to newly arrived policemen, supervising the removal of Majola's body, his face neutral, held under tight control, a man operating without thinking, automatically doing all that he knew could not be avoided.

The night had become colder and the pavement had slowly emptied as the people who had come down from the flats or stopped their cars to see a dead man had gone back to their flats and cars and forgotten what they had seen without ever understanding it. Finally just before the body had been removed and the crowd had shrunk to a few black workmen and domestic servants Nieuwenhuysen and Dippenaar had arrived to assure themselves that it was indeed Majola who had died. They had come away from the body unable to disguise their pleasure. Nieuwenhuysen had nodded to him, his soft fleshy mouth smiling, a grimace that was clearly intended to suggest that he was satisfied, both with the night's work and that Yudel could be trusted. As they passed into Weizmann's place Dippenaar had stopped in front of him and, taking hold of his

223

shoulder, had squeezed it in a gesture that was intended to convey that now he was one of them. Past doubts were forgotten.

Eventually the security policemen had left, the names of witnesses had been noted, measurements had been recorded and photographs taken, and they had been free to go home.

A man had died. Standing on the pavement in the cold Yudel had wondered if Majola's death counted and the cycle was now complete. Or would it only be complete when the tormented old shopkeeper had done the job himself? Would there have to be another victim to complete the score?

He did not want to think about it, not for a long time. Yudel feared the answer.